One Winter in Blue Sky

by

Margot Johnson

One Winter in Blue Sky

Cover Art by *Teddi Black*

The Wild Rose Press, Inc.
PO Box 708
Adams Basin, NY 14410-0708
Visit us at www.thewildrosepress.com

Publishing History
First Edition, 2025
Trade Paperback ISBN 978-1-5092-6292-2
Digital ISBN 978-1-5092-6293-9

Published in the United States of America

Dedication

For Laura & Lindsay, my favorite former figure skaters

Chapter 1

Dragging a big red suitcase, Krista burst through the doors of the cute white church on Main Street in the smallest town she'd ever visited. She'd barely heard of Blue Sky in the Canadian prairies, and here she was in the middle of almost nowhere—breathless, flustered, and late for Amy's wedding rehearsal. The bride was allowed to keep everyone waiting but not the maid of honor.

The big day was tomorrow with sunny and mild autumn weather in the forecast. Thanks to a ridiculously long flight delay, Krista landed at the nearest airport at exactly the time the rehearsal was due to start. With no better option, she jumped into a cab and paid a small fortune for a forty-five-minute ride out to the country. Finally here, she paused and took a deep breath.

Scanning the crowd of family and friends milling around in the lobby, she spotted Amy heading her way. "I'm so sorry I'm late." Krista dropped her suitcase, threw her arms wide, and encircled Amy in a bear hug. They were still best friends, even though they lived thousands of miles apart. From a distance, Amy had been there through everything—the good, the not-so-good, and the plain horrible.

"I forgive you." Amy hugged her just as tight. "But as punishment, I might throw my bouquet right into your hands."

"Don't even think about wasting it on me." Now, Krista could laugh most of the time. Amy knew the whole story of all the hurts of her bumpy past and usually just nudged her to move on with her life. Mostly, Amy accepted she would do it when she was ready. "I'm so excited for—" Before she could finish, someone very good looking appeared at Amy's right elbow.

"I'd like you to meet Tate Harris." Amy performed the introduction, sweeping her left arm with a flourish. "He's our best man, Matt's buddy from nursery school days. He actually lives here in Blue Sky, unlike the rest of us."

Tall, dark, and handsome! Krista had never seen a guy in real life who so perfectly matched the cliché. Meeting his gaze was like diving into two vats of rich dark chocolate—and she loved chocolate. The sight made her heart flutter in a very surprising and unsettling way. Smiling, she held out her right hand. "I'm pleased to meet you." Warmth from his handshake travelled up her arm, and she glanced around for a distraction.

"His twin daughters, Gracie and Ella, are my flower girls," said Amy. "They're adorable." She pointed toward a pair of little girls with bouncy chestnut ponytails and snub noses dusted with a smattering of freckles.

"What a sweet pair!" Krista smiled at their energy, overflowing so it practically bounced across the lobby.

Since the wedding attendants all lived in different locations, Krista barely knew the groom, Matt, and had never met the rest of the wedding party. In her calls leading up to the big event, Amy hadn't mentioned anything at all about the gorgeous best man, probably because he was a happily married dad. Even if for some reason he was a single guy, why would Amy bother matchmaking anyway? Krista lived on the other side of the country. In texts and calls, she made it abundantly clear after escaping a toxic relationship, she wasn't interested in becoming anybody's girlfriend, let alone wife.

Listening to a flurry of introductions and instructions from the pastor, she stood next to Amy at the front of the church for the mock ceremony and studied her petite, pretty friend. Amy's glossy black hair fell in a straight sheet to her shoulders, and she glowed with anticipation. She was lucky to have met the man of her dreams and know exactly where her life was headed. Krista could not say the same thing.

Glancing around, she admired the tall, narrow stained-glass windows on both sides. The ancient building wafted the not-unpleasant musty smell of history and tradition, and it reminded Krista of the church her grandma had attended. Tomorrow, white flowers and matching bows would soften the edges of the wooden pews.

"Do you like weddings?" Tate murmured after the rehearsal as he escorted her down the aisle toward the lobby.

She felt slightly awkward with her forearm tucked through the crook of his arm. "I do." She almost laughed at her choice of words and glanced over to see if he noticed. His tanned face, blue jeans, and brown sweater made him look strong and outdoorsy. The dark shadow gracing his chin only added to his rugged appeal. He'd probably look even better in the suit he'd wear at the wedding service tomorrow. But seriously, why did she choose the words *I do* at a wedding?

"Does that mean we're married?"

He quirked an eyebrow in a charmingly irresistible way. Instantly, butterflies fluttered in her stomach, and she wished she could bat them all away and return to her normal, in-control self. "I hope not." She glanced over and laughed. The idea was so far-fetched it was funny.

"Whew." With his free hand, he wiped his brow. "You scared me for a minute."

"Aren't you already married? You have two beautiful daughters." She shouldn't pry but couldn't resist finding out more. Not that she was interested in a man right now.

"Nah."

His voice sounded almost wistful and trailed off like he might have a story he didn't want to share. She recognized the vague signs of weariness and disappointment she carried inside too. He must be divorced, and maybe he still felt the pain of the split.

"I'm a single dad. I take it you're unattached too?" His statement was more of a question.

"Definitely. Happily. But I love other people's weddings." After what she'd been through with Zach's continual barbs, she wouldn't open her heart to another man for a very long time, if ever. How could she find the energy? Did she have the confidence? How could she trust she wouldn't get hurt? Now, all she wanted…well, what did she want? She could use a break in her life, like intermission in a play, to regroup and find a new path. She needed a fresh start, plain and simple.

"Whoa. Slow down." He applied gentle pressure to her arm. "We're not supposed to sprint out of the church."

"Oh, right. Sorry." She inhaled a deep breath. She needed to remind herself to slow down and, as her grandma always said, smell the roses. Hurrying was a habit. She'd spent too many years racing from off-ice training to on-ice practice to coaching to performing.

They reached the end of the aisle, and Krista backed two steps away while the twins bounced over and threw their arms around Tate's hips.

The rest of the wedding party trickled into the lobby, chatting animatedly. Excitement about the big event buzzed throughout the crowded space.

"Meet my little darlins." Tate placed an arm on both girls' shoulders. "This is Ella." He tilted his head toward one of the identical pair. "And this is Gracie." He nodded to the other side.

Both girls grinned and showed off gaps from their missing front teeth.

"I'm very pleased to meet you. You look like expert flower girls." Krista smiled at their sweet faces. Tate must be very proud of them, understandably. A wistful pang flitted across her middle. She might never experience the joy of parenting.

"Thanks." Gracie bounced in place.

"How old are you?" They were so cute she wanted to hug them.

"Seven." Gracie held up her fingers.

Ella nodded.

"Amy told me you're a figure skater from Toronto." Tate glanced from his girls to Krista and back.

"True. I love skating." Krista spoke right to the girls.

"Ella and Gracie take skating lessons," he said.

"I'm going to be a champion." Grace grinned.

Her toothless smile would charm anyone, and her spunk would serve her well, no matter what she decided to do. "Awesome. That's a great goal." She flashed a thumbs-up. "What about you, Ella?"

"I want to win a gold medal like Gracie."

Ella didn't sound quite as confident as her twin, and Krista wondered if they were equally talented.

"I'm glad to hear that. Good luck to both of you." Krista scanned their eager faces, shining as smooth and bright as a fresh sheet of ice. "Keep practicing hard, and maybe I'll see you on TV someday."

"Really?" Gracie stared up and batted her dark eyelashes.

"Really." Krista nodded. Anything could happen, and she might as well keep the girls' dreams alive. They didn't need to know yet how hard they'd have to work, how reaching the podium was so difficult, and how competition judges could make or break their future.

"Can we go downstairs now?" Gracie blinked up at Tate.

Anybody could see how much the twins loved their dad, and no doubt the feeling was mutual.

"I s'pose so. But stay out of trouble." He shot them an exaggerated mock glare.

"Daddy." Gracie rolled her eyes.

She was obviously used to Tate's teasing.

"Don't get into the snacks until an adult says

okay," reminded Tate.

Gracie sighed. "We know. Right, Ella?"

Ella nodded and trailed her sister, who was already clattering down the stairwell to the reception hall below.

"So, you're a big-city woman?" Tate faced her.

"Only partly. I grew up a few hours' drive away from here. But after high school—that's where I met Amy—my mom shipped me off to Eastern Canada to train and compete. I'm still based there." Krista's stomach squeezed around the lump of shame and disappointment she continually worked to overcome. Failure and criticism could beat down a person.

"Do you coach?"

He focused on her like she was the only person in the room, even though the small space was crowded with the wedding party, and conversation hummed around them. "What did you have in mind?" Something about the glint of amusement in his eyes made her want to tease. "Do you want to take figure skating lessons?" She quirked an eyebrow and took great pleasure in seeing his quick grin.

"Thanks, but I'll pass. I played junior hockey back in the day." A sudden wistful expression flitted across his face. "But I followed my dad into the family business." He shrugged. "It was a long shot, but I shelved my chance to aim for the National Hockey League."

"Oh. I hope things worked out okay." A wash of empathy filled her chest. She knew the feeling of dreams squashed like a bug. His eyes, the color of chocolate syrup, held uncertainty and a touch of weariness.

7

"Yep. All's well." He paused. "Mostly."

"Oh, good." She paused and smiled. "Mostly." She examined the way his sudden stiff expression didn't exactly match his words. Underneath his good looks and light banter, Tate Harris held a bit of mystery.

****

The next evening at the wedding reception downstairs in the church hall, Tate gathered his courage and asked Krista to dance. These days, he didn't spend much time around women, except Mom and his sister, Carly, who didn't really count. Despite his outer confidence and bravado, he felt less sure on the inside. Major loss like he'd experienced could crush a person.

But now, he wanted to run his fingers through Krista's tumble of reddish curls. He struggled to tear his gaze away from her eyes shining as deep blue as a summer sky. And her slim shape, outlined in a satiny dress the color of raspberries… He hadn't felt a spark like this in years.

The room smelled faintly of perfume from the yellow, pink, and white flowers on round tables. White netting and fairy lights swooped along the cream-colored walls and transformed the basic room into a fancy wedding venue. Voices and laughter mixed with the music. He glanced around and recognized a lot of the crowd from here in his hometown. His best friend Matt, the groom, had grown up here too. Even though he had long since moved away, he and Amy had opted for a blast from his past for their celebration.

How many events had he attended in this very place? Weddings. Team fundraisers. Christmas parties. Funerals. Now, five years later, he remembered Whitney's memorial service with only a fleeting thickening in his throat. He'd worked hard to get past the devastating loss of his wife, his first and forever love.

"After you, ma'am." His timing could not have been better. With the varied playlist, he just happened to have suggested a dance and followed her to the center of the dance floor right in time for an old-fashioned waltz. His heart quickened as he set an arm gently on her waist and felt one of her hands on his arm and the other slip softly into his hand. They fit together like puzzle pieces. Their dance steps flowed. But why was he torturing himself this way? She lived on the other side of the country. She'd fly away tomorrow, and he'd never see her again.

"You know how to dance," she murmured.

"Are you surprised?" He inhaled a deep breath and another. Her hair smelled faintly like vanilla and lemon deliciousness. The room spun into a blur of color and lightness better than anything he'd felt in a long time.

Other couples swirled around them.

Gracie and Ella twirled in their fancy, light-pink flower-girl dresses.

"I thought hockey players were too rough and tough to dance well. She tipped her head back to glance at his expression.

"Are you hockist?" He smiled downward and met her gaze.

"Hockist is not a word. What do you mean?" She stifled a giggle.

"It's a person who prejudges a former hockey player.

"I see. My mistake. You are proving me wrong." She twirled in his arms.

"I'm not your average hockey player." Her hair brushed his cheek.

"Apparently not." She laughed softly.

He danced with her to another song and another and another, waving at Gracie and Ella and occasionally pausing to chat with other guests. He was enjoying this far too much. Not dating much, he hardly knew what he was missing. But now Krista reminded him. He'd like to get to know her better—a lot better.

Finally, he led her to a table and brought them cool drinks. "Do you teach skating to people who actually want lessons?" With all the hubbub and the busyness of the rehearsal party, he never got around to hearing her answer yesterday. He shifted his chair to almost face her and leaned forward so he could hear her answer over the blaring music.

"I'd like to get back into coaching. Right now, I perform in ice shows on cruise ships." She crossed her legs and tilted toward him.

"Oh! A star." He widened his eyes. "I'm in elite company."

She laughed and brushed a curl off her cheek. "I'm glad you think so. Now that I've visited every port in the Caribbean, the novelty is wearing off."

"Did you ever compete? Are you a champion?"

"I came close but just missed out on the medal part."

"An almost champion?" Maybe he should have just dropped the topic. Her voice suddenly tightened around the mention of her competitive record. "You could say so." Did he detect a bit of a wince? "Why not coach if it's really what you want to do?" He heard his own tone dissolve from teasing to serious.

"It's complicated." She sighed. "Maybe someday."

He sensed her heavy disappointment verging on bitterness. What was her story? Much as he wanted to know, now was not the time to nudge her for more details. He knew the pain of lost dreams and a lost relationship.

He studied her face and traced her firm expression. Was there a chance? Would she possibly consider a new opportunity? "Are you locked into a contract with the cruise line?" A rush of anticipation bodychecked him in the chest. Was she open to a dramatic life change?

"More like a standing offer from sailing to sailing. Why do you ask?"

The winter skating season started in two weeks, and the Blue Sky Figure Skating Club desperately needed a temporary coach to replace the one who decided at the last minute to extend her maternity leave. So far, they'd had no luck recruiting anybody. Most coaches wouldn't even consider a short-term position that would only last for this winter. Life in a small prairie town wasn't for most people either. But the club was desperate. Running on a shoestring budget, the local rink relied on revenue from the skating club and its major annual ice show to stay afloat.

He glanced at Krista. Her determination showed in her vivid blue eyes and the set of her sculpted jaw. If she could be convinced to accept a term job in Blue Sky, she could get back into coaching like she wanted. His little darlins would benefit. So would the rink. So would the whole town and surrounding rural area.

Janine Horner, the skating club president, would be more than a little impressed.

He cleared his throat. He could at least broach the topic. It never hurt to ask. "How do you feel about small town life?"

She widened her eyes. "Uh, I'm sure it's great…for other people."

"Blue Sky is bigger than a cruise ship." He held his breath and studied her face for any hint of encouragement. With her furrowed brow and tilted head, she looked slightly puzzled yet curious. He inhaled a deep breath. A country song blared in the background, and dancers two-stepped by. "Seriously, here's an idea…"

Chapter 2

Two weeks later, Krista Reynolds glided onto the ice surface of the Blue Sky skating rink. The way her legs trembled, she felt like a beginner instead of a full-fledged figure skating professional.

Since the wedding, when Tate broached the idea of becoming Blue Sky's temporary figure skating coach, her insides had whirled faster than a corkscrew spin. Within days, she had arranged a leave from the cruise ship cast, packed the essentials, and driven clear across Canada—all on a whim. She could practically hear Amy cheering her on all the way from her honeymoon in Jamaica. She'd make the most of her short stay over this one winter until spring and use the time for some serious soul-searching. After all she'd been through, she needed time, space, and something new.

Was it excitement, nervousness, or the combination making her feel so shaky? Inhaling deep breaths of cool rink air, she mustered her determination and warmed up with knee bends and swoops. The more she lapped the ice surface and focused on the skaters whizzing in all directions, the more her jelly legs steadied and gained strength. She could do this.

With her blades crackling over the ice, she curved and waved the entire group of skaters to cluster around her at center ice. Stopping with a spray of snow, she swiveled and watched the group skid into place. "Hi,

Ella. Hi, Gracie." She smiled at the pair, the first to slide to a stop. "Hello, everyone. You can call me Krista. I'm your new coach, and I'm happy to be here to help you become the best skaters you can be." They didn't need to know she wouldn't stay long. She came to dodge bad memories and regroup…just a stepping stone to…to where she didn't know.

Upbeat music floated through the chilly air and provided a background soundtrack for scratching blades and kids' voices. She spun twice and planted a toe pick to stop. Why were her knees so shaky? Determined to relax, she wiggled her legs to ease the tension. Accepting the challenge Tate had thrown out at the wedding better not be a big mistake.

Smiling, she swept her gaze across the skaters. Her job was to build skills and inspire future champions. From all reports, she had a tough act to follow. The parents and kids all loved their regular coach, Lauren, so filling her skates would not be easy.

Still, the club president, Janine Horner, had hinted Lauren was sometimes a bit too lax to help skaters reach their full potential.

No fear. Krista would not make the same mistake. She dropped her smile into a firm expression and pressed her gloved hands together. "Champion skaters never give up, and I want to see you have fun but work hard out here. No standing around chatting. No sitting on the benches. No slacking off. Does everyone understand?" She rotated and nodded, encouraging them to nod in return. She'd set clear ground rules right up front so the skaters knew she meant business.

Even though she wore her favorite green ski suit to keep her warm for hours of teaching, she shivered.

Glancing toward the sidelines, she spotted parents clustered in the stands and knew they would scrutinize every move she made. If they were like her mother, they would harbor high hopes for their children's skills and even higher expectations for the new coach to produce results. Did Tate feel the same? "Okay, everyone, time to get back to practice. I'll call you when it's your turn for your lesson. If you are seven, eight, or nine years old, please stay right here."

A semi-circle of Ella, Gracie, and four other fidgeting little girls stared from eager faces. "We are going to have fun and work hard so you can become really, really, really good skaters. First, I'd like to meet you." She swung her warm mitts together into a muffled clap. "Please tell me your name and what you like best about figure skating." Sweet little kids warmed her heart, and she could make a difference in their lives. She pointed at the girl at one end of the line. "Let's start with you."

Other skaters dipped and twirled by in a colorful blur on the busy ice surface.

She filled her lungs with rink air and took comfort from the familiar mix of smells from the ice plant, leather skates, and rubber mats.

"I'm Charlotte, and I like skating fast."

"I'm Natalie, and I like spins."

"I'm Zoe, and I love everything about skating."

"I'm Haley." She paused, stared at her skates, and shrugged.

"Hi, Haley." Krista gave the shy girl a reassuring smile. "You can tell me another time. Now, your turn, Gracie and Ella." She glanced at the others. "I met them at my friend's wedding."

"I'm the oldest." Gracie nodded and bounced her thick chestnut ponytail.

The girls were just as cute on the ice as they were dressed as flower girls. They wore matching purple skating skirts with cozy pink-and-white fleece jackets, and their toothless smiles were contagious. "What do you girls like best about skating?" Krista flipped her gaze between Gracie and Ella. Before they could answer, a flash of recognition jolted straight to her heart. She knew those wide eyes, so dark brown they verged on black and fringed with dark lashes. Soft yet determined, they reflected an unmistakable glint of mischief—just like the eyes of their handsome dad. Suddenly, she couldn't take a deep breath. But just as quickly, she scolded herself for thinking about Tate. Her short time here in Blue Sky was to find herself, not him. They could be friends but nothing more.

"I like to glide to music and do spirals," said Gracie, straightening to her full height.

Clearly the more extroverted of the two, she liked to take charge.

"Toe loops are my favorite." Ella flickered a smile.

Krista studied their expressions, and her chest squeezed hard and achy. If things had turned out differently, maybe she would have her own family by now. Falling under Zach's spell and letting him batter her confidence had been a huge mistake. But now…she didn't need to be squashed by his criticism anymore. She didn't need to let Mom's disapproval echo in her head. Now, she would stand firm on her own two skates and build the life she wanted, one step at a time.

"Wonderful. I can see you all love skating for different reasons. Now, let's get started." She scanned the girls' faces and made sure they all paid attention. "I'd like you to skate around the whole rink and listen to your feet. Try to make your skating quiet by pushing with the edges of your blades." She demonstrated a few silent strokes. No scratchy toe-pick noises." She scuffed her toes and made a scratching sound. "Ready, set, go." She pointed away from the center to the edge.

Krista traced the girls' paths around the ice while her thoughts spun to the past so fast they made her as dizzy as a layback spin. With a hefty push from her mother, she had moved away from the prairie city she grew up in and headed for bigger and better things in Toronto.

"Shoot for the moon, dear," Mom insisted. "You'll end up with the stars."

In Toronto, the smooth, sharp-featured skating judge named Zach had pulled her aside and crushed her dream of standing on the podium. Like a sharp skate blade, she could still feel his biting assessment of her artistry. Mom's overwhelming disappointment hurt almost as much.

Krista realized too late Zach was no kinder in everyday life than on a judging panel. Now, from a distance, she still couldn't believe she fell for his superficial charm and then had endured his daily criticism for far too long. Her insides still twisted with regret.

Gliding along the boards, she slid her gaze to the sidelines and raised her right hand in a small wave. She couldn't miss Tate's burning gaze, and she almost lost her balance at the fleeting sight of his broad shoulders, chocolate eyes, and handsome face. Her instant attraction hadn't faded one bit since the wedding, and alarmingly, it collided deep in her stomach with her usual common sense. Feelings would only complicate her mission here in Blue Sky.

****

The moment Tate set foot in the rink, he felt her presence. Pausing, he inhaled, and a rush of rink air jetted him back to his youth. His head filled with the timeless smells of damp air and lingering exhaust from the ice resurfacing machine, just like way back when he played countless hours of hockey. Every rink he'd ever been in smelled the same. The atmosphere reminded him of fun, carefree times in his growing-up years when life was rosy and full of promise.

Taking time to brace himself, he sauntered to the sidelines. He wanted to see Gracie's and Ella's progress, but they weren't the only thing that drew him to the edge of the ice surface. Usually, he sat with other parents in the stands, but right now, he leaned his forearms on the boards for a close-up view. Why he didn't keep his distance he couldn't explain, and he immediately regretted his decision to stand so close when she swept by like an autumn breeze, waved, and sent his heartbeats into a breakaway.

Trying to look calm and casual, he backed away from the boards to the safety of the passageway from the ice to the lobby and changerooms. From there, he could still see the rink, but he wasn't such an obvious spectator. Nobody could tell he was wound tighter than a pair of skates.

Shifting, he jammed his hands into his jacket pockets. Thanks to his spontaneous invitation and rink board approval, Krista was the new figure skating coach. He couldn't avoid her and didn't want to, even though romance was the furthest thing from his mind. They proved at Matt and Amy's wedding they got along, so he expected they could be friends. But he had no idea his mouth would dry and his pulse would rev into overdrive the instant he saw her. Even from a distance, he could tell she was as gorgeous today as she was as maid of honor at the wedding.

Following her movements, he shifted, rubbed his chin, and then forced his attention to Ella and Gracie. No sense torturing himself with temptation. His girls were his number one priority. He thanked his lucky stars he had family help in the years since he lost Whitney forever. A single dad had his hands full—way too full to think about a woman and risk his heart all over again.

This morning, Tate's parents delivered Ella and Gracie to the rink so he could squeeze in a few household chores and miscellaneous errands. Now he'd spend the rest of the day with his little darlins. At least, he wasn't exhausted like sometimes. His business, Snow & Grow, kept him plenty busy, but today's workload was manageable. He had finished fall cleanup at a bunch of locations around town and dumped leaves and branches at the town compost site.

"Hi, Daddy." Gracie bounced off the ice onto the rubber flooring. "I practiced crossovers, and I only fell twice."

Her spunk would carry her far in life if it didn't get her in trouble along the way. Loitering a few feet back from the opening in the boards and still riveted on the greenish blur swooping over the ice, he yanked his attention away and smiled at Gracie's flushed face. Her eager grin always warmed his heart.

"Only two falls? Good work." He flashed her a thumbs-up. "How was your skating time, Ella?" He made sure his quieter twin got a turn to report too. If he didn't ask, then she would happily fade into the background, but she deserved to be noticed too.

"Krista said we had to work hard, so I did." Ella wrinkled her forehead and wiped her nose with the back of her purple mitten.

He pulled a tissue from his pocket and handed it to her. "You darlins will soon be superstar skaters." Grinning, he squeezed their shoulders. "Now go ahead to the dressing room and take off your skates. I'll come help you in a minute." Pride rising in his chest, he watched them toddle down the hallway. No doubt about it. He loved them more than anything. They lit his lonely life. Rotating to follow his girls, he spotted Krista waiting to step off the ice.

Feet planted on solid ground, she froze less than six feet away and glanced sideways like she wanted to dash. She lowered her gaze to the rubber floor and back to his face. Did she feel the same trepidation he did? At the wedding, she liked him well enough. He was sure. But why her reaction now? He was the one who should fear getting involved. Losing her was inevitable. She only planned to stay six months.

He forced his shoulders back, even though they weighed so heavy they wanted to cave around his chest. He wasn't a carefree, young guy anymore. Painfully, he'd given up his hockey dreams to join the family business. Dad's multiple sclerosis really left him no choice. What kind of son wouldn't pitch in to help a disabled parent? Then he married Whitney and became a doting dad until her cancer destroyed his perfect life.

He'd grieved a devastating loss and moved on as best he could. But he wasn't about to knowingly invite more trouble into his life. Right now, he couldn't handle the upheaval. Definitely, he couldn't face another loss.

"Hello, Tate. How are you?" Krista smiled and held out her right hand.

He whipped off a mitt and shook her hand, which felt too formal when he had already held her close on the dance floor. He couldn't say for sure, but she might have flushed darker pink behind the rosy glow from the rink air. "Welcome to Blue Sky! I'm all right, thanks. And you?" He glanced over his shoulder and shuffled sideways out of earshot of the other parents trickling out of the stands. The truth was he was uncertain, nervous as heck, and still afraid of what her presence around town would mean. He forced himself to breathe.

"I'm fine, thanks." She shifted and met his gaze.

The tinny music from the rink hung in the space between them.

"Still adjusting to the minor shock of all that's happened in the last two weeks, but I'm excited." She flashed a smile. "Your girls are very cute, and they show a lot of potential."

He grinned and straightened. "Yeah, they're pretty special." His girls were a safe topic. He'd talk all day to anybody who'd listen about darn near anything to do with Ella and Gracie.

"You and their mom should be very proud."

"Uh...yeah... I sure am." At the mention of Whitney, he felt his throat dry, and he fumbled for the right words. When he ran into people he hadn't seen for a long time, he hated the way this kind of awkwardness always happened.

Krista must have assumed he was divorced. Truth be told, they had danced at the wedding more than they talked about much except skating. Bringing up his devastating loss was hardly a casual conversation topic. "Their mom...I should have explained...she, uh, passed away five years ago. The girls were only two at the time." He swallowed.

The cancer that stole his wife and the mother of his children was cruel and quick. He'd shed his share of tears over the whole heartbreaking situation, but he'd dealt with the pain, picked up the pieces of his life, and forged ahead. He had twins to raise and a business to run.

"Oh, I'm so sorry." Blinking, she rested her right hand over her heart. "I didn't know. I just assumed..."

Her smile dissolved into a stiff, somber expression, and he hurried to ease her discomfort. "It's okay." He meant it. Gracie, Ella, and he were thriving. The girls had been so young at the time they hardly knew what they were missing. His pain had gradually faded into acceptance. But life had left its mark. His heart had recovered but was nowhere near invincible yet.

Krista glanced past him toward the hallway. "I'm just on a short break, so I better excuse myself." She paused. "Nice to see you again."

He blinked and nearly choked on his heart pounding in his throat. "You, too." Maybe she said so just to be polite, but he meant it. Waving an arm to usher her ahead, he followed her down the hallway to catch up with his girls. Her ski suit hinted at her shapely body underneath. He forced his gaze to the mint-green walls, anything to distract him from the temptation. He needed to keep his distance. Attractive and nice as she was, he'd never welcome any woman into his life unless he was darn sure he could handle the ups and downs. Being friends might work, but nothing more.

Chapter 3

Finally, after a long day of coaching, Krista stepped off the ice exhausted, took a deep breath, and snapped on her skate guards. Suddenly dizzy, she straightened and gripped the boards until the rink stopped spinning.

Why had she allowed Tate to entice her into spending six months way too close to him in a town so small it was barely a dot on the map? She had known his daughters figure skated. Why hadn't she realized she couldn't avoid him, even if she wanted? Overcoming the past and heading in a new direction was much easier without a major distraction.

From the moment she had bumped into him after Gracie and Ella's lesson, she couldn't concentrate. Thanks to the wedding dance, she already knew how she fit into his arms and how good he smelled of fresh air and clean laundry. The skaters deserved her full attention, and she fought to keep her focus where it belonged. She really did. But images of Tate's wide smile and muscular arms kept elbowing their way over top of split jumps and sit spins.

After a full day of teaching skaters of all ages, she yearned for a long soak in a hot bathtub. Instead, she just had time to hurry home to her rented duplex, change into casual clothes, and freshen up. The club board had arranged a meet-and-greet gathering for the new head coach, and of course, it was a command performance.

"You've had a busy day." The club president, Janine, stopped in the hallway off the ice surface and greeted her with a smile.

Janine's clipped tone didn't hold much warmth, though. Her short hair, pointy features, and precise movements reminded Krista of a blackbird. "Busy but good."

"I'll see you back in the lounge here within an hour for the welcome reception." Janine glanced from Krista's feet to her face. "Don't worry if you don't have time for dinner. We ordered plenty of hot appetizers."

"I'm looking forward to meeting all the parents." Krista gathered her remaining energy and forced a smile. She did want to meet them all—eventually—and she'd make the best of this evening. When Janine interviewed her over the phone for the job, she made the coach's role crystal clear. She expected Krista to work wonders with the skaters and the ice show.

This evening's gathering was a chance to let parents know they could count on her to set the bar high and achieve results. Her breath caught in her throat. Parents included Tate Harris, so at least she'd know one familiar face in the crowd. "I'll see you again soon." She waved at Janine and beelined for her combination office and changeroom to remove her skates before she headed home.

Outside, a full moon lit her way as she crunched over stray dried leaves the two blocks to her place, conveniently located close to the rink. Pulling her scarf higher against the biting wind, she let her mind drift back to her short encounter with Tate Harris earlier today.

Their exchange had been pleasant enough, but a draft of awkwardness hung in the air—a touch cool like the temperature in the rink. This was real life now. It was nothing like dancing the night away at a romantic wedding reception. But at the thought of his tall stature and the hint of stubble on his handsome face, she felt a flutter inside. The same unsettling sensation had been coming and going for the past two weeks since they walked down the aisle together as maid of honor and best man.

She pulled out her house key and took a last breath of the clean, sharp air to clear her head of any trace of Tate. The teaching job in peaceful Blue Sky was supposed to be a manageable step toward her future, wherever it lay. For the next six months, she would focus on the skaters and the club. Her plans did not include getting involved with a man, even if he was nothing like Zach. How else could she protect her heart from more battering?

As she stepped inside, she felt the hug of inviting warm air, just what she needed. Flopping into an armchair, she gathered a deep breath and savored a brief reprieve from the flurry of activity at the rink, the uncomfortable role of newcomer, and the awkward encounter with Tate.

She scanned the cozy living room, furnished with hand-me-downs from local residents. She'd never have chosen an overstuffed floral sofa, but it gave the room a country-cottage feel, and she could add personal touches over time. The walls were freshly painted cream, awaiting her eclectic collection of artwork. Where not covered in pastel area rugs, the wood floors gleamed like her mother had just polished them. Although far from the sleek décor of her former condo in Toronto, she would be comfortable here encircled in the retro vibe. Anything beat a cruise ship stateroom the size of a closet.

She closed her eyes for a few seconds and, at the sound of the doorbell, jerked them wide. She wasn't expecting a visitor. Dragging herself to the door, she swung it open and faced a short woman stuffed into a blue parka and clutching a large pottery container.

"Hello, Krista." The woman grinned. "I thought you should meet your landlord."

"Come in." Krista waved her into the entranceway. "You must be Mrs. Nicol." Janine had arranged her accommodation on behalf of the rink board, so she hadn't spoken with the owner since she arrived in town yesterday.

"Call me Daisy. Mrs. Nicol was my mother-in-law, not me." She nodded and extended the steaming pot. "I brought you some of my homemade corn chowder to welcome you to your new home. It's one of the most popular soups on the menu at Daisy's Diner. I'm *that* Daisy. By the way, I live right next door, if you ever need anything."

"Thank you, Daisy. I'm pleased to meet you." She breathed the sweet, creamy aroma and felt a pleasant warmth creep into her chest. Small town life had its benefits. "Let me set the pot in the kitchen." Hurrying back to her guest, she caught her peering around the living room.

"I hope you'll be comfortable here. The furniture's not new, but it's comfy enough."

"I'm sure it will be just fine." Krista shifted. She

should be polite and invite Daisy in for tea, but she didn't have time to spare. "I'm sorry I can't..."

"I know you can't visit now." Daisy smiled, showing a crooked front tooth.

Her wiry silver hair poked under the edges of her woolen hat, the same royal-blue shade as her coat. In her vibrant garb, she'd show up in a snowstorm.

"You have a party to attend."

"You know about the reception at the rink?"

"Honey, I know everything that goes on in this town." She winked and chuckled. "You might as well tell me your secrets before I hear them at the lunch counter."

Krista forced a small laugh. Everyone knew everyone else's business in small towns, so Daisy was only half joking. Townsfolk would be curious about the new coach and what attracted her to Blue Sky. Well, they'd soon learn part of the truth. Believe it or not, she came to make a difference, plain and simple. Nobody would know she really needed the time to find inner peace and regroup.

"Make sure you reconnect with Tate Harris at the party." Chuckling, Daisy raised her eyebrows. "He's the most eligible bachelor in town. Come to think of it, he's the only bachelor your age in town. You won't find a kinder, more hardworking guy or a better dad. His looks don't hurt the eyes either."

"Reconnect?" Apparently, Daisy really did know everything that went on in this town.

"News travels. I heard you met at a wedding, and he recruited you." Daisy scrunched her pudgy cheeks into a grin. "How else would a professional skater from a cruise ship land in little ole Blue Sky? Now, take the opportunity to get to know that gentleman a lot better!"

"I'm not really looking for—"

"Oh, I've heard that line before. You're not in the market for a partner. But an attractive young woman like you should have a husband and kids."

Krista swallowed and shifted her gaze from Daisy's intense stare to her clunky boots. No use arguing. She'd never change the woman's mind, and she didn't have time to linger anyway. Glancing up again, she waited, wondering how she might end this surprise visit.

"Those two little cuties of his need a mother." Crinkling her eyes, Daisy rambled on.

Krista opened her mouth to protest and closed it again. The image of Tate's tall presence next to her at the rink raced in circles in her mind. Heat rose in her cheeks, and she hoped Daisy wouldn't notice.

"You don't have a cat, do you?" Daisy scanned the room.

"No, I…" Daisy's conversation jumped around like a grasshopper in the sun. Still, even though she tried to let go, she couldn't erase Tate from her thoughts. Her stomach spun like it skated on ice. Not only was he irresistibly handsome, he was a good person, if Daisy was any judge.

"Good." Daisy swept her gaze to Krista. "Not that I don't like cats. I have three of my own. It's just I'm looking for a good home for a lovely, gentle dog. She's a golden retriever named Pearl."

"A dog? Pearl?" Krista shook her head. Much as she loved dogs, she didn't need a pet any more than a man.

"The kids named her after their late grandma."

Daisy smiled. "She's two years old, house-trained, and everything. Trouble is the family's moving to a place without a yard in the city, so they can't take the dog. Maybe you could use a pet for company? A young woman living alone…you might like a furry companion." She studied Krista's expression.

"I love dogs, but my schedule's pretty full. I'd feel bad if I couldn't give the dog enough attention." Krista glanced at her watch. She appreciated the friendly welcome, but she really needed to get ready for the social at the rink.

"Won't you have free time during the day when the kids are in school?" Daisy tilted her head, her gaze never leaving Krista's face.

"But evenings and weekends…" Krista shifted and folded her arms. She would spend long stretches at the rink. How could she finish this conversation and usher Daisy gracefully out the door? "I, uh…"

"Pearl could go with you and roam around the rink." Daisy bobbed her head. "Where there's a will, there's a way."

"But I don't know if—" She'd leave town in six months. A dog would only tie her down.

"Think about it." Daisy reached for the doorknob. "You and Pearl would even match with that lovely copper hair of yours. If you decide you'll take her, then I'll get permission from the rink board to give her access any time you like." She smiled. "I have a bit of an in there, you know. Janine's my daughter. And my late husband's estate—bless his heart—endowed the town with enough cash to pay for a good chunk of the rink. You just say the word, and I'll take care of everything."

"Oh." Krista swallowed and pursed her mouth in a small circle. What else could she say and not promote more conversation? Big as her heart was, Daisy didn't easily take *no* for an answer.

"Well, I really must go." Daisy turned, paused, and glanced back over her shoulder. "I'm sure I'll see you again soon, neighbor. She grinned and crinkled her intense eyes.

Now that Krista knew Daisy was Janine's mom, she could see a faint resemblance. But Daisy was a warmer, rounder, softer version of her daughter. "Of course." Krista hugged her arms tighter around her middle. What had she gotten herself into?

"Hmmm. Okay, stop by the diner next week, and we can have a longer chat." Daisy opened the door.

A chilly blast whooshed in.

"Ta-ta, honey." Daisy stepped outside.

"Thank you so much for the soup." Krista pressed the door shut behind her, spun, and leaned on the wall. For sure, she would never need to worry about making conversation when her path crossed with Daisy's.

Now slightly rushed, she slid into skinny jeans and a teal sweater and glanced at her reflection in the bathroom mirror. At this point, she couldn't do a thing to tame her stubborn curls squiggling to her shoulders. She'd long ago quit trying to disguise the dusting of freckles across her nose and cheeks. With a dash of lip gloss, she was ready for her first Blue Sky social event.

Striding back to the rink, she replayed Daisy's running commentary. She whooshed a cloud of air into the cold and hunched her shoulders. Right now, she needed to focus her attention on the challenge she had accepted—to teach budding champion skaters and lead a successful ice show to help keep the rink afloat. Simple. She wouldn't complicate matters by getting involved with a man or a dog.

Lit by old-fashioned streetlights on tall posts, the street lay quiet. Tidy homes in assorted colors lined her route. She glanced up at the bare tree branches arched in a spindly canopy over the sidewalk. Her chest filled with an odd combination of unsettled and comfortable here away from the charged atmosphere of big cities and cruise ships.

Crossing the parking lot toward the entrance, she shivered, not so much at the weather but at the crowd awaiting her arrival, even though Janine had assured her they were a mostly congenial bunch. Nearly all the parents would be there, anxious to meet the new coach. She and Tate Harris already knew each other, so would he attend or skip? If he didn't show up, then at least she could avoid any awkwardness.

She squeezed her cold fingers inside her mitts. As long as no one criticized her inaugural day of coaching, she'd be just fine handling the many introductions and small talk. If asked why she came to such a small town, she'd offer an honest but suitably vague explanation. She was ready to give up performing for coaching. Nobody needed to know about the degrading relationship and exhausting lifestyle she left behind.

At the door, she paused, heartbeat tapping from the brisk walk. She refused to admit her feelings had anything to do with who she might see inside. Her skittish heart had no business reacting to the very thought of Tate Harris.

****

"Now scoot and get your pajamas on." After the

twins' evening bath, Tate pulled the plug on a tubful of bubbles and bent to mop up the puddles on the bathroom floor. The blue-and-white tile and matching blue fixtures filled the room with a 1960s vibe. Renovating was on his long to-do list, far behind being a good dad and keeping his customers happy.

Straightening, he glanced in the mirror. He'd shaved while watching the girls slosh in the tub. He ran the back of a hand along the smooth skin of his jaw. Now, he'd just change his shirt to be presentable for the reception at the rink.

"See my cape, Daddy." Gracie clutched a navy-blue towel around her shoulders. "I'll fly to my room."

With her towel wrapped around and tucked neatly under her arms, Ella backed out of the room. "I love my new skating teacher. She's bluuu-tiful."

"You mean beautiful." Gracie spun to face her sister.

"Isn't she, Daddy?" Ella stared at Tate. "Krista's the prettiest teacher I've ever seen. And she's sort of nice too."

"You mean when she smiles?" Grace demonstrated a wide grin.

Tate sat back on his heels and chuckled. "I'm glad you like her. And sometimes, teachers need to be firm and not smile so kids work hard and learn more." He agreed with his daughter's assessment of Krista's attractiveness, but he wasn't about to admit it. "Hey, I asked you two to get into your pajamas. Hurry! Grandma and Grandpa will be here soon." He pulled himself up and chased them to their bedroom.

Returning to the bathroom, he surveyed the chaos the girls left behind. He shook his head and rotated his stiff shoulders. Inside and outside, he always found plenty of chores to consume his energy. Right about now, he'd gladly read a few stories, tuck in his darlins, and flip TV channels. He'd happily skip tonight's social at the rink if…if he wouldn't be conspicuous by his absence. He'd do anything for the sake of his girls. Then again, the slight surge tickling his chest told him his motive for attending might extend beyond the interests of Gracie and Ella.

"Ready, Daddy." Ella zipped into the doorway behind him. "I beat Gracie."

"Put her there, princess." He held up a hand for a high-five.

Gracie zoomed into view beside her sister. "Ella pushed me out of the way."

He ignored her whine and held up his other hand to high-five her as well. "You were both speedy." Cozy in matching flannel pajamas dotted with pink and yellow flowers, they looked so sweet and innocent he swept them into a group hug on the spot. "You can choose two stories each."

Smiling at their continuous banter in the background, he hung towels and tidied the last of the mess. He wouldn't trade his busy life as a dad for a minute. Swallowing, he straightened and allowed a brief wistful memory to flit by. With support from a bereavement group and the healing power of time, he had mustered strength and overcome his raw grief. These days, he rarely thought of how life might be better if he had a wife and his girls had a mother. "I'll be right there to read."

A prickle of annoyance and regret rolled across his chest. Krista's appearance on the scene reminded him what he was missing, and he didn't like the feeling. He inhaled a deep breath and yanked himself back to the present and away from the memories threatening to drag him down. He threw on a clean plaid shirt and strode to the kitchen to slice apples for a bedtime snack.

Glancing out the window at the deserted street illuminated by wide circles of light, he expected to see Mom trudging beside Dad toward the house from their place on the next block over. He glanced at the clock. When they knew they had the chance to see their precious grandchildren, they usually arrived early.

Just then the phone rang, and as he answered, he spotted his parents' number on Call Display. "Hi, Mom."

"It's Dad." His deep voice rumbled, and he cleared his throat. "Sorry we're late. Your mom came down with one of her migraines. She insisted she could fight it off well enough to babysit, but I just sent her to bed."

"Oh, okay." Spirits sinking, Tate grimaced. Now that he was dressed and ready, he looked forward to the party and seeing Krista again more than he'd admit. "Stay put and keep Mom company. I don't have to go out tonight."

"Of course, you do." Dad delivered a no-nonsense answer. "I'll wheel my way over in a few minutes." Cole Harris had used a wheelchair for a few years since his multiple sclerosis attacked his legs, but he never felt sorry for himself for a minute and didn't let using a chair stop him.

Fifteen years ago, the chronic disease was already interfering with Dad's mobility, so Tate knew his place was behind a lawn mower and snowplow, not at the end of a hockey stick. His future belonged in Blue Sky, supporting Dad and the family business. Family did those things for each other. "Thanks, Dad. The ramp out front is clear." Tate hung up phone and strode to the living room. "Girls, come to the window and watch for Grandpa."

True to his word, a few minutes later, Dad arrived and brushed dirt off the wheels of his chair in the entrance way. "How are my favorite seven-year-olds?" He threw an arm around them on either side of his chair.

Gracie hopped onto one of his knees.

Ella climbed onto the other. "Will you please read us stories?"

"If your dad says I can."

"Two stories each and then off to bed. Understand?"

"Yes, Daddy." Gracie twirled a lock of hair around a finger.

"Yes, Daddy." Ella rubbed Grandpa's arm.

"C'mon give me a hug. I'll see you in the morning." He squatted and swooped them into a bear hug. He was lucky. When he needed a sitter, he could almost always count on Mom and Dad or Carly. Finally, he was free to pull on his parka and catch up to the party about an hour late. As he jogged the few blocks to the rink, he scanned the yards he looked after. They were tidy and well kept, just the way he wanted. Satisfied customers, large and small, were the heart of his successful business.

Face tingling from the evening chill, he paused just inside the rink doorway to catch his breath. The smell of melted cheese and spicy chicken wafted from the appetizers at the party. Already, he could hear the buzz of conversation and laughter floating down the hallway.

An instant, strange combination of nervousness and anticipation collided like a couple of hockey players inside his belly. He'd soon see Krista, and she would be the center of attention. Mouth drying, he headed for the activity room with several long strides. Would she avoid him or strike up a conversation? Did he want to keep her at a distance or pursue a casual friendship? He had no idea.

Taking a deep breath, he stepped into the wood-panelled room and felt the heat from a gas fireplace at the far end. The sudden coziness and glowing light reminded him of a ski lodge. After hanging his jacket, he paused and scanned the crowd of fifty people, chatting and laughing. He recognized almost everyone. A couple of people raised a hand in greeting, and he nodded and lifted a palm in return. Then his breath got all jumbled in his chest.

On the opposite end, in the flickering light of the fire, Krista smiled and gestured in a circle of women. When she nodded, she bounced her curls around her shoulders. He liked the way they glowed as orange as the flames behind her. For an instant, he made eye contact before she turned to the woman on her right.

The back of his neck tingled, and a fierce tug-of-war erupted in his chest. He needed to move closer. He better stay away. She had barely acknowledged him. He wouldn't give her the choice. Could he make her smile at one of his quips? Should he risk rejection? Despite his own best advice to steer clear, he took a tentative step in her direction.

Distracted by whole scene, Tate didn't see his buddy until Brett slapped him on the back. "Thought you decided to pass."

"Nah. My sitter ran late." He shifted and watched people slide in and out of the group around Krista. Everyone wanted to introduce themselves to the new coach.

"I saw you met her at the rink." Brett chuckled and tapped Tate's upper arm with a fist.

"Re-met. She was the maid of honor at Matt and Amy's wedding. I convinced her to come."

"Very convenient. Maybe it's time you ventured back into dating?"

"Nah." The trouble with a friend like Brett who he'd known since elementary school was he felt qualified to give unwanted advice. Tate shifted, shoved his hands in his jeans pockets, and straightened his stiff shoulders. "Have you introduced yourself yet?"

"I'll wait until the crowd clears." Brett ran a hand over his balding head. "She's definitely the center of attention tonight."

"No kidding." He pulled his attention back to Brett. "Hey, catch you later. I could use a hot apple cider." The beverage station sat at the side of the room, closer to Krista.

"Gotcha." Brett grinned. "You've got more important people to talk to." He glanced in Krista's direction.

Tate chuckled and headed toward the refreshments.

Krista looked at her watch, excused herself from the group, and wove away in the opposite direction.

Was she avoiding him or just mingling with the other parents? He paused and sipped the hot beverage. After he'd moved past the pain of bereavement, he'd dated once or twice, but his interest soon fizzled. His life was just too full of work and parenting to make the effort...until Krista appeared. What was wrong with his head? He needed to protect his heart from yet another loss, so why did he feel a push as strong as his front-end loader?

Maybe they could become friends. Against his better judgment, he circled the room while she rotated just out of reach. He inched closer, saying "hello" and shaking hands along the way. She was so close but so far. Hopes fading, he paused and watched.

Janine cupped Krista's elbow and murmured in her ear.

Krista nodded and straightened without a glance his way.

Her face appeared slightly flushed, possibly because of the warmth of the fireplace or the crowded room. Were Janine's words unsettling, or did Krista sense he was heading her way? Heat like a flame burned in his chest. He needed cool water instead of his hot drink. He should backtrack and chat with Ian from the town council since they were one of his largest clients. Instead, he gave him a quick nod and concentrated on Krista.

"Could I have your attention, please?" Janine's scratchy voice rose above the din, and she gave three sharp claps.

Nobody messed with Janine. She liked being in charge and made sure everyone knew it.

The crowd quietened.

Tate edged backward to give Janine and Krista some space.

"Thank you all for joining us this evening." Janine smiled and swept her gaze across the room. "In case you haven't met our new head coach yet, I'm very pleased to introduce Krista Reynolds. As you might know, she has spent a number of years competing, coaching, and performing, so she comes to us very well qualified direct from a cruise ship." Gesturing toward Krista, she led the applause.

Krista's resumé sounded impressive all right. No wonder she set her sights far beyond this small town. He sighed. Life might not be exciting here, but it was satisfying in its own way.

"I'll invite Krista to say a few words in a moment, but first, I want to remind you the Winter Wonderland Ice Show is only twelve weeks away. To make the show a success and live up to our tradition, we need all of you to volunteer to help in some way. Remember, the rink depends on revenue from this event. And the town depends on the rink. So, please put your name on the sign-up sheet by the door, or Krista and I will pester you until you do." Janine pinched her face into an exaggerated wince.

Krista half smiled and widened her eyes.

The crowd chuckled.

Then Janine pointed at the coach. "But I know Krista is the person you really want to hear from, so let's welcome her." She clapped and started another loud round of applause.

Krista smiled, and the flush on her cheekbones deepened a shade. "Hello, everyone. I'm not one to make long speeches, so I'll just say how much I appreciate the opportunity to work with your children and help them reach their full potential. Skating is my passion and my first priority. I came to Blue Sky to lay the groundwork for future champions and coordinate a first-class ice show." She scanned the room and landed her gaze squarely on Tate. "I promise I won't let anything detract from those goals."

Tate bowed his head and jammed his hands into his pockets. Did she mean even friendship? Her message felt like a firm slap on the cheek. She might as well have told him to back off and leave her alone.

"Thank you for the warm welcome and enjoy the rest of the evening." Krista tucked a wayward curl behind her ear and launched into a conversation with a group of women.

She didn't give a second glance his way. Clenching his jaw, he spun and headed for the coat rack. Suddenly, he was very tired—way too tired to hang around waiting for his turn to talk to a woman who wasn't interested.

Chapter 4

The next day, Tate's chest still smarted from Krista' snub last evening. In his truck, on the way to Carly's place for a family brunch, he struggled to focus. But pretty soon, his little darlins snatched his attention to the present, exactly where it belonged.

Within minutes, they arrived at Carly's. In the doorway of her modest two-story home, Gracie and Ella held his hands and jiggled, one on each side.

"What a pair of wiggle worms." Tate grinned down at their impish little faces.

At the same time, his lookalike sister smiled a welcome.

"Where's Sam?" Gracie peered at her aunt.

Both girls loved their slightly older cousin. For a time, Tate had hoped his nephew might turn into a hockey player like him, but Sam was the studious type with round glasses and a slight build. He was happy with books and science experiments.

"He's helping Uncle Will set the table." Carly waved them inside. "Come and warm up. Grandma and Grandpa are here already."

"Oh goody." Ella slipped out of her coat, handed it to Tate, and scooted into the living room. "Hey, Grandpa, can I ride on your knee?"

Grandpa Cole wrinkled his brow. "I guess so. Good thing I have two knees. C'mon, hang on tight, and I'll give you a lift." He wheeled his chair in a circle around the room.

"Hi, girls. Hey, slow down, Grandpa, before you break something." Mom held up both hands.

Within a few minutes, they were all seated around Carly and Will's large wooden dining table. The worn wood floor and deep beige walls encircled them with a cozy atmosphere that chased away the autumn chill.

"How do you like your new skating teacher?" Carly passed a casserole of eggs, ham, and cheese.

"Krista's her name. She's pretty, and she's a really good teacher." Gracie grinned and helped herself to a slice of orange.

Ella nodded, her mouth too full of toast to speak.

Inhaling the savory scent of bacon and eggs, Tate felt Mom's and Carly's stares. Even though he resisted, he couldn't stop their attempts at matchmaking. They never gave up. He steeled himself for the pressure he knew would come.

"What do you think, Tate?" Will gulped his coffee. "Hey, I heard she might be single." He raised his eyebrows and drilled his gaze into Tate.

Tate glanced over at his brother-in-law's round face and toothy grin. He was a good guy, but Tate didn't appreciate his teasing right now. "She'll do fine as a coach." Ignoring the pointed reference to her marital status, Tate stabbed a bite of egg and searched for a way to change the subject. "She and Janine are looking for volunteers for the ice show. I didn't sign up, because I'm not sure how I'd fit in another job between work and time with these two." He gripped his fork as tightly as a shovel.

They could be friends. Nothing else. Even that was

questionable. The pilot light inside him had surged into a flame the moment Krista whizzed by him on the ice. He'd find it tough enough to keep things at the friend level at the rink, let alone working with her on the ice show. She'd signalled she intended to keep her distance. Deep down, he knew her decision was smart. If he needed a woman at all, he wanted someone who would stick around for the long haul and not somebody who would leave come springtime.

"You know best." Mom reached behind Dad and squeezed Tate's shoulder. "But you might like to get out and socialize with the other parents. You know we'll always take care of our sweet granddaughters."

He didn't need to worry a bit about the kids eavesdropping on the adults' conversation. They chattered like cheeky squirrels at their own end of the table, goofing around and oblivious to anyone but each other. "Thanks, Mom." Tate swiped his chin with a napkin. "You and Dad and you two"—he glanced from Will to Carly—"give me too much help already. I couldn't manage without you." Carly generously offered before-and-after-school care and refused payment. She genuinely loved her nieces like her own and made them feel almost like younger sisters to eight-year-old Sam. The kids even teased and argued like siblings.

"Yeah, you owe me big time." Lifting her coffee mug, Carly laughed and wrinkled her nose. "Of course, mowing our lawn all summer and plowing snow out of our driveway all winter makes a pretty fair trade." She pursed her lips and stretched them sideways. "But Mom's right. You could use a little social life now and then."

Here we go again...the dreaded talk about life balance. Tate had heard it all before. Carly had even set him up with her next-door neighbor, but he'd run out of conversation after five minutes. She was nice enough but nobody special and nowhere near as attractive as Krista. But why was he thinking about her again? Chest tightening, he swallowed. He'd socialize when he felt like it, not when his well-meaning but overly persistent older sister decided he should.

"I know, I know. You might have mentioned once or twice I should have a little more fun but—" Tate threw up both hands with open palms to call a truce. When he saw the impish expression on Carly's face, he opened his mouth and clamped it shut. He'd learned a long time ago she knew how to provoke a reaction, and there was no point arguing.

"Gracie spilled." Sam shouted and burst off his chair out of the way of a fountain of orange juice streaming off the table from Gracie's tipped glass.

"I'm sorry." Gracie frowned. "I didn't mean to."

"Don't worry, sweetheart." Carly pushed back from the table and dashed to the kitchen for a cloth. "We'll clean up in no time."

"You almost got me wet." Sam grinned and poked Gracie's arm.

"She splashed me." Ella pointed to a blotch of orange on her sleeve.

"Oopsie, doopsie, daisy." Gracie hid a smile with a grimace.

Tate blotted the pool on the table with a napkin. Normally, he might have admonished his lively daughter for fooling around at the table until she caused a mess. Today, he could have hugged her for grabbing

45

the attention away from his social life. "Better slow down and be careful, darlin."

Returning with a damp cloth, Carly wiped away the mess.

Good. Carly dropped the topic of his social life. "What say we take this crew to the playground this afternoon?" Tate raised his voice over the clamor at the kids' end of the table and glanced at Will and then the trio. Household chores could wait, and he might as well enjoy playtime outside before a big snowfall hit. The weather forecast predicted clear skies for the next couple of days, but in late October to early November, you never knew for sure. By next weekend, he could be up to his knees in snow, which meant nonstop work.

"I don't think they'd want to go and have fun at the playground." Will's eyes twinkled as he downed the last of his coffee.

"Yes, we do." Ella clapped and bounced in her chair.

"Dad…" Sam bumped the table with both fists.

"Uncle Will, I love the slide and swings." Gracie jiggled and caught her glass before it tipped again.

"I guess we better take them then." Will shrugged.

Tate laughed. "Let's clear the table, and then maybe the women will give us a pass on dishes."

"Hmmm. Just like when you were little." Carly stood and placed her hands on her hips. "Always finding a way to skip out of dishes."

Mom shook her head and clucked her tongue. "I remember. But I recall his older sister wasn't much better."

"Ha. Gotcha there." Tate smirked over a pile of plates.

"Mom, he's bugging me." Carly laughed and faked a whiny tone. "Leave me alone, little brother."

"Never." A wave of affection washed over Tate. His family might push too hard with opinions and advice once in a while, but they meant well. He was lucky to have such a loving circle around him. Overcome with gratitude, he set down the plates and slung an arm around Carly's and Mom's shoulders and pulled them close.

"He does love me." Carly tickled his side until he released her.

"Sort of." Then balancing a full load of sticky plates, he shuffled to the kitchen.

"Let's go, Daddy." In the kitchen, Ella and Grace tugged on the back pockets of his jeans.

"Thanks for brunch, sis. Your cooking was better than usual." Tate waited for Carly to react to his teasing and ducked out of reach to avoid her playful swat on his arm. Then he gave his girls a pointed look to remind them of their manners.

"Thank you, Auntie Carly." Chorusing their thanks, they hugged her around the hips, then hugged Grandma and Grandpa goodbye too.

"Bet I can get my jacket on before you." Ella zipped her jacket and yanked on her hat. "I won."

"It's a tie." Gracie straightened. "We both beat Daddy."

Tate gave a final wave. "We'll go home and change into warmer clothes. Then we'll meet Will and Sam at the playground in the school yard." On the short drive home, Tate passed Daisy's Diner and spotted a woman stepping outside the doorway.

"Hey, I see Krista." Gracie tapped on the car

window. She and Ella both waved.

Krista raised a hand.

Glancing sideways, he smiled at the sight of her shapely body and her springy hair blowing in all directions. Instantly, his pulse tripped. Like it or not, in a place this size, he couldn't avoid her. Inevitably, they'd bump into each other at the rink and around town. Dating was out of the question, but he could be her friend, couldn't he? No strings attached. No complications of romance. No fears of painful loss. Just friends.

****

After an early lunch at Daisy's Diner, Krista escaped the curious glances and murmurs about the newcomer in town. A few patrons stopped by her stool at the lunch counter to introduce themselves and welcome her, but others hung back, examining her as she savored the vegetable quiche. With both feet planted to keep the stool from swivelling, she jiggled a leg. An unfamiliar mix of comfort and uncertainty stirred inside her. She'd meet all the locals in time. For now, they could wait and wonder what the new coach in town would bring to the figure skating club.

Outside the sharp, brisk wind caught her breath, and she braced herself to walk several blocks to the rink for afternoon lessons. Glancing at the street, she waved at a passenger in a passing vehicle, even though she wasn't sure who it was. Small-town people were friendly that way.

Charging along the empty sidewalk, she passed a bakery, gift shop, florist, and hardware store. The colorful storefronts all displayed welcome signs in the windows. At the end of the block, a small grocery store advertised the weekly specials. Unlike the big city, the local businesses closed on Sunday, so she'd need to stock up on groceries tomorrow.

The air smelled like autumn with a trace of smoke from someone burning crisp leaves or dry stubble in a field. As she approached the rink, she felt her cheeks tingle from the chilly air and a touch of embarrassment. She hadn't intended to avoid Tate at the meet-the-coach reception at the rink. True, she wouldn't get involved with him—or anyone—in the six months she'd stay here, but she hadn't intended to appear rude. She just needed to prove to the board and parents she was dedicated.

Last evening, scanning the crowded lounge as she spoke, she had spotted Tate just as she assured the crowd she would make coaching her top priority. Regret twirled through her stomach the moment she saw his focused, hopeful expression crumble into disappointment. Even in the subdued lighting, she could see he had shaved, and his caramel-and-brown plaid shirt flattered his deep complexion. When she encountered him at the rink, she couldn't deny her instant attraction, but she also knew spending too much time in his company would be a tempting and dangerous distraction. They could be friends but nothing more. Still, she hadn't intended to reject him in public with her accidental eye contact. When she saw him bow his head and step back like he'd been pushed, she felt her throat squeeze.

She ended her short remarks and briefly considered reversing the damage by approaching him with a comment about his talented daughters. But before she could gracefully excuse herself from a conversation with Janine, she spotted him bolting for the door without pausing over the sign-up sheet. Apparently, he wasn't an eager volunteer for the ice show.

"You made a good first impression." Janine had tapped Krista's shoulder.

Dressed in black pants and white sweater, Janine wore color choices that somehow suited her personality. Krista already knew she had precise opinions about everything.

"I like your attitude. We need tough standards to help our skaters win, and the rink badly needs revenue." She shook her head. "Our regular coach was way too soft, and the results show." She clicked her tongue. "By the way, Tate Harris just left. Since you met at the wedding a couple of weeks ago, I presume you know he's the dad of those talented little twins."

"Yes, I know. I intend to bring out the best in all my students." Did Krista imagine Janine's probing gaze examined her reaction to the mention of Tate? Could Janine sense an attraction, even from a distance? She hoped the flush in her cheeks didn't show. She didn't want anyone to get the wrong idea. She would focus on the job above all else.

Inhaling a deep, crisp breath, she stopped her rehash of last evening. It just unsettled her, and she had more important things to worry about. Within minutes, she reached the rink, and excitement glimmered in her middle. Over the next six months, she'd lay the groundwork for future champions. She'd coordinate a sold-out ice show. Her experience performing on cruise ships would come in very handy. Maybe by springtime, her former life would be a distant memory, and she would know where to head next.

Inside her office changeroom, she laced her skates, then hurried to the ice and motioned the advanced group of skaters to gather round. "You have talent, but you need to work harder." She drew in a deep breath of the familiar scent of rink air. Placing her hands on her hips, she made eye contact one by one. "When you fall on a jump, get up and try it again. Quitters don't turn into winners. Ready? Let's see you all practice your double jumps."

Later, during a private lesson, Olivia, one of the teenage girls, glided backward to the rink boards and leaned both elbows on the edge behind. "My tailbone hurts. I'm tired of falling on my double loop jump. Lauren let me quit after five tries."

"I'm not Lauren." Krista swung an arm to motion Olivia better get moving. She wouldn't allow the skaters to slack off like her predecessor. "Try again and pull your arms in close to your chest this time."

Music floated above, and other skaters whizzed around the rink in a colorful blur.

"My mom's the president, you know." Olivia rocked forward onto her toe picks.

She had her mom's dark hair, but hers was long and swept back into a ponytail. Dark eyeliner framed her piercing brown eyes, and she wore gray leggings and a magenta sweater. If she softened her makeup and her facial expression, she would be pretty. The sharp toss of her head and her defiant smirk weren't flattering at all.

"I know. She wants me to help every skater improve as much as possible." Clearly, Janine had high hopes for her daughter with her sights set on a medal at the spring provincial competition. Likely neither of them had any idea how hard Olivia would need to work to achieve her goal. Early indications were Olivia didn't share her mom's drive, but time would tell. Krista would work hard to motivate the girl and help her believe in herself. "Your mom hired me to build top skaters, and success starts with a strong work ethic. Champions never give up." She gave Olivia a scant smile. "Now, let's go."

Olivia huffed and skated away.

Krista blinked and pressed her lips together. Unlike Olivia, she had always wanted to do her best. She didn't mind hard work. In fact, she actually enjoyed it. With her mother's relentless prodding, she set her sights on a national medal...until... Krista shook away the bitter memories and glared at Olivia.

Frowning, Olivia gave an extra thrust, swept up her arms, and landed the double loop.

Krista caught a hint of a smile but wasn't surprised it didn't last.

Olivia turned away and then circled back. She stopped in front of Krista with a spray of ice.

"See." Krista tapped Olivia's arm. "You can do it. Believe in yourself."

"Yeah, I guess so." Olivia tossed her ponytail.

Krista nodded, and a rush of satisfaction warmed her chilly limbs. Sooner or later, she would learn to follow her own advice. Criticism, unlike constructive feedback, had a way of wearing a person down, but she could overcome the hits to her confidence from Mom and, worst of all, Zach. Maybe this winter in Blue Sky doing something she loved would help.

The rest of the afternoon of lessons and practice sessions flew by. Some of the girls and the single boy in the group exhibited a bit of attitude and resisted her techniques, but she'd stand firm and win them over before long.

After five hours of steady coaching, she plunked onto the bench in her office changeroom. The ice resurfacing machine hummed in the background, and the murmur of skaters' voices and laughter drifted down the hallway. Now, she could relax and regroup after a busy day.

She scanned her surroundings and sized up the basic black desk and unadorned cement block walls painted mint green to match the rest of the rink's color scheme. The black rubber flooring protected it from skate blades. Four black chairs on rollers rounded out the furniture, just enough that she could hold private meetings with skaters and parents. How convenient green was her favorite color because she'd see a lot of this place for the next six months. By then, she'd know where her future lay.

Outside the window, the wind whipped loose dirt and stray leaves across the parking lot. Winter would arrive soon and then Christmas followed by the ice show. She whooshed a deep breath. The next few weeks would be jam-packed with activity. Tired but encouraged by the potential she spotted in several skaters, she unlaced her skates and gathered her remaining energy. She'd hurry home and warm Daisy's homemade chowder for dinner. Shivering, she pulled on a woolen hat for the brisk walk.

"Bye, Krista." In the hallway, several skaters smiled and waved.

"See you tomorrow." She nodded and raised a hand. After a good rest tonight, she'd look forward to the next session.

In the hallway, Janine flagged her down with a grumpy-faced Olivia beside her. "Do you have a minute?"

"Sure." Janine likely observed the interaction between Krista and Olivia, and maybe she wasn't impressed. Krista steeled herself for feedback and hoped Janine would stand behind her. "You caught me just in time." She twisted to view Janine's birdlike features. She resembled her mother, Daisy, with her fast-paced speech and movements.

"I reviewed the list of volunteers who signed up last evening, and we're short in a few areas." Not responding to Olivia's impatient huff, Janine waved a piece of paper. "We need to get to work now because we have a lot to do, and Christmas always interrupts things."

"I agree." Krista stopped and faced Janine. From past experience, she knew local ice shows demanded hundreds of volunteer hours.

"So I was thinking…" Janine clutched the paper so hard it wrinkled. "We'll divide up the list and recruit more volunteers. You take *A* to *M*, and I'll take *N* to *Z*. This is your copy. Beside each name, I noted which committee I thought would be the best fit."

"Uh, sure." Krista stiffened and forced a smile. Janine was in charge and definitely a hands-on club president. She might be hard to please. "Whatever you need. I'm in."

"Good. I thought you wouldn't mind." Janine hurried to the door where Olivia waited glowering and tapping her foot. "I better get this girl home for a late supper."

Striding toward home and reflecting on the day, Krista made a mental note to check her email for Janine's request. As she clomped up the front steps, she felt a sudden realization hit her as hard as the wind. *H* for Harris—Tate Harris—landed smack-dab in the middle of her half of the phoning list. Like it or not, she'd just committed to call him. Her stomach rose and fell like a double jump. What would happen when he answered his phone and heard her voice? She was the coach. He was a parent. The call would be all business and nothing more.

Chapter 5

At home, Krista turned up the heat and changed into thick black leggings and a zip-up sweater. After so many hours on the ice, she finally felt deliciously warm again. She'd eat a bowl of Daisy's hearty chowder and decide whether to start the calls to recruit volunteers this evening or tomorrow morning. She didn't mind the job, except for one particular name on her list. Thinking about the *H* names, including Tate Harris, jostled her stomach into a nervous flutter, which was not helpful at all.

The kitchen in her new home was compact but cheery with its cream walls, white cabinets, and pastel polka-dot curtains. As she stirred the soup on the stove and inhaled the rich buttery scent, she heard her phone ring in her pocket. After a glance at Call Display, she answered. "Hi, Mom."

"Hello, Krista dear. I've been waiting for a call. I want to hear everything about your new job."

Krista kept stirring. From long experience, she knew Mom wouldn't pause to listen for a while.

"I still can't quite picture you in that tiny place. Blue Sky isn't much bigger than a postage stamp. I always hoped if you left Toronto and performing on cruise ships, you'd come home to Saskatoon. Why do you want to live in a small town on the bald prairie when you could live in a decent-sized city close to your mother and father? Somebody sure twisted your arm."

Disapproval hung in the air. Would Mom ever give up? She meant well but always had her own vision of the right choices for Krista and didn't hesitate to pass judgment. Mom was the driving force behind eighteen-year-old Krista moving to Toronto to train with a national-calibre skating coach. Krista tightened her grip on the wooden spoon and took a deep breath. She craved a conversation without guilt or blame. She needed a connection with no hint of criticism.

Mom just proved why Krista avoided a job in Saskatoon. Living in Blue Sky, a few hours' drive away, was close enough. At least now, she didn't have to catch a flight from Toronto to visit Mom and Dad, but occasional visits were plenty. She took a deep, calming breath. Bracing for more, she turned down the temperature on the burner, sniffed the sweet scent of corn, and continued to stir.

"Your dad and I want to know when you're coming to visit."

Mom's tone hinted at a whine. "I promise I'll come at Christmas." Of course, Krista wanted to celebrate with her parents, but she had the perfect excuse to make the visit brief because of all the ice show preparations. She could prove she cared without wearing herself out listening to strong judgments and unwanted advice. "The rink closes for a few days over the holidays, so I'll see you then."

"Well, I guess I have no choice but to wait." Mom sighed. "Too bad your brother won't be able to join us this year. It's the in-laws' turn."

Krista ignored Mom's pouty tone. "Blue Sky is a cute little place." She turned off the burner. "I have some very talented students, but the rink is struggling with revenue. The club is under pressure to raise a significant amount of money through the ice show."

"Oh, it's unfortunate you stepped into a financial mess." Mom paused and clicked her tongue. "A city club wouldn't have that problem. Now, what about friends? Don't be a hermit when you're not at the rink."

Mom would never understand why she came here to regroup and not to socialize. "Tell you what." Krista reached into the cupboard for a bowl and filled it with steaming soup. "I'm starved and just about to eat dinner. I'll call you tomorrow for a nice, long chat." Tomorrow, she'd be more rested and patient and maybe in a better frame of mind to contend with Mom.

"Make sure you don't forget. You let things slip your mind sometimes."

Mom's voice turned firm, almost scolding. "Don't worry. I could never forget you, Mom." Krista widened her eyes and shook her head. It was the truth, but the reasons weren't all positive, as much as she loved her mother. Mom was like a dog gnawing a bone. She wasn't easily diverted from her agenda. "Good night. Say hi to Dad."

Krista set down the phone and put an orange placemat on the round white table in the corner of the kitchen. Grabbing a spoon from a drawer, she sampled Daisy's soup. It tasted as good as it smelled. Plopping onto a chair with a magazine spread beside her on the table, she dipped a spoon into the hot, creamy concoction. After exactly three bites, she jumped at a sharp knock at the front door and set down the spoon. This time, she had a strong hunch who she'd find on the doorstep. Her chatty neighbor and landlord, Daisy, must be back. Maybe she came bearing more homemade food.

Dragging herself to answer the door, she wondered if drop-in company would become a daily ritual. She swung open the door, and as she swept her gaze from Daisy down to her companion, she snapped her smile into a startled *O*.

"I brought Pearl to meet you." Daisy grinned.

She offered no hint of an apology for arriving unannounced.

The golden retriever wagged her tail so hard her whole hind end swayed.

"Pleased to meet you, Pearl." Krista bent and ran both hands along the dog's reddish-gold head and velvety ears.

"Do you mind if we come inside? I feel like a human ice cube out here." Daisy drew in her shoulders and shivered. "I feel snow in the air."

"Uh, not at all. Come in." She backed up to make space.

Jostling and bumping the walls, Daisy and Pearl squeezed into the tiny entranceway.

Krista squatted, pressed her cheek again the dog's smooth face, and received an enthusiastic lick. Laughing, she straightened and studied Daisy's bright eyes and wide grin. "This is a surprise."

"Yes, well, I know you said you didn't want a dog, but I thought you might change your mind when you saw what a lovely pet she would make." She set a hand on the dog's head. "Imagine having this cute, furry companion here to greet you and accompany you to the rink."

"She's beautiful but—" Krista squirmed under

Daisy's jovial but unmistakeable pressure. Right now, the woman acted as single-minded as Mom. How could she get her to take *no* for an answer?

"No *buts* until you think over the possibility." Daisy blinked and stared. "If I gave up every time I hit a roadblock, I could have never built a successful business. Think about it. That's all I ask."

"But…" Krista sighed. Why argue? It was pointless but didn't mean she had given in and agreed. In the end, she would stand firm. Nobody, no matter how nice, would push her around. Those days were over. "Are you babysitting, or should I say dog sitting Pearl?" Krista stroked the dog's back, enjoying the soothing motion. "Don't you have cats?"

"I promised her former family I'd find her a good home. She came to stay at my place for a few days while they pack for their move. Turns out Pearl loves the cats, but they don't feel the same way." Daisy winced. "So I have a request. Please, could Pearl stay here until tomorrow? I can't ask Janine because she's allergic. You and Pearl can get to know each other, sort of like a test drive. And if you still don't want her, which will shock me, I'll leave you alone about the idea. Maybe." She punctuated her words with a tinkly laugh. "I mean, who could possibly resist this bundle of canine joy?"

Krista flipped her gaze from Daisy to Pearl and back. Hearing Pearl pant and thump her tail on the wall, she felt a rush of affection. "Okay, she can stay. But just for tonight. Tomorrow, you need to find her a new home."

Pearl whined as though she didn't like what she heard.

Daisy's dark eyes lit.

"Thank you, honey. You won't be sorry." She unhooked the leash and handed it to Krista. Then she wrestled into her left pocket and thrust a small bag of kibble into Krista's other hand. "She ate supper. She'll eat this food in the morning. Now, be a good girl, Pearl." With a final pat, she spun and left.

What just happened? She hadn't owned a dog in years, but the sensation of total comfort and undying loyalty hugged her like a long-lost friend. "You're a pretty girl." Krista softened her voice to baby talk and bent to pet Pearl. She'd enjoy the company for one evening and then say goodbye tomorrow. Resting her cheek against the dog's gentle face, she took a deep breath of the mild musky smell. For one evening only, she'd pretend she was a contented dog owner.

Pearl followed her to the kitchen and curled under the table.

Krista savored her reheated soup, then rustled in the cupboards and found a plastic bowl for a water dish. The dog's day must have tuckered her out because after a long drink and a quick trip to the backyard, she stared while Krista tidied the kitchen and then flopped on the braided, pastel area rug in the living room.

Nestled on the sofa and rubbing her feet along Pearl's side, Krista examined the list of potential parent volunteers. Some of the names were familiar, but the only one that jumped out like it was written in red was *Tate Harris*. Instantly, her heart fluttered another warning to proceed with caution. Even Pearl's calming presence didn't help.

She closed her eyes and considered the options. Work her way down the list, building confidence with each call. Sleep on it and start calls in the morning, although she suspected she'd catch more people available to chat in the evening. Procrastinate as long as possible, or bravely jump right in and tackle the most challenging call first.

Pearl thumped her tail.

Clearly, she supported whatever choice Krista made. Snapping her eyes open, Krista knew what she had to do. Sitting forward, she spread her fingers wide and trailed them along Pearl's shiny coat. Emboldened by the dog's steady presence, she glanced at the time and picked up her phone. She paused, then entered Tate's number.

Unprompted, Pearl shifted to a sitting position and rested her chin on Krista's knee.

How did the dog know she needed moral support? Should she have waited until morning to place the call? With the phone ringing on the other end, she couldn't change her mind now, even though her hand trembled. Waiting to hear his deep voice, she petted Pearl's velvety ears and held her breath.

****

"Hello." Tate rushed to grab the landline in the kitchen and didn't check Call Display. Probably his mother or sister wanted to confirm childcare details for tomorrow morning. With light snow already falling, he planned to start early to sand the slippery patches on Main Street and would need a babysitter to get his girls ready for school.

"Hello, Tate."

The voice was not Mom's or Carly's, but he'd know it anywhere.

"This is Krista. Krista Reynolds." She cleared her

throat. "Do you have a moment to talk?"

She didn't need to identify herself. Her voice had been stuck in his head for the past few weeks since the moment he met her. "Yes, but not for long." His heart pumped an extra beat. "I need to read stories and tuck in Gracie and Ella. What's up?" Might as well get right to the point of her call. Waiting for her to continue, he pointed at his sleepy twins and motioned for them to go and brush their teeth.

"I'll just keep you a minute. Or would you rather I call in the morning?"

She sounded so halting and hesitant he decided to let her continue. In a town this small, he couldn't afford to add any tension. "Nah, now is fine. I just want to keep my little darlins well rested for school tomorrow. But this'll give them time to goof off without me getting in the way." Hearing their giggles echo down the hallway, he couldn't help a quick smile. They certainly kept his life interesting and fun.

"Janine asked me to call. We need to recruit parent volunteers for the ice show."

"Ah. I should have known you weren't calling to invite me out for dinner." He could hardly believe the words tumbled out of his mouth. He didn't feel nearly as confident as he sounded. The younger, carefree Tate flirted all the time, but now, he tended to keep up his guard. If he didn't expect much, he couldn't lose.

"Not tonight, anyway." She laughed.

At least, she sounded amused and not repelled by his quip.

"This is what Janine wrote beside your name...are you ready for it?" She paused, creating an exaggerated dramatic effect. "By the way, she drew a big star beside your name. The note says: *Set construction—knows his stuff. See if he'll lead the construction committee.*"

"Knows his stuff, eh? That's what she said?" He chuckled and gave a thumbs-up to Gracie and Ella bopping in his line of vision and flashing their clean teeth. The faint minty smell of toothpaste floated around them as proof they did the job. Mouthing instructions to choose two stories each, he mulled over his answer. "A little flattery never hurts."

Automatic *no*? Or *yes*? Should he answer on the spot or promise to call her back tomorrow? One answer would leave his little free time open. The other would thrust him into contact with Krista all the time. He needed to pause and calm his whirling thoughts. "I have a few questions, so might be best if I called back. Can I catch you in about twenty minutes? I need to put some tired girls to bed."

"Of course. Call back when you're free."

He'd bought himself a few minutes to slow his racing thoughts. He set down the phone and followed his girls to their bedroom while a flurry of thoughts chased him down the hallway. "Hop onto Ella's bed, and I'll read." Every night they huddled on one of the girls' twin beds in a froth of pink and yellow created by their Auntie Carly.

"Who called you, Daddy?" Gracie yawned and covered her mouth.

"Your skating teacher, Krista." Although he'd been tired, now he buzzed with anticipation. "She wants me to build the backdrops for your ice show."

"Will you?" Ella widened her sleepy eyes. "Please, Daddy."

"You're a good builder." Gracie snuggled under

the fluffy pastel quilt.

"I'll see." He didn't know the answer. "While you're in dreamland, I'll decide and tell you tomorrow." After stories, he kissed their firm rosy cheeks, tucked the covers under their chins, and turned off the light. For a second, his throat squeezed. He was so lucky to have his twin packages of love.

Returning to the living room, he sank into his favorite gray leather chair, gripped the armrests, and shut his eyes. Normally, his comfortable, neutral furnishings and matching area rug created a calm oasis, but this evening, he couldn't relax. He needed to make a decision and place a call.

Tapping his palms, he beat soft smacking sounds on the arms of the chair. Thinking of his twins' welfare and the small pool of potential volunteers, he should help, even though he already donated more than enough time to the skating club's outdoor maintenance. Considering his busy schedule, he should decline the additional, time-consuming commitment.

Leaping to his feet, he imagined working next to Krista, and he wanted to accept. Anticipation boosted his pulse and lifted his heart to his throat. Definitely, he shouldn't feel this way about a friend. For sure, he should decline. The temptation to get closer would continually tug, and his wounded heart couldn't take indifference or worse—outright rejection.

He opened his eyes, stared into the darkness out the front window, and then picked up the phone. He knew the club needed help, but he must decline. No sense asking Krista any questions when he already knew his answer. He'd get right to the point. Ready to respond, he punched the numbers on the phone.

She answered on the first ring. "Hello, Tate. Are those lovely girls of yours fast asleep?"

Krista sounded bright and breezy, yet firmness underlined her tone. How would her attitude change when he gave his answer?

"As I was saying, we'd love to have you and your construction skills on the ice show team. Can we count you in?"

"I know the pay's lousy, but do you s'pose the job offers any added benefits—like all-you-can-drink hot chocolate?" He chuckled and flushed, glad no one was there to see his red cheekbones. Why did he make a joke about the perks of the job when he was about to turn it down?

"Hmmm. We might arrange something, especially if you're a strong performer like Janine predicts."

"I'm really sorry." He intended to say he couldn't volunteer, but somehow, his tongue defied his brain. "I can't guarantee the results, but I'm willing to take a crack at the job." His mouth dried, and he swallowed, suddenly desperate for a cooling drink of water. Now, he couldn't avoid Krista. He had placed himself way too close for comfort.

"You will? Oh, thank you!" Her voice rose and turned into a giggle. "I just got a kiss."

"Pardon?" Puzzled, Tate waited for an explanation. He thought she lived alone. Still facing out the window, he rocked heel to toe.

"I'm babysitting a golden retriever, and she just gave me a big lick on the cheek."

Relief tickled the back of his neck. "Pearl?" He shouldn't care, but if she had a boyfriend, he couldn't stand it.

"You know Pearl?"

"Everyone in town knows Pearl." He chuckled. "Her family isn't exactly attentive, so she runs free once in a while. I s'pose Daisy roped you into looking after the mutt."

"How did you guess?" Krista laughed. "But only for one night."

"You don't know Daisy." He was only half teasing. Daisy was plenty determined and didn't take *no* for an answer.

"Don't scare me. Okay, back to business. I want to meet and talk about the ice show theme as soon as possible. The sooner you know what materials you'll need, the better. I have no idea how much time the project will take, but you'll know when you hear the details."

Already, the wheels were in motion. Why didn't he stand firm and decline when he had the chance? "I'd rather not leave Gracie and Ella with a babysitter any more often than necessary." He racked his brain for options. "You could come here tomorrow evening, or I could take a coffee break and meet you at Daisy's Diner sometime during the day. Assuming the snow holds off or stays light. If there's a big dump, I'll be stuck to the plow all day."

"Hmmm. I'd love to see your twins, but I teach until nine tomorrow evening, which would probably be past their bedtime. So, let's say Daisy's tomorrow afternoon at two. If you can get yourself unstuck."

She sounded amused like she pictured him plastered to his snow removal equipment. "Okay. It's a date." He felt his face flush again. His choice of words caused an awkward innuendo in his mind. He would definitely never take Krista on a real date, and he hoped she didn't take his innocent comment the wrong way. "See you tomorrow."

"Perfect. Thank you, Tate."

Her voice firmed into a businesslike tone. He ended the call and paced to the kitchen sink for a glass of cold water. Running a hand through his hair, he massaged his tense scalp. He had just agreed to spend his precious free time helping a woman he needed to avoid. The way people talked, pretty soon his frequent time with Krista would spread all over town. Nobody would believe it was all business. He couldn't change his mind now, but he better guard his heart before he skated down a very slippery path.

Chapter 6

"Well, Pearl girl, I did it." Krista slid to her knees, nuzzled the dog's neck, and was rewarded with a reassuring tail wag and lick on the cheek. She had called Tate Harris and recruited him to the ice show team. Now, she just had to thicken her skin against his raw masculinity. Even his deep, measured voice made her insides feel like jelly. The charming best man would now continually tempt her as they consulted on details of the ice show sets. What had she done? Why had she subjected herself to such sweet temptation?

The next morning, after a fitful sleep with Pearl sprawled next to her on the yellow-flowered comforter, she woke determined to attack her long to-do list. First, she'd return Pearl to Daisy. Adopting a dog, even as gentle and well behaved as this one, would add a responsibility she didn't need right now. She stroked Pearl's soft wavy coat. "Don't worry, girl. Daisy will find you a good home."

Instead of unpacking more boxes and hanging pictures, Krista walked Pearl a few streets over to the edge of town. Gazing across the open field covered in a dusting of snow, she felt unburdened and free. All the pain and turmoil of Toronto and Zach and her escape to the cruise ship already felt a world away. She had left it all behind and would find her new beginning.

Judgmental and verging on cruel, Zach couldn't

shake her confidence any longer. She'd make sure she'd never again live in that kind of hurtful environment. Filling her lungs with the fresh, clean smell of the first snowfall of the season, she stretched her arms wide and stared above at the wide blue canopy that gave Blue Sky its name. Spending the winter here would help her grow stronger and ready for a fresh start wherever she found the right opportunity.

Unfastening Pearl's leash, she watched the dog grab mouthfuls of snow, flop on her side, and slide like a penguin. Krista laughed harder than she had in a long time, and she shook loose worries about pleasing Janine, managing her mother, and seeing Tate. Even so, she couldn't keep her thoughts from drifting right back to him, and butterflies fluttered in her stomach.

This afternoon when she met him, she would stick to ice show details and steer the conversation away from anything personal. After escaping a relationship that crushed her spirit, she wasn't ready to try again. She'd focus on her skating students and the ice show until the end of the season. With any luck, six months from now, she'd move her rejuvenated self onward and upward to…to what she wasn't sure.

Krista romped with Pearl for fifteen minutes until the cold seeped through her jacket and her cheekbones tingled. What a difference in weather since Amy's wedding just a few weeks ago. Shivering, she snapped on Pearl's leash and circled back to Main Street. She really must find Daisy at the diner and get instructions on where to leave Pearl. Rounding the corner, she ducked her head against the wind. Half a block down, she poked her head in the door and asked to see Daisy. No one knew where she was, so Krista had no choice but to return home with Pearl still in tow. Tightening her fist around the leash, she trusted Daisy would drop in and pick up the dog soon.

At home, Pearl followed her every move as she unpacked boxes and personalized the décor with her own favorite items.

Krista didn't bother to bring along many things, but she treasured a few pieces of artwork collected in her international travels and a few ornaments passed on from her grandma. Pictures of Zach had hit the garbage long ago. She left him far behind in Toronto and hoped the unhappy memories would stay away too.

While she sat at the kitchen table, listened to music, and made notes of possible choices for students' individual skating programs and the ice show group numbers, she warmed her feet on Pearl's thick coat. When her imagination wandered to Tate's firm jaw and stubbly chin, she reached down to pet Pearl and stayed grounded in reality.

Her stomach growled for lunch, and Daisy still hadn't reappeared. "Guess it's you and me, Pearl girl." She bent and placed a hand on either side of the dog's furry face. Tongue lolling out of the side of her mouth, Pearl appeared fully content like she knew she belonged. "You look like you're smiling." Talking to Pearl was as natural as chatting with a good friend. Her presence was warm and soothing. But to adopt a dog now when her life was so uncertain? The whole idea made no more sense than getting involved with Tate.

As she ate her grilled cheese sandwich with Pearl propped against her legs, she felt a slow realization sneak into her heart. Forget reason. Forget common sense. Some things were meant to be. Without a doubt,

Pearl was home. She belonged right here at Krista's side. Determined Daisy must have sensed she could make a match. She was staying away long enough to encourage the pair to bond and clinch the deal.

"You were right." By the time she greeted Daisy on the doorstep an hour later, Krista headed off another sales pitch. Waving her neighbor inside, she nearly hugged her. "You knew, didn't you? Pearl and I belong together."

"I'm a pretty good judge of people…and animals." Smiling, she winked.

Krista forgave Daisy's smug expression. "How do I finalize the adoption?" She rested a hand on her new pet's head.

"It's all final and official, honey. Pearl's family said their goodbyes and left the rest to my good judgment. She's all yours."

"Thank you." Krista heard her own voice waver. "Can I hug you?"

"Of course. I love a good hug."

Krista threw her arms around Daisy's chubby waist and squeezed.

Pearl circled them, panting and batting her tail.

With a dog's intuition, she understood the significance of the moment. Krista dropped her arms and backed up. "I'd invite you in to celebrate, but I'm meeting someone at your diner in just a few minutes." Instantly, she felt a rush of heat in her face. But why? She was headed to an ice show meeting, not a social event with the very handsome Tate Harris. She bent and petted Pearl. "You'll have to lie down for a nap."

"Oh, good. We can walk together because I need to hurry back there and bake a batch of chocolate chip cookies." Daisy petted Pearl. "You're going to like it here, pup."

Krista bolted upright. "Hey! Wait a minute. You said hurry back? You mean you were there at the diner all along? Your helper claimed he didn't know where you were."

Daisy clucked her tongue and shrugged. "Maybe he didn't see me with my head stuck in the oven."

Krista laughed. "Sure, Daisy." She was one smart woman to avoid her all morning. If Krista couldn't find Daisy, she couldn't return the dog. After tossing on her warm clothes and giving Pearl a final pat, she hustled beside Daisy to the diner.

"Do you mind if I ask who you're meeting? Of course, I'll see for myself in a minute." Daisy's breath puffed out in a cloud.

Staring down the street, Krista spotted a couple of parked cars and a few shoppers. Monday was a quiet day in town. Actually, probably every day was quiet here. She took a few more brisk steps, and uncertainty swooped in and nearly smothered her words. "Tate Harris. About the ice show."

"Good, honey. You recruited the right guy to help. He's probably one of the handiest men in Blue Sky. Definitely one of the nicest too."

A nervous flutter rippled across Krista's middle. First, a dog. Now, a man. She better watch out for Daisy's wily ways, because she had absolutely no intention of allowing her interactions with Tate to turn into anything but friendship and a necessary business arrangement.

****

Tate hurried through the doorway of Daisy's Diner

and inhaled the warm, moist air filled with the delicious scents of chocolate and cinnamon. The place reminded him of summertime all year round with its yellow walls, white tables, and flower artwork. Mouth watering, he scanned the room and spotted Krista at a table for two off to one side. In front of her sat a small teapot and a notepad, clear signals this was a business meeting and not a casual date. The sight of her pretty face shot a small jolt of electricity through his limbs.

He'd daydreamed all morning about the time they'd spend together. At the wedding, they both felt a spark. Over the phone last evening, they easily bantered like friends. But today was business. Feelings would only complicate everything. "Sorry to keep you waiting." Puffing slightly, he unzipped his jacket and draped it over the back of his chair. "I parked the truck down the street out of the way and jogged from there."

He'd lost track of time while grooming the parking lot of the seniors' center and rushed to make their two o'clock appointment. Plunking into the chair opposite Krista, he rubbed his hands together and flexed them to ease the stiffness from the cold and get the blood flowing.

"No problem. I just settled in with my tea." She cupped her mug in both hands. "What would you like? I called this meeting, so I'll buy."

Her smile softened, and her crisp tone mellowed. In her gray-and-white-patterned cardigan, she looked like a healthy, outdoorsy model who wasn't fazed in the least by the start of a prairie winter. The lighting tinted her eyes to the color of the sky outside, and she sized him up, sweeping her gaze over his face and upper body.

Instantly, he felt self-conscious in his work clothes. He probably didn't look his best with his face ruddy from the biting wind, hair scrambled by his woolen hat, and more than a day's growth shadowing his face. But she couldn't expect any better when she had interrupted his workday. She'd have to take him rumpled and all.

Just then, Daisy appeared from the kitchen wearing a hair net and white apron and set down a mug of steaming hot chocolate without even asking his order. "I assumed you'd want the usual."

"You're absolutely right, ma'am." He chuckled. Good old Daisy, bustling around as efficient as ever. He grew up under her eagle eye just like the rest of his friends. Nothing got by Daisy, and if she spotted any shenanigans by the youth around town, she was never afraid to speak her mind and snitch to a parent.

"How are those little sweeties of yours?" She paused, hands on hips, then pulled a cloth from her apron pocket and wiped a drip off the table.

"Full of beans as ever." He glanced up at her inquisitive eyes. "They love their skating lessons and gave good reviews on the new coach." Tensing his shoulders, he wanted to suck back his words. Hard as he tried to make normal conversation, he couldn't resist pulling Krista into the conversation. He didn't intend to flirt, but his words suggested otherwise.

"Janine's impressed so far too. That granddaughter of mine, Olivia, might be a little tougher to please. I love her to bits, but she wears a bit of an attitude." Daisy winked and tucked the washcloth into her pocket.

"Okay, you two. Quit talking about me like I'm not here." Krista smiled and wagged a finger.

"I'll leave you to sort out things without my help."

Daisy laughed. "I have cookies to bake." She took a couple of steps toward the kitchen and then paused. "Be sure to tell Tate about your new baby."

"Pearl?" Tate raised his eyebrows. "I figured Daisy had something up her sleeve when she asked you to dog sit."

"She didn't make me do anything against my will." Krista raised the mug to her lips and peered over the rim. "The truth is I love dogs, and Pearl made herself right at home like she belonged. I really had no other choice."

Tate smiled at her brisk explanation. It came across as slightly defensive, but if she wanted a pet, who was he to judge? "I'm sure Pearl will be good company. Maybe I can borrow her when Ella and Gracie pester me to get our own dog. It happens at least once a week."

"I'll keep you in mind when I need a dog sitter." She laughed. "As long as your rates are reasonable."

"You might get the friends and family discount." The joking back and forth felt good, and he chuckled. "If you're lucky."

"I'll hold you to the offer." Krista nodded, set down her mug, and placed both hands on her notepad. "You probably don't have much spare time in the middle of your workday, so let's get down to business."

"Yes, ma'am." Tate leaned forward in his chair, thumping a fist on the table. He only half successfully contained a smirk. He better listen to the boss. "What do you have in mind?"

"Have you ever worked on an ice show?" She pressed her lips together and stared into his eyes without a waver.

"Never." Muscles tugging hard across his chest, he shifted and sat straighter. She really had no business treating this like a job interview. He was doing her and the club—really the whole community—a favor. She didn't need to trot out her big-city attitude and make him feel like a junior employee.

"Not an ice show, but I got an *A* in shop class in high school."

"Impressive." She barely cracked a smile.

Did a hint of amusement flit across her face? Where was her usual sense of humor? She must know he was joking.

"When I have time, I do odd jobs and renos around town." Toying with the salt and pepper shakers on the table, he noticed she had the grace to lower her gaze and soften her expression. Now she looked like she wanted to withdraw her question or at least change her tone.

"Good. I don't want the ice show to be the same old event." She tapped her pen on the notepad. "Janine tells me the theme is winter wonderland. But I'd like to do something new. I can't just recycle the same old ideas and the usual sets. People here get plenty of real winter, so I think a hot theme would be a lot more fun."

"Whatever you say, ma'am. I'm here to serve." He tried to imitate her serious expression but suspected his amusement might reflect in his eyes. He flicked his gaze to the froth on the top of his hot chocolate. She must want to make a name for herself as the new, improved coach full of fresh ideas.

"I want to stage a Mexican fiesta." She flipped a page and held up rough sketches of ocean waves, palm trees, and bright costumes. "You know, big sombreros and full skirts."

He leaned to examine the details. "Yup. That's Mexico. You want the whole nine yards. You're talking what—beach scenes, colorful backdrops, mariachi music?"

"Exactly." She raised her voice and glanced sideways.

"I'm no artist." He shook his head. A small knot of hesitation in his stomach told him this project loomed bigger than he had anticipated.

"I'll sketch, if you build and paint." She pointed to the drawings in her notebook.

"Okay, but my time is limited." He resisted the determination burning in her eyes. He had young daughters and a demanding business. They gobbled most of his time.

"Sunday mornings would be a good, quiet time to work uninterrupted. I don't teach lessons until the afternoon—"

"Hold it right there." He raised a hand like a stop signal and watched her widen her eyes. He needed to fill her in. She really had no business scheduling his time. "Sunday morning is family time. I work every other day of the week, and I won't leave my girls on Sunday, too. We usually have brunch with my parents and sister."

"Well, how about Saturday evening? We'll start then." She searched his face and sipped her tea. "These things always take longer than a person thinks, and time is ticking."

Mostly, weekend evenings meant popcorn and a movie with Gracie and Ella. But he was pretty sure his parents would babysit, especially if they thought they would help give his social life a much-needed boost. "I s'pose I could make Saturday work." He drew out his words. She didn't need to rush him into an answer, and he sort of enjoyed seeing her wrinkle her forehead. "If I can arrange a babysitter." Watching her lips dip at the corners, he could see she might not be the easiest person to work with. She better remember he was a volunteer. The next few weeks would be quite interesting.

"Let me know as soon as you can." She scribbled a quick note. "I'll plan to meet you at the rink at seven."

"Yes, ma'am." She was his little darlins' skating coach. She was a fun dance partner at the wedding. They were friends. Spending time together on a project was pretty harmless, but still, anticipation jostled his insides like a hockey bodycheck.

"Now, I'm sure you need to get back to work." She reached for a napkin from the dispenser on the table and knocked over her water glass with her forearm.

"Whoa." Tate shoved back his chair and leapt to avoid the waterfall off the edge of the table. Grabbing a handful of napkins, he blotted the splotches of water off his coveralls.

"Oh no. I'm sorry. I'll grab a cloth." She slapped a hand to each cheek and then darted between tables to the counter and returned with a rag to soak up the mess.

"Was it something I said?" He laughed. With the rush of air, he caught a whiff of her faint floral scent. It threw him back to the wedding dance and sparked a twinge of desire in his chest.

"I'm so sorry." She stood opposite him and smothered a giggle. "I hope your pants are waterproof."

"Yeah, mostly. Maybe they won't freeze solid on

my way back to the truck so I can bend my legs to sit."
He couldn't help teasing and sending her slightly off
balance. She didn't seem quite so in-command with a
light blush tinting her cheeks. He loved the sound of her
stifled laughter. "Nah, don't worry. Just get out of here
before you cause more trouble." He rooted in a pocket
for enough coins to cover the bill.

She waved him off and set down a five-dollar bill.
"Remember, I'm treating today. Thanks for coming."
She grabbed her notepad and pen.

"Thank *you* for the coffee break, ma'am." He
couldn't wait to see her again, but he wasn't about to let
her know. "I'll see you tomorrow when I pick up
Gracie and Ella from their skating lesson."

"Oh, right. I'll see you then." Smiling, she brushed
a curl off her cheek. "If I'm not too busy on the ice."

He reached to help with her jacket.

"That's okay, thanks." She slipped it over her
shoulders.

He only meant to extend the same courtesy he'd
offer anyone, but he recoiled at her slightly edgy tone.

Blinking, she stepped back behind an invisible
fence. Maybe she saw his innocent gesture as a little too
familiar. Well, good. He felt the same way. Friendship
could work but nothing else. He wouldn't get too close.
She was only here for a few months. "I better run." He
raised a hand and should have just walked away, but he
couldn't resist a second glance at her deep-blue eyes.
"Maybe you should consider a Hawaiian theme
instead."

"No, I—" She straightened, then froze.

His teasing smirk worked. It stopped her for a beat,
just like he hoped.

Shaking her head, she waved him off and led him through the doorway.

Outside, he burst into a run toward the safety and predictability of work. Adrenaline shot through his body. He accelerated until his heart pounded like he'd made a hockey breakaway. Back in his truck, he caught his breath and revved the engine. Checking for traffic, he eased onto the street toward his next job.

If only the situation was different and he had met the gorgeous, strong-willed redhead when the time was right. But now was all wrong. His days of romance were past. He had already suffered the pain of lost love, and he wasn't about to risk it again. These days, he was tied down to the max. Besides, he knew she wasn't here to stay.

If everything was different, he might carve out time from his family obligations and suggest a dinner date. He might invite her to join him on an evening walk. In another world, he might use the ice show as an opportunity to get to know her better. Regret twisted his chest the way he rung out a wet cloth. Now, he just had to figure out how to keep his commitment to the ice show without falling for the woman in charge.

Chapter 7

All the way home, Krista replayed the coffee break with Tate. She scuffed snow along Main Street, glancing in store windows and barely seeing a thing. The way he took her breath away, she could barely concentrate on the ice show details.

When he had arrived, his face was as red as an apple, and his eyebrows tinged gray with frost. Working outside all day wouldn't be easy and must test a person. She had nearly gasped when she swept her gaze from his ruddy complexion with a hint of a whisker shadow to his navy fleece sweater with the faint outline of biceps underneath. He had run a hand through his rumpled hair and rubbed his broad hands together to warm them. Her heart had beat approval at the evidence of his good, honest work.

Back at home, she got a greeting from Pearl like she'd been away for a year.

The dog wagged her whole body and flopped onto her side for tummy rubs.

She was a little on the chubby side, and regular exercise would do her good. Krista hung up her outdoor clothes and sank to the living room floor. The warmth felt good, and the cozy pastel furniture reminded her of a country cottage. "Oh, Pearl girl, what is wrong with me?"

Tail swishing, the dog leaned close.

Was Pearl reassuring her everything would be just fine? "I came here for six months to coach and reflect but not to get involved with a man." Slinging an arm around Pearl's shoulders, Krista bent her legs and rested her forehead on her knees. Right now, she should be obsessed with evaluating skaters, choosing music, and planning the ice show. Instead, daydreams of Tate's funny quips and muscular body crowded out everything else. She didn't understand herself anymore. Within a week of arriving in Blue Sky, she already felt her priorities slipping out of her grip.

Determined to remain on track and focus on the reasons she came, she took a deep breath, sprang to her feet, and unpacked the last of the boxes from the move. Pausing, she soaked up the familiar fragrance of her homemade potpourri scented with orange and spices. With a few personalized touches, the place felt more and more like home.

The rest of the afternoon passed in a flurry, and when she was ready for a break, she grabbed her notepad and curled up in the flowered armchair. Outside the large front window, tree branches trimmed with snow and a wide blue sky created a pretty and peaceful scene. She knew she'd find the space here to forget the feelings of failure following her everywhere.

When she first met the opinionated skating official, Zach Drake, she convinced herself his sharp edges were nothing to fear. After all, he was the skating expert. Too angular to be considered classically handsome, he had attracted her with his edgy charm and stylish image. Sadly, as their relationship developed, she experienced his true colors—a harsh critic of people. Not only a skating official on the ice, he judged everything in his sight, including her. Even now, she winced at the sting of anything that felt remotely like disapproval.

Starting long before that disastrous relationship, she had struggled her whole life to stand up to her difficult mother. Mom might mean well, but she called her frequent criticism *just trying to help*. The memory of Mom's pained expression when Krista repeatedly missed the podium still stabbed her in the stomach.

Zach only made things worse. In his own biting way, he had chipped away at her confidence until she nearly cracked. She took longer than she cared to admit gathering her courage, but finally, she ended their relationship. How long would she have struggled without Amy's gentle, steady long-distance counsel and encouragement? When Zach told her the decision to leave was her loss, he only confirmed she had made the right choice. Finally, she escaped to the cruise ship to perform for tourists and dream of a new life.

Krista shuddered. Shaking her head free of unpleasant memories, she shifted to rest her notepad on the wide arm of the chair. She stared at the blank paper and forced her mind to the ice show. She doodled until a costume idea materialized in her head, and then she sketched the image. Only the picture wasn't a traditional Mexican dance costume. It was a hula skirt. Tate would get a kick out of how her unconscious had listened to his joking suggestion. She flipped the pencil and erased all evidence of Hawaii. The ice show would transport the audience from the frigid prairies to hot Mexico, whether Tate liked it or not.

Half an hour later, she changed into her warm teaching clothes and headed for the rink with Pearl trotting at her side. Daisy said the dog was welcome at the rink, and now was as good a time as any to try out the idea. From four o'clock until nine or later, Krista would teach group and individual lessons, and Pearl could amuse the kids coming and going throughout the evening.

"Who do we have here?" Janine paused just inside the rink doorway.

Popcorn scented the bright lobby area and blended with the rest of the familiar rink smells.

"I'll stand back so I don't start sneezing."

"Your mom mentioned you're allergic. She introduced me to Pearl, and I fell in love at first sight." Krista bent and rubbed the dog's thick coat. "She assured me no one would mind if Pearl hung out at the rink while I teach."

"That mother of mine." Janine smiled and rolled her eyes. "She pretty much owns this place, so usually, what she says goes. I guess Pearl is welcome. Most of the kids already know her from around town, and everyone knows she wouldn't hurt a flea." She put a hand on Krista's arm. "How did your recruiting calls go? I signed up nearly everyone I called."

"I did well too." She smiled at the cluster of kids smothering Pearl with hugs and pats.

"Did Tate agree to handle sets?" Janine narrowed her eyes.

At the slight edge in the question, Krista stiffened. Janine didn't overlook a thing. "Yes, he did." She forced her voice to remain steady as though Tate was any other parent, but at the sound of his name, she felt her pulse jump. "I can give you details later, but I need to put on my skates and shoo the kids onto the ice. Don't ever worry. When I set my mind to something, I deliver."

She didn't feel so sure inside but remembered Dad's advice to *fake it until you make it*. She turned but not before she saw Janine press her lips into a tight smile.

"You must have worked some magic." Janine raised her eyebrows.

Looking back over her shoulder, Krista shrugged. She wouldn't let Janine know she felt the same way. Not everyone could have persuaded Tate to give up family and work time to volunteer. A warm glow radiated from her cheeks, and she hurried to the changeroom before Janine could notice.

All evening as she coached, she swept her gaze from the skaters to the sidelines. *Don't be ridiculous, Krista. He won't appear tonight when his girls' lessons are tomorrow evening.* Still, she couldn't tame the buzz vibrating up and down her spine whenever she pictured Tate's chocolate eyes and hesitant grin. "Girls, the boards can hold themselves up." Partway through the advanced session, she skirted the ice and smacked her hands together. A core group of dedicated skaters practiced new skills, but a few slacked off. "Back to work." Ignoring the eye rolls, she scraped to a hard stop next to a group with Janine's daughter, Olivia, at the center.

"We just need a break." Olivia straightened and dug a toe pick into the glassy surface. She blinked and met Krista's gaze.

The teen was used to getting her own way, and she didn't back down easily. She led the way, and the girls on either side imitated her stubborn attitude. Krista took a deep breath and didn't bother to smile. Their defiant attitude called for immediate action. She ran the skating school. The students did not. If she needed to do something dramatic to send a message she was in charge, she would. "I really want to see you all become the best skaters you can be. When you stand around and chat, you waste your time and mine. You also set a bad example for the younger kids." She dragged out her words and made eye contact with each of the girls except Olivia, who stared across the arena during the lecture.

"Now, let's get back to work. Choose your toughest jump and try it ten times. Olivia…" She paused until the group leader lifted her gaze. "I suggest you work on your double flip." Krista flashed the briefest of smiles. "I expect everyone to cooperate." She swiveled to sweep her gaze around the whole group. "If you don't, I will have no choice but to ask you to leave the ice for the rest of the practice."

The group split, and the teens skated in different directions, leaving Olivia standing alone.

Music blared overhead, and the sound of blades cutting the ice swirled close.

Frowning and wrinkling her nose, Olivia pushed and glided away at a leisurely pace.

She either liked to challenge authority or just didn't have a passion for the sport. Either way, Krista might soon need to meet with Janine to discuss the situation and enlist her support. During short breaks, Krista checked on Pearl. The dog appeared to be thoroughly enjoying the evening between pats from adoring kids and circuiting the outside perimeter of the boards around the ice surface. "Good dog." She bent to stroke Pearl's rounded sides before returning to the ice.

All evening, every time Krista turned her back, she sensed a couple of the older skaters pausing to chat. Repeatedly, she hustled the loafers back to practice. "Champion skaters don't slack off." She raised her eyebrows and sent a stern look their way. Clearly, the regular coach had allowed plenty of socializing to detract from practice time. Well, she'd soon fix bad habits and get the skaters on track to real improvement.

Five hours later, she arrived home with Pearl, tired and hungry. After a late dinner, she ran a hot bath and slid in. A long soak in the soothing vanilla bubbles would work wonders. Rewarding as she found coaching, it took buckets of energy, especially when not all her students were eager to please. Her thoughts jumped between the frustrating interactions with Olivia and pleasant musings about Tate. Sighing, she sank lower and let the hot water steam away her chilled and tense muscles. She needed this time to recharge and clear her head of thoughts that didn't belong. She could daydream about anything but Tate Harris.

Not two minutes later, her cellphone rang from her bedroom. She had tossed it onto the bed before her bath. She groaned. "I don't want to talk to anybody except you, Pearl."

Resting her chin on the edge of the bathtub, Pearl thumped her tail.

Pearl understood she needed reassurance. Chances were the call was from Mom. Who else would call this late on a Monday evening? She considered ignoring it, but just in case it was urgent, she jumped out of the tub, wrapped a robe around her damp body, and dashed to answer. "Hi, Mom." She didn't check Call Display before she answered but was certain the caller must be her mother.

"Hello, ma'am." A deep voice greeted her. "I hope you're not too disappointed. I'm not your mother." He chuckled. "This is Tate. Did I call too late?"

The rich sound was as delicious as milk chocolate. A surprising and unsettling tickle of anticipation ran up her spine, and she used her free arm to hug her robe closer around her waist. "Not exactly, but you lured me out of the bathtub." She had wished for his presence all evening at the rink but didn't expect a call. Why now? Did it concern the twins? Or did he just want to connect again? She plopped on the edge of the bed and tucked the robe over her damp knees.

"Pardon me. I didn't mean to interrupt an important event. I could call back later or wait until tomorrow."

She heard the smile surrounding his words. Of course, she wanted to talk to him anytime. "No, I'm almost dry, so I can talk for a minute."

"I'll set the timer."

She laughed and savored the warm burst his gentle humor caused. His tone was humble like he didn't mean to intrude, but he must have a purpose for his call. Was it business or pleasure? She really couldn't tell. Unless he wanted to hear about the twins' skating or the ice show, she shouldn't be so interested in what he had to say. Drooling over a man was not part of her plan. She needed to contain her feelings so he wouldn't suspect his call sent her heart racing. She paused. "Okay. Your allotted time starts now. On your mark, get set, go. Do you have a question about the ice show?" She moistened her lips. Why did she hope he wanted to discuss something more personal? Whatever the reason he called, he couldn't wait until tomorrow. What was so important he called her so late?

****

"I need your advice." Tate jumped right to the point. Krista likely couldn't wait to sink back into the hot bath. Pulse skittering, he forced away images of her shapely body wrapped only in a towel. She sounded more curious than upset about the interruption, but he didn't want to push his luck. Now that he thought about the time again, he probably should have waited. Almost ten o'clock was pretty late to call someone he didn't know very well.

He gripped the phone and swallowed. He felt a bit foolish. The trouble was his impatience and attraction were hard to ignore. For some reason, his jumbled feelings propelled him toward her instead of away. "Nah, not the ice show."

"Oh…okay then…"

He heard her hesitation with a hint of a question. Ever since the afternoon coffee break when he sat opposite Krista, admired her wild curls, and imagined kissing her full lips, he could think of nothing else. She had sparked his energy and consumed his thoughts for the rest of the afternoon while he roared around parking lots and town streets with his snowplow. He hardly felt the nippy air.

Later, as he'd stirred spaghetti sauce for dinner, he daydreamed.

"Daddy, you're not listening. Look what I brought home from school." Gracie waved a colorful soft-covered book. "After supper, I have to read it out loud, and you have to listen."

"I'm supposed to read a book too." Ella tugged on the back pocket of his jeans.

90

"You bet, my little darlins." Tate snapped back to his role as attentive dad. Looking down at his lookalike daughters, he felt a rush of love. He couldn't imagine life without their busy minds and endless energy. They definitely kept him on his toes. Gracie was right. He'd drifted a million miles away from their cozy kitchen, barely aware of the tempting scents of tomato, garlic, and oregano wafting from the stove. "Time to put away the books and set the table, please." He assigned a chore and served plates of steaming spaghetti with meat sauce, Caesar salad, and fresh bread. Settled at the white wooden table, he made sure they tucked napkins under their chins over their sweaters. "Guess who I saw today."

"Grandma and Grandpa." Ella twisted a knot of pasta.

"Nope," he said.

"Miss Daisy," Gracie shouted her answer.

"Guess again." He shook his head.

"I give up." Ella wrinkled her forehead and stuck a finger into her temple.

"I saw Krista." His heart sped, and he wound spaghetti around his fork at top speed.

"Where?" Gracie swigged her milk, set down her glass, and stared with wide eyes.

Tate grabbed a napkin and swiped at her milk mustache. "I met her at Daisy's Diner and talked about the ice show. I'll build the backdrops to make the show really special."

"I wish I could see Krista." Ella tore bread and dipped a piece into the red sauce.

A string of spaghetti winding over her chin, Gracie nodded. "Me too."

"You'll see her tomorrow at your skating lesson."

"Goody gumdrops." Mouth rimmed with orangey-red, Gracie grinned.

He smiled at her old-fashioned expression. He never knew exactly what Gracie and Ella would say next, but their outlook was almost always bright and positive. Glancing at their sweet faces, he scolded himself. He needed to switch away from the topic of Krista. She didn't belong anywhere in his imagination when he should focus on family.

"Tell me a highlight of your day. Ella, go first." He stabbed bites of salad and chewed while he listened to stories about school and friends. After dinner, he sat between them on the sofa and helped them read some simple books. "I'm proud of you both for learning so many new words." He placed an arm around their shoulders and hugged them close. "Time to brush your teeth."

At the bathroom sink, the girls giggled and used their toothbrushes as mini swords.

Their laughter bounced into the hallway. Smiling, Tate tidied the living room and kitchen. They could enjoy a little sisterly fun for a few minutes before he stepped in. He wasn't exactly a housekeeping whiz, but he got by, and the results weren't too important anyway. His twins didn't notice, and his parents and sister forgave him a few dust bunnies.

"We're ready, Daddy," Ella called from the bathroom and waited in the hallway for him to appear.

After stories, he tucked them into bed. Then he stretched, flopped on the sofa, and flipped TV channels. But the more he tried to relax, the more he felt his chest vibrate with a restlessness he couldn't contain. Leaping up, he paced from the living room to the kitchen and down the hallway. He listened to the soft breathing of his sleeping twins, retraced his steps, and stared at the moon high in the inky sky outside the picture window.

He usually headed to bed soon after the girls to recharge after his demanding workdays. The steady physical work and the harsh elements drained him in a way hockey never did. Hockey shot him full of adrenaline and chased away fatigue. It spurred him on to the next challenging game. Blood percolating, he needed action. Tonight, an early bedtime held no appeal at all, so he had called Krista before he changed his mind.

Now, feeling slightly awkward, he rushed to explain the reason for his impromptu call. "I have a question you're the best person in town to answer." He tried to calm his breathing enough to hide the sound.

"I'm flattered you consider me the resident expert."

Hearing her sound mildly amused encouraged him to forge ahead. "You know more about figure skates than me." He cleared his throat. His specialty was sturdy hockey skates with curved blades. What did he know about girls' skates with toe picks?

"I agree."

He heard her smile around her words. Feeling slightly foolish at her teasing, he sensed his face warming and was glad she couldn't see his discomfort. "I wanted to ask about the twins' skates." His excuse for the call sounded lame. The question could definitely have waited for a consultation at the rink, and now she'd probably think he'd use any old excuse to connect. "Do you think their skates give enough support for jumps and spins? They need the right equipment to do their best." He sucked in a breath, waiting for her opinion.

"I'm glad you understand the difference proper ankle support makes."

"Yep. Hockey taught me that much." He felt the pain like a stab of how much he missed the days when he rocketed across the ice and launched a puck at the net.

"At the first lesson, I didn't look carefully at the calibre of skates they wore, but I'll take special notice tomorrow. I'll catch you after practice and let you know."

"I'd appreciate it. Thank you."

"That's my job. I only wish all parents were as committed to their children's success." She paused. "Was there anything else you wanted to discuss?"

As businesslike as she sounded, she might have given him a compliment for his parenting. A wave of pride washed through his chest. He did his best. "Nope. Nothing else tonight. Next time, who knows?" Argh. There he went again with a comment that surprised him. He should make sure another call didn't happen. "Okay. I'll let you dive back into the tub. See you tomorrow."

"Good night."

Her voice floated soft and happy. Tate clicked End, mimed a quick flick of a hockey stick, and threw his arms high like he just scored. Crazy, he knew. Maybe someday, he'd be strong and confident enough to handle a little romance. For now, he'd pretend. The idea warmed him from the toes up. Only twenty hours to go until he saw her again.

Chapter 8

On Tuesday, snow fell like a white curtain, and the wind whipped it into such a blinding swirl many of the out-of-town skaters couldn't travel to the rink. The miserable weather left Krista with time to extend lessons for the smaller number of students and take more frequent breaks to pet Pearl.

Before Gracie and Ella's group lesson, Krista pulled them aside. "I promised your dad I'd see if your skates are sturdy enough for jumps and spins."

"What's sturdy?" Gracie looked down and examined her feet.

"Yeah, why are you looking at our feet?" Ella bowed her blonde head.

"Sturdy means strong, so your ankles stay straight and don't flop sideways when you skate." She kneeled and squeezed their ankles. "Your daddy and I think you girls are very good skaters already. And you're going to get even better." She smiled up at the eager pair and felt a small surge of excitement mixed with trepidation. Why did she speak for their father as though he was her partner? She shook off the inappropriate rush of emotion. Tate and she were partners only in wanting Ella and Gracie to excel on the ice.

"Now wiggle." Krista straightened and demonstrated the motion, turning her ankles in and out. "Let me see what happens when you try."

Gracie giggled and held out her arms. "I'm a ballerina."

Ella imitated her exaggerated pose and forced her ankles back and forth.

"Now, show me a spiral." She watched as first Gracie, followed by Ella, took several big pushes, extended her arms, bent, and curved a leg up behind. They both performed the move with hardly a wobble.

Krista instructed the twins to try a few more moves and assessed the situation. Now she could offer Tate a professional recommendation. Gracie and Ella both wore skates ideal for recreational skating and adequate for novice figure skating moves. Tate didn't need to invest in new skates right now, but by the start of next season, he would. Both girls would likely have progressed to the point where they should upgrade to competitive-calibre brands.

She was ready to report to Tate whenever she had a chance. "Your skates look good. Now, off you go. Work hard and have fun." Krista waved them away and swept her gaze along the boards and up into the stands but didn't spot Tate yet. Maybe in the stormy weather, he'd need to clear snow and would send someone else to pick up his daughters.

"Thank you, Krista." Ella swiveled and caught her balance before she glided toward a clear patch of ice.

"Can Ella and I play with Pearl after practice? I love her cute face and soft ears." Gracie slid her blades forward and backward like scissors.

"Maybe, if your dad says it's okay." Krista clapped her mitts together. "But first, you need to practice your toe loop."

"Okay." Gracie grinned, hopped, and slid away.

Nearing the end of the two-hour session, she still saw no sign of Tate. "Time to clear the ice." She and her teenage helpers, Molly and Brandon, ushered the kids toward the changeroom.

As the kids tottered by wearing skate guards on their blades, they passed Pearl.

She batted them with her tail, and most of them stopped to admire her.

Gracie fell to her knees and threw her arms around the dog's neck. "I want you for my very own."

Pearl grunted, plunked into a sitting position, and gave Gracie wet licks on the cheek.

She was a big dog, even a little overweight, but exercise would get her into shape.

"My turn." Ella bent to hug the dog.

Pearl used her gentle retriever mouth to pull a mitten off her hand.

"Hey! Give it back." Laughing, she tugged from side to side.

Pearl released her hold and dropped the mitten at Ella's feet.

"Good dog," said Ella.

"Where's Daddy?" He's supposed to come and get us for supper." Gracie crinkled her forehead.

"Gracie, don't worry." Ella patted her sister's arm. "He'll come."

Krista glanced around and still couldn't spot Tate. Faint concern and disappointment nudged her chest. She needed to return to the ice any minute with the advanced group, but she wanted to see Tate first. Where was he? Talking about the girls' skates was a good excuse, but the truth was any reason to gaze into his deep-brown eyes was enough. At the last moment, she got her wish.

Tate rushed in, brushing snow off his shoulders. He looked both ways, checked his watch, and made a beeline toward the open gate to the ice surface next to where she stood.

She swallowed a sharp breath. Every time she saw him, he awakened feelings she didn't believe were possible.

"Sorry I'm late." He breathed heavily. "On the way here, I pushed out three stuck vehicles. The roads are icy, and the drifts are piling up."

"Don't worry." Krista wanted to ease the strain around his eyes. "Ella and Gracie's lesson just finished, and they headed off to the changeroom with the other kids. I don't think they've missed you too much yet." She smiled and touched a hand to his snowy forearm, then retracted it like a spring. She didn't want to send the wrong message she considered him anything but a parent just like any other. Besides, she only had a few spare moments between lessons to chat anyway. "Everything is fine."

He flicked his arms, and flecks of snow fell to the rubber mat. "I intended to get here earlier so I'd be ready and waiting as soon as you took a break. I didn't want to interrupt or make Gracie and Ella wonder when I'd get here."

"Let's step into the hallway."

He turned and led the way.

She followed, swallowing and forcing herself to divert her gaze from the rear view of his broad shoulders and thick legs. She shivered, not just from the chilly environment and the cold radiating from his clothing. His physique, even through his parka, tempted her thoughts away from figure skating into distant and risky territory. Veering right, she allowed a trickle of senior skaters to pass toward the ice. Olivia should be part of the group but didn't file by.

In the hallway, he faced her and waited. His cheeks beamed red, and he swiped a hand across his face where drops of melting snow glistened.

"This won't take long." Even though she breathed damp, cool rink air, she felt her face grow warm. Wishing she had enough time for a longer conversation, she avoided small talk. "I don't think you need to buy new skates at this point. The ones the twins are wearing right now are pretty good quality. They are fine for their level. As long as their feet don't grow too quickly, their skates should last for this season." Aware of the time and the chatter of the skaters, which meant socializing and not practising, she glanced over her shoulder. "When I have more time, I can make some suggestions on what to look for when you upgrade ahead of next season."

"Great. Thanks for the advice." He nodded and held her gaze for a beat.

Was the topic of skates the only reason he wanted to connect today? Her heart thrummed in her chest at the idea his interest might extend beyond skating equipment. "I better go, but I'll see you Saturday."

"Right. See you then." Smiling, he backed up a step.

"Oh, one more thing. I told Gracie and Ella they could play with Pearl if you say it's okay." She tilted her head.

He flashed a grin.

As she spun and hurried to the ice, she resisted an

unexpected pull like an elastic band tugging her back. Right now, Saturday seemed forever away.

****

"Got weekend plans?" On Friday afternoon at quitting time, Tate's assistant, Nick, propped a scoop shovel inside Tate's storage shed.

Located on the edge of town, the large metal-clad building housed all the equipment for Snow & Grow. "Yep. For once I do." Tate wouldn't share details with just anyone, but he knew Nick was a steady guy with lots of life experience. Best of all, he knew when to listen and never gossiped about anybody.

Nick raised his heavy gray eyebrows under the brim of a thick knit hat with ear flaps reaching to his chin. "Yeah?"

"Yeah. Besides spending time with Ella and Gracie, I got roped into building sets for the ice show." An image of Krista whisked by, and Tate blinked and cleared his throat. "I have to meet with the new skating coach to make some plans."

Nick grunted. "Hope she won't work you too hard." He crinkled his weathered angular face into a grin. "Heard she's one tough cookie. Pleasant enough but doesn't let the kids get away with anything."

Tate pushed away an uneasy tug in his gut. Nick was probably right. She set high standards on the ice and in everything she did. "Have a good weekend. Forecast says no snow, so I shouldn't need to call you back to work."

"I'll be around. If you need me, call." Nick straightened and slapped Tate on the back. "Have fun on your date."

"It's not a—" Tate cut short his protest when he

caught a glimpse of Nick's wrinkled wink. All evening, Tate counted down the hours until Saturday. He'd been eagerly waiting all week. Every time he closed his eyes, he pictured every single detail of Krista's faintly freckled face. Her eyes shaded from the color of a summer sky to royal blue like a January sunset.

Cozied under a patchwork quilt on the living room sofa, he read five stories to Gracie and Ella. Anticipation flipped in his stomach, and he worked hard to focus on story time rather than on seeing Krista tomorrow. Hands practically vibrating as he turned pages, he imagined running his fingers through her lush curls.

"Daddy, you're not listening again." Gracie tapped his thigh between stories. "Guess what Sam did today?"

She yanked his attention back to reality. "I'm sorry, darlin. What did Sam do now?" The twins admired their older cousin and frequently shared stories of his latest escapades.

"He made a model volcano. Right, Ella?"

Ella nodded.

Gracie spread her figures upward. "And then all this gooey stuff spilled all over Auntie Carly's floor." She giggled. "It was really messy."

"Cool." He smiled at first one girl and then the other. He was so lucky to have such bright lights in his life. They seemed happy in their extended family and thrived in school and at skating. But even with a dedicated grandma and aunt to love them, they still lacked the presence of a devoted mother. A pang clutched his stomach, and he drew them both close in a hug. Swallowing a lump in his throat, he sighed. He hated to think about what they had all lost when

Whitney passed away.

As a Friday treat, he switched on a movie and served Gracie and Ella their own bowls of buttery popcorn. He chuckled at the mischievous dog in the show and even more at their shrieks and giggles.

"Daddy, can we please get a dog?" When the show ended, Ella tapped his knee.

"Yeah, Daddy, please." Gracie jiggled and pulled the quilt under her chin. "Can we get a puppy just like Pearl?"

"Maybe when you're older and can take the dog for walks and brush him and feed him."

"You mean *her*." Ella tugged her share of the blanket. "We want a girl dog."

"We'll see." He stood and gathered the quilt. "It's bedtime for two tired munchkins." After tucking in Gracie and Ella, he tidied the kitchen and let his thoughts drift back to Krista. The smell of popcorn and butter hung in the air, and he popped open a window and let in a puff of cold air. Now, he smelled burning wood from a neighbor's fireplace, and he quickly shut the window again.

He'd love to spend time with Krista in front of a cozy fireplace—talking, laughing, and cuddling. Should he dare risk his heart? Tomorrow, he'd see her twice in one day. In the morning, he'd take the twins to their skating lesson, and in the evening, he'd meet her back at the rink to get down to serious plans for the ice show. Fingers crossed a surprise snowfall wouldn't hit and bury him with too much work to get away.

Under a wide, sunny sky the next morning, Tate hustled the twins through a biting wind into the rink. "Hi, Janine. Hey, Brett." Following Gracie and Ella, he inhaled the familiar rink smells and lifted a hand to the folks sipping coffee in the lobby. "Catch you in there shortly." He nodded toward the rink. "Promised the twins I'd watch their lesson."

Errands could wait. If he accompanied Gracie and Ella into the arena, he might snatch a few words with Krista. His entire body hummed like he bumped along a gravel road. Even though he knew she couldn't possibly share the same attraction, a guy could still hope.

"Morning, ma'am." After tying the twins' skates, Tate nearly collided with Krista in the hallway. Bending to pet exuberant Pearl, he wracked his brain for something profound and witty to say. "How are you this fine winter day?" Even to himself, he sounded like an eager car salesman.

She widened her eyes and took a step back at the boisterous greeting. "Fine like the weather, thank you." Curving her lips into a bare hint of a smile, she lifted her gaze to meet his and then swept it toward the collection of skaters gathered beside the gate to the ice surface.

"Have a good practice session." Tensing inside his jacket, he shuffled sideways to let her pass. Today, she wore a red ski suit with black trim, and it suited her as well as the green one.

"Will do. I better go put these kids to work." She hustled away.

"See you later." She was in clear business mode, and he wouldn't interfere any longer. From behind, he watched the curve of her slim waist to her rounded hips and longed to trace her womanly shape with both hands. "Looking forward to meeting you later, ma'am." She likely had no idea of the intensity his words held.

For an instant, he needed a drink of cold lemonade more than hot chocolate.

Instead, he opted for the usual hot beverage and joined Brett and Janine huddled in the stands. The wind outside had a way of increasing the chill inside, and he left his jacket fully zipped. "What's new?"

Brett shrugged. "Same old. No errands today?"

"Nah, not today. I figured I should lounge around the rink doing nothing like you." He elbowed Brett in the ribs. His buddy wore a gray beanie to keep his bald head warm.

"Ha." Brett gave Tate's shoulder a playful punch. "Real men know how to relax."

"You guys remind me of my brothers when they were about twelve." Janine tutted her tongue. "You want to know what's new, Tate?" She glanced both ways. "I'll tell you." Leaning closer, she lowered her voice. "The new coach has been at the club two weeks, and already, I've received three complaint calls. People say she should ease up and get to know the kids before she cracks down. I asked her to be firm. I didn't expect a drill sergeant."

"I hope you told them to give her a break." Tate clamped his jaw. How could people judge so quickly? The back of his neck grew hot. Sure, Krista had high standards and came across as strong and in charge. If he wasn't mistaken, the whole reason the club had hired her was to produce results. He felt a compelling urge to defend her actions. "Ella and Gracie like her."

Janine twisted her head and blinked. "Why so defensive?"

She reminded him of a curious blackbird. "Krista deserves a fair chance." Tate gulped his hot chocolate, and it stung his throat.

"I hate to say, but I think they have a point." Janine wrinkled her nose. "My Olivia refused to come to skating last Tuesday. The first practice session with Krista didn't go well."

Tate kept his mouth shut and tried to contain a judgment fighting to the surface of his mind. He noticed Olivia strutting and tossing her hair around town and suspected she might be a tad spoiled.

"I'm with Tate." Brett wrapped both hands around his disposable coffee cup. "Give the poor woman a chance."

"I won't do anything dramatic yet." Janine crossed her arms over her coat. "For now, the problem will stay our secret. But I came today to evaluate the situation. If I see any issues, I'll nip them in the bud."

"Take your time, Janine." Tate thumped a fist on the arm of his seat. "The club wants to build a reputation for excellence. Don't lower standards just because some kids can't handle hard work."

"Are you saying Olivia is afraid of work?" Janine stared at Tate.

Janine's indignant tone didn't faze him. "I'm saying nobody should jump to conclusions about Krista. The committee agreed she was the best choice."

"Thanks for your input. Excuse me, fellows." Janine stood, plastered on a stiff smile, and eased out of the row of seats. Moving quickly, she disappeared down the stairway toward the lobby.

"You chased away Janine in a hurry." Brett chortled and rubbed his hands on his thighs. "I'm impressed."

"She'll get over it." Tate chuckled but inside, his

irritation simmered. He had no doubt Krista was a talented coach and knew what was best for the skaters. Sure, she demanded a lot, but she deserved a fair chance. Skaters' parents shouldn't label her as too tough and criticize her methods so soon. A lot of people agreed Lauren, the coach she replaced, had been a little too nice.

He turned his attention to the motion on the ice. Krista led the group in a zigzag pattern around the perimeter, bending, stretching, and posing her arms in different positions as she glided. True, she wore a stern set to her face out there and didn't allow any of the kids to dawdle on the way to their lessons or to linger on the sidelines. But when she smiled…she lit the arena.

Discipline was a good quality. Better to set the right tone right from the start. Wistful memories skidded into his chest. He'd played enough hockey to know athletes needed to push themselves beyond their limits.

"Hey, want to drop by the rec center this evening and play some pool?" Brett glanced at Tate. "Been a while since I beat you."

"Ha. Have you ever beaten me?" Tate laughed. He traced Krista's every movement on the sheet of ice below. "Sounds like fun, but sorry, not tonight."

"No babysitter? Hilary might not mind taking care of Gracie and Ella at our place for a couple of hours. Annie would love to see them."

"Uh, naw." He paused and decided how much to say. Brett wasn't the type to gossip. As a doctor, he knew how to keep secrets. "I'm getting together with Krista." He motioned his head toward the ice.

"Didn't take long. Nicely done." Brett elbowed

him in the side.

"It's a business meeting." Tate swallowed a mouthful of his drink. "About the ice show."

"Sure it is." Brett injected a hint of innuendo into his tone and chuckled. "Why else would you book a free Saturday night with an attractive, single woman? Especially when you could play pool with yours truly." He planted a thumb in his chest.

Why did Tate wish it was more than a meeting? Usually, he didn't really miss dating and didn't have the energy or desire to even try. But ever since he had danced with Krista, his life lacked a little excitement and companionship.

Krista stirred a loneliness that kids, family, and friends couldn't fill. He craved more time with her, and for an instant, he dared to imagine she'd stay. But he knew better. A future together was nothing but a futile daydream. A glamorous figure skater wasn't the right match for a hometown guy who mowed lawns and shovelled snow for a living. Neither was a woman who would move on as soon as the snow melted. "A pool game would probably be more fun." Tate shifted on the bleachers and slid his gaze from Ella to Gracie to Krista in quick succession and then let it linger on Krista. "She twisted my arm. I agreed to design and build sets for the ice show. She has some fancy Mexican theme in mind."

"Olé." Brett elbowed Tate's side. "You have your hands full."

"Yep." Lesson time was nearly over. He watched Krista motion the kids into a circle around her and give final instructions. He wouldn't try to chat with her now, but he'd spend plenty of time with her later. An unfamiliar sensation skittered across his stomach. He should hurry home and tidy the house just in case after the meeting at the rink, he invited her back there for refreshments.

Standing next to Brett, Tate stretched to his full height. Clutching his empty paper cup, he headed down the steps to greet the twins.

"Adios, amigo. Have fun." Brett jostled along behind him.

Tate flashed a smirk over his shoulder, and his stomach jumped like a battery charger. Fun might be too much to hope for, but the evening would prove interesting, if nothing else.

Chapter 9

Saturday evening, Krista paced in her office changeroom and counted the mint-colored cement blocks in the walls encircling her. Focusing on something besides her meeting with Tate helped calm the butterflies in her stomach. The slap of hockey sticks and pucks against the boards drifted down the hallway and mixed with soft country music playing in here. She remembered from the wedding Tate liked it, and she didn't mind it either. She listened to all kinds of music as possibilities for skaters' programs.

Batting her tail against Krista's legs, Pearl tracked her every move.

"You're a good girl, Pearl." Krista squatted and hugged her dog. She hadn't known how much she needed her furry companion, but already, she had no doubt.

Krista's vision of the ice show backdrop and decorations stared from diagrams on her desk. She might put up with Tate's teasing, but she would not compromise on the non-traditional theme. She came to the club to make a difference in everything she touched.

Tate would arrive soon. She glanced down and surveyed her outfit for the meeting. Instead of throwing on any old thing, she chose beige skinny jeans, a cream cable-knit sweater, and tall brown boots. The effect was casual but classy and, judging by the reflection in the mirror in her bedroom, accentuated her trim shape.

She spun and changed direction again. Why did she want to see Tate's eyes light when he walked in the door? She shouldn't care so much how she looked for a business meeting. But he wasn't just anybody. He was the most attractive eligible bachelor in town, and from all appearances, he was nothing like Zach. He was a dedicated dad. He was hardworking, intelligent, and funny. He knew how to dance. She ticked a list of positives in her head. Was he truly as perfect as he appeared? Why test her heart in the short time she'd stay?

As if thinking about him made him materialize, she heard a tap at the door, rotated, and faced it. "Come in."

Grinning, Tate swung the door open. "At your service, ma'am."

"I like the sound of that." Krista's breath caught in her throat. His velvety brown eyes glinted with spunk. The cleft in his chin burrowed deep. His masculine good looks made him one of the most ruggedly handsome guys she'd ever known. Maybe the faint scar under his left eye was a lasting reminder of a run-in with a hockey puck. Drifting her gaze from his face to his down jacket to his faded jeans, she drank in his casual, outdoorsy style.

Krista tossed her hair and placed a hand on her hip. "Thanks for being willing and able to help. I admit I tend to expect a lot." She laughed, but a grain of truth tiptoed under her words. In the past, she'd been criticized by skating parents more than once for her firm approach. She called it reinforcing high expectations.

They called it demanding too much of their

children.

"Can I buy you a coffee or hot chocolate from the machine in the hallway? It's the finest rink blend I've tasted." Smirking, she tilted her head toward the doorway.

He laughed. "You need to get out more. But hot chocolate sounds good right about now." He pulled off his gloves, tucked them under one arm, and rubbed his hands together. Unzipping his jacket, he revealed a charcoal-and-brown flannel shirt.

She liked the way it hugged his chest and painted his eyes to nearly black. "Have a seat. I'll be right back." She returned a couple of minutes later with two steaming drinks in paper cups, set them on the desk, and dropped into her chair.

"Thanks." He rolled forward to face her. "Let's get right down to business. I don't want to leave my parents babysitting for too long." He claimed a cup, sipped, and flinched.

"Yes, sir. I agree." She gave a mock salute. "I'll launch right into details then." Keeping their interaction to work only had been her intent all along. He didn't need to tell her. Clutching a sketch, she rotated so he could examine it.

"What? Not Hawaii?" He laughed and pushed slightly backward, then forward on his chair's rollers.

"Mexico, all the way." She wouldn't give him the satisfaction of cracking a smile.

"Fine, señorita. Mexico it is." He quirked an eyebrow.

Pearl flopped on the floor next to Krista, groaned, and curled up.

She must sense she was in for a bit of a wait. Krista

spent the next thirty minutes pointing out highlights of the backdrop she had designed and glancing at his expression to see if he was interested, bored, or amused. Judging by his wrinkled brow, muffled yawn, and twitching lips, which came and went in turn throughout her instructions, he jumped between all three.

He focused, nodded, and finished the rest of his drink.

"So, that's the plan." Finally, she took a breath and leaned back in her chair. Twirling a curly tendril of hair around a finger, she met his gaze. The more she visualized the results, the more she liked them. The club leadership committee, volunteers, and parents would be impressed. She was sure. "What do you think?"

Waiting for his answer, she tried to rein in her impatience. His slow, easy pace must be a far cry from his speed manoeuvring a snowplow or stickhandling a hockey puck. She breathed and told herself to relax.

The room heater kicked in with a clunk and blasted hot air throughout the room.

"Very creative, señorita." He nodded, widened his eyes, and spread a slow grin across his face. "You have some good ideas there. But—"

"Good? They're great ideas," she burst out. Who was he to downgrade her inspired theme and label it plain good? And what did his *but* mean? "Sorry. Just had to clarify. Continue."

"I have a business to run and two little girls to raise." He rolled backward, crossed a boot over the opposite knee, and slapped his hands on the arms of the chair. "Your plan turns set building into a full-time job. So, unfortunately, I'm not your guy." He quirked an eyebrow and shook his head.

Krista leaned forward, planted her hands on the desk, and clamped her jaw so it didn't drop so far she'd trip over it. He said *no*. How could he? He had already committed to the job. She took a deep breath and cooled the agitation she wanted to spit out of her mouth. "I'm surprised you would decide not to follow through at this point. I already told Janine you agreed."

His eyes darkened, and the last trace of a smile dropped off his face.

"At the time you twisted my arm, I didn't know your expectations were higher than the rink roof. I can see that now, and I don't want to let you down with the quality of my work. Better to quit now than deal with an awkward situation later."

The situation was already awkward. Krista had a vision, and if he would agree, he could get her there. She didn't want to go back to Janine and report she'd failed in her first task related to the ice show. She couldn't admit Tate backed out. "I'm sorry to hear. From what Janine said, I'm sure you'd be an asset to the ice show team. Of course, it's your choice" She wouldn't grovel. She wouldn't let him know her spirits just plummeted like a nasty fall on ice. "Can you recommend anyone else for the job?" She clasped her hands on the desk and pictured his cute little twins. Of course, he didn't want to steal too much time away from his family. But still...she had expected him to keep his word. Obviously, she couldn't rely on him like she thought.

"Not offhand." He uncrossed his leg and smacked his hands on his thighs. "But I'll let you know."

"All right. I guess this meeting is a wrap." And a

waste of time. She shuffled her diagrams and notes into a neat pile, thrust back her chair, and shot to her feet. "I'll see you around the rink."

"Yes, ma'am, señorita." He rose, and his chair creaked. He straightened until he was nearly a foot taller than her. He smiled down. "No hard feelings?"

Breathing his subtle, fresh-air scent, she felt her heart flutter in a most annoying way. She shook her head. "Everybody can be replaced." The trouble was her words might not be true in a small town. The pool of volunteers to draw on wasn't very deep, and she couldn't guarantee she'd find anyone else to take the job.

He glanced at his fitness tracker. "My parents don't mind babysitting until nine. Care to join me at Daisy's for a snack?"

She wanted to, more than anything. The pull was so great she took a step backward to resist. But she couldn't go. He had disappointed her, and she wasn't impressed. Tucking a curl behind her ear, she glanced at his eyes and then away. The heater hummed, and suddenly, she felt hot in her heavy sweater. She needed to escape with her feelings intact. "Thank you, but no. I better get home."

"Okay. You'll miss a good time. Daisy's is the place to be on Saturday night in Blue Sky." He laughed and threw on his jacket.

She smirked. On her first visit, she quickly determined Daisy's was a popular diner filled with chatty locals and home-cooked food, but it was hardly a happening nightspot.

"If I can't interest you in joining me, I'll walk you home," he insisted. "I doubt you've had enough of my charming company."

****

"Please."

Tate hadn't even said hello yet. Leaning on edge of the kitchen countertop that held his landline, he instantly recognized Krista's voice. Surprise and anticipation jumped in his stomach. Gracie's and Ella's voices and giggles trickled down the hallway from their bedroom where they were playing a game. He was free this Sunday afternoon to talk to Krista but hadn't expected to hear from her. She should be busy with skating lessons.

He chuckled. "Please, what?" He glared at the stack of dishes piled in the sink of his compact kitchen. Housework in a home with two busy girls was a never-ending task. This mess was next on his list to tackle. The sun glinting in the windows warmed the kitchen and beamed cheeriness but also highlighted the crumbs on the white wooden table. Light country music drifted through the room, and he lowered the volume so he didn't miss a thing she said.

"Tate, I'm just on a quick break between lessons." She inhaled an audible breath. "I talked with Janine, and we both agree you will be hard, if not impossible, to replace."

"So, you figure you really need me?" He couldn't resist teasing.

"For the ice show. Yes."

If she picked up the innuendo, she ignored it.

"We need your building skills. You're the best in town. And think of the benefits to your dear little daughters.

He paced to the living room and scanned outside

115

the wide window at the sparkly ice crystals blowing across the street in front of his house. Matching his love of ice, snow, and everything winter, his living room surrounded him with shades ranging from light gray to navy blue.

Peering up at the thickening sky, he sensed another blast of winter headed this way. Fingers crossed the snow in the weather forecast would hold off until at least the morning so he didn't need to call on his parents or Carly for overnight babysitting service. When snow fell, he jumped to work. "Uh…" Truth be told, he had felt slightly guilty since last evening when he backed out. She was practically begging. How was a guy supposed to react?

"Please, say *yes*. When I'm not teaching, I'll even babysit. If you need to work in the evenings, you can count on me to look after your girls."

"Now there's an offer that's hard to refuse."

"So, is that a *yes*?"

"It's a definite *maybe*. Can I call you later?" Tate's pulse quickened. He should stand strong—not fall under her spell.

"It's not a *yes*, but okay, I guess."

"You sound like a poet." He laughed at her rhyming reply. He shouldn't joke and drag out the call, but he couldn't resist. Her laughter softened his resolve. "I'll think about your request on one condition." He wasn't a total pushover.

"Name it."

"You trade in the Mexican fiesta for a winter wonderland."

"The winter theme is old and boring. We get enough of winter in real life."

"We're a traditional bunch here in Blue Sky. If we recycle the usual theme, we'll reuse a lot of the materials from previous years. My job will be a lot easier and less time-consuming. Think about it." A few snow flurries whipped from the sky past his kitchen window, and he glanced up at the thick billowing clouds. Proof of his heavy workload floated right there.

"Daddy, Gracie won't let me use her doll clothes." Ella's squeal echoed down the hallway.

"They're mine. Let go." Gracie screeched.

The argument erupted in a noisy flurry. "Excuse me for a moment." Tate covered the phone, padded to the girls' room, and stepped into a world of fluffy pink like cotton candy. Gracie and Ella were best friends but had the usual sibling squabbles now and then. Of course, the minor conflicts always happened at the most inopportune times. He furrowed his forehead and threw a stern look at the pair huddled between their twin beds. "I'm talking to someone. Please, lower your voices and share. Both of you."

They glanced up.

"But…" Gracie stuck out her chin.

"No *buts*," he insisted.

They lowered their heads and quietly resumed their negotiations.

He retraced his steps to the living room. "Sorry. I'm back. I'll call you later and let you know." The girls' exchange underlined how much he was needed on the home front. It wasn't fair to Gracie and Ella or to his parents and sister for him to be away too often.

"Thank you. I'll wait for your verdict."

A little extra warmth coated her words, and attraction hit him as fast as a flying puck. Why did she stir feelings he should keep parked on ice? "Bye for now, Krista."

"Almost goodbye, Tate. One more thing…"

"More?" He chuckled and breathed to relax his churning emotions. He turned away from the window and eyed the sports magazine and early-reader books strewn on the round gray ottoman in front of the sofa. The ever-present clutter was his reality. Totally organized Krista didn't fit.

"I'll take you up on your invitation to join you for snacks at Daisy's."

"You will? What if my offer didn't allow for rain checks?" What was wrong with him? Flirting was dumb. Why act like he could actually date her? She probably suggested Daisy's as nothing more than a friendly, no-hard-feelings gesture.

"Then we're both out of luck, aren't we?"

"Would be very unfortunate, señorita." He chuckled and paced in front of the sofa. His dark blue jeans were almost the same color.

"Hey, don't call me señorita when you want to change the ice show theme. Are you rubbing salt in the wound?"

She sounded more amused than indignant, which was encouraging. "Good point. Maybe I'll call you Snow Queen." He couldn't resist bantering, and she didn't seem to mind. Friends did that kind of thing all the time.

"I like the regal sound. But it's a bit cool."

"Maybe it suits you." He made his voice sound light and teasing so she didn't feel insulted. He suspected she came across as unapproachable when she felt uncomfortable or fought for something she believed.

She breathed a sharp intake of air. "Ha, Snowman."

"At least they're round and jolly." He chuckled to show her he didn't mind her teasing back. "Seriously, you won't find a nicer guy."

"I can't be too sure."

He pictured a smile around her words. She sounded like she meant to tease, but did she really mean other men waited in the wings? He shouldn't care, but somehow, he did. He didn't want to picture her dating someone else. "Okay. I'll wait for a second chance to invite you to Daisy's."

"Sure. Now I'll say goodbye."

"Talk later." He barely squeezed in his words before the phone clicked off. He dropped into the easy chair at a right angle to the sofa, plunked his feet on the ottoman, and stared at the artwork on the opposite wall. He was no decorating whiz, but the winter scene, selected by Carly, tied the whole room together. Too bad his life wasn't so neat and tidy. By flirting with Krista, he opened a door that should remain firmly locked. She'd picked up his broad hint he'd like to see more of her, but now, he realized his mistake.

Leaping to his feet, he strode to the kitchen, grabbed a damp cloth, and attacked the sticky countertops and table until they gleamed. If only he could wipe away his uncertainty as easily. Ever since he met Krista at the wedding, she had invaded his daydreams. Could he work with her on the ice show? Despite his home's cozy warmth, he shivered. Grabbing a broom, he swept the kitchen floor in swooping strokes.

"Daddy," Ella hollered right behind him.

He jumped. Apparently, she had abandoned the game of dolls and jolted him from daydreams of Krista back to reality.

"Will you play the fish card game with Gracie and me?"

He examined her wide-eyed face and smiled at both girls.

They beamed, fidgeting on the spot.

Who could resist an invitation like that? "You bet I will, darlins, as soon as I hear the magic word." He set aside the broom. Housework could always wait.

"Please," they chorused in unison.

He smiled and patted their heads. They were his number one priority. Nothing—no one—should distract him for a moment. If he said *yes* to volunteering for Krista, he predicted things were about to get very interesting and maybe a little too tempting for his own good.

Chapter 10

Two weeks later, at seven on a Saturday evening, Krista scanned the faces of the ice show committee members. In the rink meeting room, they sat around a black rectangular table and clutched paper cups of coffee or hot chocolate. Located on the second level of the rink above Krista's office, the room overlooked the ice surface. Through a large acrylic window, she spotted the junior boys hockey team practicing below and heard the sharp crack of pucks *thunking* against the rink boards.

The group included Janine as club president, two mothers of skaters, Hilary and Roxanne, and Tate. Dressed casually in jeans, boots, and sweaters, they looked ready for any chill from the rink.

When Tate had called back to re-accept the role of head of construction for the ice show, he made her day. She did a small celebration spin, and just hearing his voice sent a whole flock of butterflies into her stomach.

"So, Snow Queen, how do you feel about going back to being señorita?" he had asked.

"Pardon me?" She wasn't sure she heard correctly.

"The ice show theme," he explained. "If you are stuck on trying something new, I'll support you."

"Are you sure?" Surprise and relief jumped inside her.

"Nah." He chuckled.

"Tate, don't mess with me." She huffed. He couldn't resist trying to get a reaction.

"Yeah, I'm sure."

He switched his tone from joking to sincere.

"We can't recruit a new coach, task you with improving things around here, and then shut down your ideas in the first month. I wouldn't choose a Mexican theme, but I can live with it."

"What about the extra work?" Her request tore him away from his twins and his business. He had made that plenty clear. She better hope the town escaped any major snowfall until after the ice show in January.

"Remember, you said you're willing to babysit. I might take you up on your offer."

"Right. It's a deal." She hadn't expected he'd actually ask her to babysit, but she didn't mind at all. If Pearl was allowed to come along, she would love the job too.

"I'll see you at the next committee meeting. Bye for now, señorita."

She had clicked off the call and spotted her huge grin in the hall mirror. Mission accomplished. Now she just had to win over the rest of the group. Abandoning her daydream, she breathed in air laden with the scents of the arena and strong coffee.

"Let's get started." Janine straightened and poised a pen for notes. Much thinner than her mother, she blinked and flicked her short dark hair.

She moved her head around in quick, bird-like thrusts. Krista pictured a crow ready to pounce at any moment.

"Thank you all for coming. I'll run through my checklist, and you can ask any questions." Janine tapped her pen. "Of course, Krista will handle all the show music and choreography with the skaters." With a tight-lipped smile, she nodded at Krista.

Detecting a hint of coolness from Janine, Krista felt a slight shiver ripple across her shoulders. Had she done something to offend her boss? She needed Janine on her side to make the ice show and the whole winter work out well.

"Thank you for volunteering to coordinate costumes, Hilary." Janine flashed her a wide smile.

Hilary nodded.

She was tiny and blonde, and her wavy hair swished when she moved her head. Krista trusted her gentle, positive manner. Maybe she was an ally.

"Happy to."

Her little girl, Annie, with brown hair looked nothing like her mother. She was in the beginner group with Gracie and Ella.

"Roxanne, with your outgoing personality, you're perfect to head up promotion and ticket sales." Janine pointed her pen toward Roxanne and screwed up her face into exaggerated amusement.

"You bet." Roxanne's hearty laugh shook her whole body from her frizzy black hair to her feet in chunky black boots. "Leave it to me."

"Then we have our gentleman on the team." Janine winked and swooped a hand toward Tate. "The man who'll pull together all the sets and props we need."

Tate tilted back in his chair and stretched his long legs under the table. "I'm ready."

Glancing across the table, Krista stopped a breath partway through. Could he get any more attractive? His eyes absorbed and reflected the rich brown color of his sweater, and his shadow of stubble added just the right touch of ruggedness to his handsome face.

He removed his knitted hat and ran a hand through his hair.

She wanted to trace the path with her own hand. Everything about him made her crave more, which made focusing on the meeting very difficult.

"Krista and I have already called a list of possible volunteers to work with each of you." Janine glanced around the table. "We twisted a few arms, and participation is looking good. Basically, we try to recruit at least one or two willing people from each skater's family to take on some sort of role. Sometimes, grandparents and older siblings help." Janine marked a big check next to the first item on her list. "Next on the agenda is the theme. Of course, we always create a winter wonderland, but Krista will share her thoughts on how to make the show bigger and better this year."

Krista smiled and swept her gaze around the circle. "Since I arrived, I've pictured a refresh. You've used the winter wonderland theme for many years, so I came up with another idea."

A furrow formed on Janine's forehead above her nose. Her mouth stretched into a straight line.

Maybe Krista should have given her a preview, but then again, the program elements sat squarely in her role as head coach.

"How exciting!" Roxanne grinned. "I'm all for something new."

"Well, tell us more." Janine crossed her arms. She flickered a smile but quickly let it drop off her face.

Apprehension rippled through Krista's middle. Janine didn't seem as impressed as when she welcomed her to town. Olivia's obstinate personality probably had more than a little to do with the change. "You get your fill of winter in this part of the world, and everybody loves a hot holiday. So…I'd like to create a Mexican fiesta on ice."

Hilary and Roxanne smiled and nodded.

Tate flipped his gaze from Krista to Janine and back.

Janine stared and blinked.

Plunging ahead, Krista smiled and tried to melt the chill seeping from Janine's end of the table. The heater fan whirred on, and she raised her voice over the hum. "Tate will build us a scene with beach, ocean, and palm trees in bright tropical colors." Nearly breathless, she rushed on. "The costumes will include beachwear and traditional Mexican outfits with colorful skirts and sombreros. It'll be a lot of fun." She stopped and smiled, and when Janine didn't smile back, she felt hot and awkward.

"Well, Janine's the president, of course, and she has the final say, but I like it!" Roxanne spoke first. "I can picture the girls twirling those big colorful skirts."

"The costumes would be really eye-catching and not too difficult to make. Kids could wear their own summery clothes for some of the numbers." Hilary smiled and tilted her head from side to side.

Her positive reaction added to Roxanne's enthusiasm, which was encouraging. But Krista still sensed a snowbank of resistance from Janine.

"Hmmm."

Clearly, Janine was not convinced.

"Tate, what are your thoughts? Creating an all-new theme will be a lot more work for the construction crew." Janine frowned.

"Yeah, it's true. But Krista and I talked already." Leaning forward, he rested his forearms on the table and locked his gaze on Janine. "I'm prepared to do whatever it takes. Like Krista and Roxanne said, maybe we should try something new."

The firm set of his jaw shouted he wasn't afraid to challenge Janine. Krista cheered inside. She felt Tate's strength, and in that instant, she knew she could count on his support.

Janine flushed and darted her gaze around the room. "I must say I'm surprised. Change can be good, but tradition is more important." She tapped her pen in quick clicks on the table. "My mom created the first winter wonderland over twenty-five years ago. I don't imagine she'll be too impressed to see it go by the wayside."

Krista gulped. She just unknowingly treaded on sacred ground. Daisy had already told her she and her late husband had been major contributors to the rink. Money bought influence, and Janine's family loyalty ran deep. "Oh, I had no idea." She glanced at Hilary, Roxanne, and Tate. "I certainly don't want to upset Daisy. You, as club president, need to support the idea too. But whatever we do, we need to decide soon to give us all enough time to prepare."

Krista mentally scrambled through options and landed on only two. Drop the Mexican fiesta before it caused Janine any more concern or consult Daisy. Of the two, Krista would choose a chat with Daisy. She came across as a lot more relaxed than her daughter. Then again, as the newbie on staff, maybe Krista should leave well enough alone.

Tate cleared his throat. "Leave it to me, Janine. I'll sweet-talk Daisy."

Krista contained a grin at Janine's frozen expression. Surprising warmth radiated from her chest to her face. She had found an ally.

****

A few days later, Tate roared down Main Street in his yellow snowplow with a blue flashing light on top. By noon, he should have cleared the last of the recent dump. Behind a thick white spray shooting in all directions, he almost missed the wave from a slight figure dressed in a navy-blue down jacket.

Next to Krista, Pearl trotted along, wagging her tail and pausing to scoop mouthfuls of snow.

Checking no car was travelling too close behind, he braked and threw the gear into Park. He hopped out of the truck, zipped his jacket up to his chin, and jogged to the sidewalk. "Good morning, señorita. Although today you look like the snow queen."

"Good morning, señor." She smiled. "Or maybe I should say Snowman."

He laughed, and his breath puffed out in a white cloud. "I was going to call you with the good news."

Pearl butted his leg with her shiny black nose.

"I like starting my day with good news." She stomped snow off her boots.

Bending to rub Pearl's furry side, he grinned up at Krista. "Daisy's all for a Mexican fiesta. She doesn't mind shelving winter a bit. She even said, 'I wish that grown-up daughter of mine would learn to chill.' " Straightening, he laughed. "I couldn't disagree."

"Yay! Great work, Tate." Krista pumped a fist bundled in a thick red mitten. "Does Janine know?"

"Probably. I talked to Daisy at the diner. She promised to handle Janine." Warmth filled his limbs, even in the cold. The glow on Krista's face did that to a guy. Even though he'd only known her for a few weeks, he had already memorized her vivid blue eyes, her perfect white smile, and her smooth pink complexion. She stoked a fire inside him that he didn't think possible.

"Thank you, señor." She sized him up from hat to boots. "Snowman suits you better." A curl sticking out from under her hat whipped across her face. "I'm excited about the show." She paused. "I owe you."

His chest filled like he just gave her the best gift possible. Now she had approval and could charge ahead with plans. Sure, she'd have her hands full with regular lessons and extra practices, but if anybody could handle it, she could. He just had to gaze into her intense eyes and see the firm set of her shoulders to know she would not be sent off course without a fight. Look at the way she had confronted the lazy skaters already. Whether Janine and the other parents liked it or not, she meant business.

He, of course, had just gotten himself into more work than he needed. But she was worth the effort. Seeing the smile on her face was a great exchange for a few extra hours of hammering and painting. Glancing at his truck idling, he smacked his leather mitts together. "Speaking of owing me, you did promise babysitting service. I might take you up on your offer, sooner than later."

"Of course. Just ask anytime. As long as I don't have lessons booked, I can help."

"Is tonight too soon?" He quirked an eyebrow. His

request might surprise her, but he took her at her word. He was doing her a big favor, so he didn't mind asking for something in return.

"Tonight? I teach until nine. Is that too late?"

"Nah. After I tuck in the girls, I'll have a nap until you get there. I'll go to the rink and take a good look at the props in storage. That'll tell me what I can revamp and what I need to start from scratch." His heart picked up at the thought of seeing her again this evening. He didn't really need to call on her services, but he might as well get started. He could make one fewer babysitting request of his parents and sister.

"It's a deal. I'll be there...if you tell me where you live."

He chuckled and admired the way the color of her cheeks tinted red, almost the color of her mitts. She would grab anybody's attention. She sure grabbed his. "Might help. Don't want you wandering the streets searching." He pulled his hat lower below his ears. "Two blocks over, light-blue house, third from the corner. You can't miss it. We don't bother much with street addresses in Blue Sky."

"Got it."

"Bring Pearl along too." Krista and her dog appeared to stick together, and he didn't mind a little dog hair on top of the clutter at his place.

At the sound of her name, Pearl wagged and circled until her leash nearly tangled.

Krista gently straightened the leash and pointed her in the right direction. "Thank you. Obviously, Pearl appreciates your invitation. Bye, Snowman." She hurried down the street.

He dashed back to the truck, and for the rest of the

day, he fought to concentrate on snowbanks instead of the snow queen.

That evening, Tate swung open the front door of his modest home and let a rush of cold air in along with Krista. "Thanks for coming." He waved her and Pearl inside. She must have a whole wardrobe of winter wear because he never knew what color jacket to expect.

"Brrr. I didn't get a chance to warm up after coaching on the ice for five straight hours." She shivered, pulled off her white hat, and shrugged off a gray jacket. "I'll leave my ski pants on for now."

"I turned on the fire and boiled the kettle for tea. The chair next to the fireplace is the warmest spot in the house." He pointed toward the blue armchair. "Make yourself at home." For the briefest of moments, he allowed himself to wish this actually was her home. Trying not to stare, he drank in her curves outlined in her turtleneck sweater and black pants. Her hair was tied back, but stray strands danced around her face. He wanted to kiss her full lips but forced himself to turn away.

"I'll show you the tea and snacks." He led her down the front hallway to the kitchen. Set neatly on the counter were a round white teapot and blue pottery mug. The scent of cinnamon spice trailed from the pot. Next to it sat a plate with cheese, crackers, and apple wedges. A small container of chocolate chip cookies rounded out the selection. "I figured you might be hungry after you finished coaching. Help yourself." He paused and glanced down at Pearl. "Sorry, pup. Nothing for you."

"You thought of everything, Tate." She flashed a wide smile. "Thank you."

"Gracie and Ella are asleep. You can relax. I plan to take no more than an hour." He grabbed his navy-blue down jacket off a hook near the back door, pulled it over his plaid flannel shirt, and paused. Should he tell her now or later?

Janine was the club president and responsible for communicating on behalf of the club, but concerning her own daughter, she still gossiped like any other parent about the new coach. True, around the rink, Krista wore a mostly serious expression. She made no apologies she expected a lot of the kids. Gracie and Ella had loved her on day one, but since then, they had complained a couple of times their new teacher was a little bit grumpy.

He didn't mind her pushing the twins to reach their full potential and wouldn't leap to any quick judgments. But her attitude clearly rubbed Janine and a few others the wrong way. Maybe he should mind his own business, but he wanted to at least give her a heads-up trouble might be brewing.

If he cautioned her before he left, he might lead her to sit and stew the whole time he was gone. If he waited until he returned, he'd have enough time to explain more details. Sweeping his gaze around the kitchen and her soft expression, he wavered. "Thanks for your help. See you in an hour." He zipped his jacket and strode to the front door. Right now, what she didn't know wouldn't hurt her. Later was a different story.

Chapter 11

A couple of weeks later, Krista paused and took a deep breath just inside the doorway of the Blue Sky Recreation Center. The building was old, but inside, the walls were freshly painted cream with white trim.

"Come on in and join the crowd, Krista. Welcome to your first WinDin. You're going to have a great time." Sitting at a chipped wood and chrome table, Daisy grinned in her role as greeter, gathering tickets and directing traffic. She wore her trusty royal-blue parka with furry trim to protect her against the frosty blast sweeping in every time somebody arrived.

"Oh, good. Sounds like fun." Krista stuffed her mitts into her pockets and unzipped her red jacket. Scanning the casually dressed guests drifting through the lobby area, she felt comfortable knowing she had chosen the right outfit for the occasion. Dark skinny jeans with tall black boots and a dark-gray sweater dotted with light-gray snowflakes fit in well with the informal atmosphere.

"The coat check is back there." Daisy swung her hand and pointed to her right. "You can buy raffle tickets from anybody wandering around wearing a yellow apron. Let's see... I seated you at a table with Tate, the twins, Brett, Hilary, and Annie. All the action is right through that doorway."

"Thanks, Daisy." Tate was one of her tablemates.

Did she imagine it, or did Daisy put some inflection on his name? Did she hint at a wink? The way she had already paired her up with Pearl without taking *no* for an answer, she probably didn't hesitate to dabble in a little human matchmaking too.

Anticipation rose and fell like a double jump in Krista's stomach. Tate was the whole package. He was genuinely nice, a hard worker, a caring dad, and extremely good-looking. But the timing for a relationship was all wrong, plain and simple. For two people meant to stay apart, they already spent more than enough time together working on the ice show and comparing notes on the twins' skating progress. She didn't need Daisy to force them together into what could never be reality.

Upbeat music, noisy voices, and bursts of laughter raced around her in a dizzying whirl. She said "hello" to a few people she recognized, and after leaving her jacket at the coat check, she wound toward the main doors. Community social events were not her favorite pastime because of the pressure to make small talk with people she hardly knew, but she had no choice about attending WinDin, the winter dinner and games night to raise money for rink programs. Like almost everything else in Blue Sky, it had a long history and plenty of community support. Janine and Tate both made sure she knew it was a command performance.

At the thought of giving a short speech about the ice show plans, she felt a faint, wavy sensation skate across her middle. Her part in the evening was small, but she didn't like the spotlight unless it was on ice. Still, no matter how she felt, she needed to convince more than a few people they should donate to the figure skating cause.

"Hi, Krista."

From behind, a little girl's voice grabbed her attention. "Hi, girls. Hi, Tate." She spun and faced Tate and then glanced down at Ella and Gracie, dressed in identical pink sweaters decorated with unicorns. They both flashed toothless grins. Suddenly, she felt hot, even in the draft from the entrance. "I hear we get to sit together at dinner."

"Yup." Gracie nodded. "With Annie and her mom and dad too."

"Lucky you, señorita." Tate quirked an eyebrow and chuckled. "Hey, why don't you two see if you can find Annie? Look for a table with the number sixteen on it."

"Okay, Daddy," Ella answered, and the pair giggled and buzzed away.

"Lucky you, Snowman." She eyed his broad chest. Under his blue denim shirt, a white T-shirt peeked out at the neckline. His face was freshly shaved, and his hair was gelled into place. He looked fit, masculine, and like the perfect dinner companion in a milling crowd of mostly strangers.

Just as quickly as she let her imagination dash away, she dragged it back to reality. The fun she shared with Tate at the wedding was only a short-lived blip, never intended to lead to more. She wasn't ready for a relationship now or maybe ever. For sure, she needed to settle somewhere first and learn to trust a man who would always offer support. Tate was a friendly face, the parent of two of her students, and the guy she depended on for backdrops. Nothing more.

He laughed. "I've been called worse. Should we

follow the girls to our table?" He gestured forward. "After you."

Feeling his gaze burning into her back, she led him through the crowd to their assigned table and paused before getting seated.

"Hello, Krista." Within seconds, Janine breezed up. "This isn't the time or place to discuss anything serious, but I'd like to book a private meeting at nine o'clock on Monday morning." Janine pursed her lips.

The way Janine lowered her voice hinted at an issue. She darted her head left and right, checking out the crowd like a bird hunting for worms.

Behind her, Olivia crossed her arms and glowered.

"Okay." Stiffening, Krista nodded. She glanced at her tablemates and caught Tate watching intently. "Can you let me know the topic so I can prepare?"

"Oh, just some questions and feedback about the skating program." Janine raised a hand, smiled, and waved at a woman passing by. Whipping her attention back to Krista, she dropped her smile and wrinkled her forehead.

As always, her dark hair remained precisely in place. Noticeably overdressed, she wore dressy black pants instead of jeans, and she paired them with a sparkly silver sweater.

"I'd rather save the details for our meeting. Well, enjoy the evening." Janine fixed her lips in a straight line and scooted away with Olivia trailing.

A sense of foreboding draped over Krista. Janine was the club president, and Krista couldn't afford to land on her bad side, if she wasn't already. Something about the woman's stiff expression and serious tone felt like a veiled threat.

She swallowed and told herself to erase the unsettling encounter out of her mind for now. She had plenty of time to worry later. Glancing at the table, she sized up her options and discovered the only available chairs were on either side of Tate.

"I saved you two spots." Tate pointed to either side of his chair.

She circled the table and sat between Tate and Hilary. "Thank you for saving me a seat next to Hilary. Now I'm assured of good company." She smirked and widened her eyes.

He gave an exaggerated harrumph. "That's all the thanks I get?"

"I'm sure she meant the guys too." Brett chuckled.

"Well..." Krista hunched her shoulders and pretended to consider the comment. She laughed along with the rest of them. They were a warm, friendly couple bound to make the evening a whole lot easier.

"Try to make a good impression, guys." Hilary leaned over toward Krista and pretended to confide in a voice loud enough for Brett and Tate to hear. "Once in a while, I catch them on their best behavior."

"I'll pay close attention, so I don't miss it." Krista laughed at Tate's exaggerated dropped jaw. Hilary knew how to joke and had a soft, kind look in her eyes. Maybe she could turn into a girlfriend. It would be nice to have another woman to socialize with in her free time. Her newlywed friend, Amy, lived much too far away. Hilary could probably fill her in on the local gossip, which was important here in a small town where everyone knew everyone else's business.

She scanned the table and smiled at Gracie, Ella, and Annie perched in a row like birdies chattering away. She breathed in the scent of melted cheese, oregano, and garlic wafting from the buffet, and her mouth watered.

Just then, Roxanne from the ice show committee stopped by their table. "Your turn to go and serve yourselves. Leave some for me, Tate and Brett." She grinned at Hilary and Krista.

"Ladies first." Tate swung an arm toward the long, narrow table stretching across one end of the room. It was covered with a royal-blue plastic tablecloth and loaded with warming trays and bowls of food.

His gracious attention felt good. For an instant, she imagined his warm hand resting on the small of her back the way he had held her on the dance floor at the wedding and the same way Brett guided Hilary. How good she would feel but, at the same time, how completely impossible it should ever happen.

Krista wound between tables and followed the girls and Hilary through the buffet lineup. Returning to their table with a plate heaped with steaming lasagna, Caesar salad, and garlic bread, she pushed Janine's disturbing comment out of her mind. She would enjoy the meal and save her worries for Monday morning. Janine's concerns could wait.

She paused, clasped a napkin on her lap, and regrouped before slicing a bite of the gooey, fragrant pasta. Settling into the meal with a buzz of conversation circling their table and floating over the room, she felt almost at home. Maybe she had made the right decision to spend the winter in Blue Sky after all.

When they finished eating, Hilary and Brett excused themselves to set up for the carnival games.

The girls flitted away to find their friends.

Left alone with Tate, Krista suddenly felt like she was on a date, and a spark of excitement tingled in her fingers and toes. If she ignored the prickle, maybe it would fade away. She needed to get along with the man but not fall in love. She slid her gaze sideways and considered whether to make small talk or raise the issue of Janine's obvious concern.

"Don't let Janine bother you." Tate scraped back from the table and adjusted his chair to half face her. "She's tough to please. Everybody in town knows it's her way or the highway."

"Oh?" Krista took a breath. Tate must have read her mind. But why didn't he give her a heads-up any sooner?

"Yeah, she's worse than somebody's strict mother," he said, "Always ready to suggest—or demand—a better way."

Krista inhaled a quick breath. She knew all about a rigid, critical mother. She forced a laugh. "So, I shouldn't take her comments personally?"

"No, but get used to her because you'll hear her opinions a lot." He shook his head. "As club president, she likes to throw her weight around, and she knows you'll want to keep the rink board of directors happy. As a skating mother to a spoiled daughter, she's fierce. So just be ready to get *Janined* all the time." He grinned. "But let's not let her ruin a fun evening."

"Sure." Krista glanced around the room at clusters of people talking and laughing. Amidst the hubbub, she felt a disconcerting knot yank in her stomach. Tate's take on the tension with Janine, while meant to reassure her, only unsettled her more.

****

Monday morning, Tate glanced at his watch and revved his snowplow. After a dusting of snow on Sunday night, he had started work early along Main Street and then cleared the streets in front of the combined fire and ambulance station and the local police detachment. When he swung out of the truck to refuel, he puffed out his breath in frosty clouds.

The weather was unseasonably cold today, and he hunched his shoulders under his heavy black parka. Carly would make sure his little darlins were well bundled for the short walk to school. He couldn't cope without his caring sister to fill in the gap where a mother should be. Carly frequently reminded him a wife could help share the parenting load, but right now, the idea seemed more like a dream than a real possibility.

Now, he circled the rink parking lot and scooped neat rows of snow. With any luck, he'd catch Krista after her morning meeting with Janine. They were supposed to meet at nine, so if he concentrated on cleaning up the area around the rink, he'd spot Krista when she left.

He zoomed to the far end of the lot, checked over his shoulder, and peered through billowing snow, so he didn't miss her before he turned around and headed closer to the rink door. Instead of Krista, he caught sight of a compact figure bundled into a brown coat and matching hat. Maybe he should tap Janine for insider information on the purpose of the meeting. She was always anxious to share her opinions and latest cause.

Pulling a U-turn, he roared partway toward her and then slowed to a stop. "Good morning, Janine."

"Good morning, Tate." Clutching a scarf tightly

around her neck, she paused. "Do you have a spare minute?"

Getting the lowdown would be even easier than he expected. "Sure thing. Want to hop in?" As soon as he called out the invitation, he regretted it. If Krista wandered out, he'd be tied up with Janine. Krista might think he supported Janine in whatever issues she had raised.

Janine looked both ways. "I guess so." Leaning slightly into the wind, she crossed the parking lot, pulled open the truck door, and hopped up to the seat. "The heat in here feels good."

"Whatcha up to so early on this frosty morning? Private skating lessons?" He chuckled. "I know. You want to perform in the ice show."

"Hardly." Janine sniffed and blew out a quick, strong breath. "I met with Krista about a few things. I don't mind telling you. You'll understand because you're the parent of little skaters. I know you want to keep those sweet girls happy." She shivered and held her gloved hands over the heating vents.

"You bet I do." Tate glanced over and then twisted the fan higher. Her words flew out in an agitated blast, nearly as strong as the hot air from the truck heater. "I'd give you a lift home if I didn't need to get the parking lot cleared." And if he didn't need to wait for Krista to get her take on her meeting with Janine. "What's up?"

"I met with Krista in my official role as club president and my personal role as Olivia's mom. Krista has only been here a short time, and I'm already dealing with complaints." Janine huffed and beat together her hands.

"So far, Gracie and Ella like her okay." But not as

much as their father did. Tate shifted. After the first lesson, their opinions had cooled because she made them work so hard and didn't let them take a break or talk to their friends. He'd already explained she just wanted to make them better skaters. He sure wouldn't let Janine know they'd hinted at a complaint. "What's the problem?"

"Problems." Janine corrected him with an emphasis on the *s*. "I won't even mention the ice show. Who ever heard of Mexico on ice in January? Somehow, you convinced my dear mother it was a good idea." She huffed. "I can't say I agree. The results will speak for themselves, and I'll wait to see. Anyway, that's the least of my worries at this point."

"C'mon. Give her a break. The new theme is original. What else is concerning you?"

"What else? I'll tell you what else." Janine shot him a look. "She's tough to the point of unreasonable. Olivia refused to go to her skating lesson last week. She reported that Krista's mean and doesn't let the girls have any fun."

"Didn't the board want an instructor who gets results? Hardworking folks don't pay for lessons so their kids can goof off. High standards are part of the package. Maybe it's just the contrast with Lauren. She was a bit slack with discipline."

Janine glowered. "I've seen Krista in action, and other parents have commented as well. She seldom smiles, and if one of the girls stops and leans on the boards to rest or chat for a minute, she waves her away. She's all work. She won't stand for any socializing whatsoever. And talk about tough. She made Olivia repeat a jump ten times until she was exhausted." She fisted her hands. "Maybe big city skaters are different. Here in Blue Sky, figure skating should be fun. Her hardball approach won't work."

Janine's tirade didn't surprise Tate in the least. She protected Olivia at all costs, even when the girl could benefit from experiencing the consequences of her actions. Krista was in a tough spot. She really couldn't win. If Olivia didn't pass a skating test or perform well at a competition, then Janine would blame the coach. He drew a deep breath. "How did Krista take the discussion?"

"She listened in a polite way." Janine sighed. "She doesn't hesitate to assert herself though. She maintained the board asked her to produce results, and she promised she would deliver. I chaired the meeting. I heard what she said. But she didn't mention she would run lessons like a boot camp." Janine reached for the door handle. "If she wants to keep her position here, she better change."

Tate scanned ahead through the windshield and caught sight of a greenish blur exiting the rink—Krista with Pearl lumbering beside her. Instantly, his heart lurched. Darn.

Krista stopped and stared at his truck.

She must wonder why, fresh from the meeting, Janine sat huddled inside. Did she assume the conversation between her and the club president would stay confidential?

She raised a hand in a single wave, spun, and strode away, kicking snow with every step.

He couldn't believe his bad luck. After planning his work route so carefully to end up at the rink at this exact time, he had missed the opportunity he'd been looking forward to since he rolled out of bed this morning. "Whoa there." Tate put a hand on Janine's forearm. "Breathe. Give the poor woman a chance. From what I've seen, she's just trying to bring out the best in every kid."

"We'll see." Janine yanked open the door.

A rush of cold air filled the cab.

"Maybe her behavior is easier to take because she's an attractive, single woman and you are the town's only eligible bachelor."

Tate gripped the steering wheel with both hands. Heat filled his face in an angry rush. "Okay, Janine. You just went too far. Your comment was inappropriate and unfair."

"Come on, Tate. Since when can't you take a little joke?"

Janine sweetened her voice until it nearly dripped syrup. "Oh, I can take a well-meaning joke any day. I better get back to work."

"Whatever you say." Janine leapt out of the truck. "Have a nice day." She smirked and slammed the door shut.

Tate roared the engine and bumped the gear into Drive. Janine had overstepped her bounds, and her comment stung. Still, he had to admit she might be more perceptive than he'd like. Was his attraction that obvious? He'd give anything to hear Krista's account of the meeting. Even more, he'd love to spend more time with her. Sure, a relationship was an invitation to heartache, but maybe it was worth the risk. He had learned life was unpredictable. Anything could happen, especially if, by some unlikely chance, she chose a future in Blue Sky.

Peering ahead, he watched Krista and Pearl disappear down the street in the distance, and a vague uneasiness bounced from his stomach to his chest. Krista had talent to share. She meant well. But already she faced the wrath of Janine. He threw back his shoulders and attacked a pile of snow. She could use someone to watch her back, and he was the man for the job.

Chapter 12

Janine was one hard woman to please. That much was abundantly clear. Krista breathed cold air and filled her lungs, but it didn't cool her simmering frustration. And why was Janine in Tate's truck? Did he have complaints too? Or was Janine attempting to brainwash him over to her side. On the way home from the rink, she scuffed snow and confided in her loyal furry friend. "Good dog, Pearl. You understand, don't you?"

At the sound of her name, Pearl looked up and batted her tail against Krista's leg.

The dog had quite a waddle. So far, exercise hadn't slimmed her down at all. If anything, she had gained weight, so Krista would need to be more sparing with the doggy treats. "Janine is impossible. Already she's on my case. She hates the ice show theme, and now, she doesn't like my approach with the skaters. What'll I do, Pearl girl?"

Pearl woofed, frolicked, and grabbed a mouthful of snow.

Krista would love to feel as carefree. She came to Blue Sky to help the club and reflect on her future in peaceful surroundings. So far, the coaching job wasn't working out the way she had planned at all. "I'll show her I know how to produce winning skaters. I refuse to let her push me around." Without breaking stride, she tilted and ran a hand along Pearl's back. Snow swirled around them and sifted a grainy veil between her and the tidy homes lining her route.

She'd show Tate too. If he had any doubts about her ability as a coach for his daughters, then she'd prove his girls would thrive under her tutelage. She'd likely bump into him at the rink this week, and maybe she could even hear about his conversation with Janine.

Dropping Pearl at home, she headed toward Main Street to browse in the gift store. Christmas was fast approaching, and she needed to select something for her parents. She would drive the three hours to their place on Christmas Eve, celebrate Christmas with them, and return to Blue Sky on December twenty-sixth. Along Main Street, festive wreaths hung on the light stands, and the store windows displayed glittery streamers, giant candy canes, and assorted boxes wrapped in shiny jewel tones. With each step, she felt anticipation edge out the misgivings stirring her stomach. Janine couldn't ruin her happy Christmassy feeling.

Pausing in front of Something Special, the town's popular, little gift store, she paused and then twisted the doorknob. A warm rush of air greeted her and enticed her inside. She breathed in the aroma of pine from the boughs outlining the front window. Stomping the snow from her boots, she pulled off her mitts, removed her knitted hat, partially unzipped her jacket, and glanced around. The place was packed with a wide selection of items. Christmas knickknacks, scented candles, holiday sweaters, kitchen gadgets, sweet treats, and wall hangings mingled like a party of eclectic guests. Her mother was difficult to please, but she might like a unique decoration.

"Good morning. You're the new skating teacher in

town." The woman wore a green apron decorated with red poinsettias. "Welcome. I'm Melanie, the owner." She smiled widely.

"Thank you. Pleased to meet you. I'm happy to be here." Krista smiled.

Melanie's shop radiated warmth. Christmas carols floated in the background, and the air hung infused with a delicious, comforting cinnamon scent.

Melanie straightened and examined Krista's face. Her wide brown eyes and straight brown hair suited the soothing atmosphere.

"I came to browse for ideas for my mom's gift," said Krista.

Melanie waved an arm across the crowded space before her. "Take your time. You'll find lots to choose from. I'll leave you alone, but please let me know if you have any questions or need any help." She nearly resumed her work but paused. "Have you met Tate Harris? He's the attractive, eligible bachelor in town." She winked.

"Uh." She laughed. "I teach his girls, and I'm working with him on the ice show sets. But sorry, it's all business." Was everybody in this town a pseudo matchmaker? And why did she react like she spun on ice every time someone suggested again she and Tate belonged together? Melanie's calming manner probably lulled many customers into spilling secrets, but Krista wouldn't add to town gossip. She glanced at a shelf where a rustic candle caught her eye.

"Oh, and one more thing." Melanie flicked her pink feather duster toward Krista. "I heard from Daisy you adopted Pearl. I might want one of her puppies. I bet Tate's little twins would love a puppy too."

Krista widened her eyes and swallowed. "Excuse me? What puppies?"

"Didn't you know?" Melanie blinked and suppressed a smile, but her mouth tipped up at the corners. "Pearl's going to be a dog mommy. Golden retrievers usually have around eight in their litters, so you'll have a lot of puppies on your hands."

Krista cleared her throat. "I just thought she was a little chubby." Her voice sounded shaky to her own ears. How had she not known? Did Daisy really insist she adopt a pregnant dog without telling her? Confusion and annoyance shot like fireworks across her chest. Like Melanie said, big dogs had big litters. Sweet and persuasive as Daisy was, she had no business unloading a large dog with a belly full of baggage.

Now what was she supposed to do? She loved Pearl and couldn't imagine giving her away. But still. Eight puppies were a lot of work, and she had no idea how to care for a pregnant dog or her litter. She knew nothing about helping a dog give birth, and she definitely did not want to deal with a houseful of puppies, even if they were the cutest things ever. Suddenly, her mellow Christmas spirit evaporated, and shock dropped onto her like a chunk of ice. "Uh, thanks for the heads-up on the situation."

"No problem. I gather you're surprised. But don't worry. We Blue Sky folks like to help." Melanie reached for a shelf with her duster. "Now, I really will let you get on with your shopping."

Krista wanted to turn, slam the door, and run. How could she possibly enjoy a leisurely browse and think about gifts when issues piled up around her faster than snow? First was the presence of Tate Harris, as big a heartthrob as she'd ever met. Then came Janine's opposition to a new theme for the ice show and her concerns about Krista's coaching standards. And now, the bad news about Pearl. Wait until she found Daisy!

Since she arrived in town, nothing had gone quite the way she expected. Life in quiet, innocent Blue Sky wasn't so simple after all.

****

That evening, Tate recruited his parents to babysit, tucked in his girls, and headed to the rink. Officially, the reason was to work on sets, but unofficially, he felt a burning urge to talk with Krista. At the last minute, he tied his skates together and dangled them over his shoulder. If the ice was free after he completed his business, he might do a few laps and get some exercise.

"Have fun, son." Dad wheeled to face the door. He didn't mention the skates, but his eyes twinkled.

"I won't stay too late. Thank you." He nodded at both his parents. His understanding mom and dad, along with Carly, made single parenthood bearable. For a glimmer of a second, an image of a family of four lit his imagination. A loving partner for him. A caring mother for his twins. Maybe someday...

The icy blast outside chased away his momentary daydream. If he didn't bare his heart, he wouldn't get hurt. Striding down the quiet snowy street, he filled his head with air so cold it tingled inside his nose with every breath. His boots crunched over snowy patches on the sidewalk and then fell silent over the pavement shovelled clear in front of most of the homes. A few blocks over, he spotted gold stars, silver bells, and striped candy canes sparkling over Main Street. A surge of peace and anticipation filled and warmed him.

Christmas season with the circle of family around was the happiest time of year.

His breath puffed around him in a foggy plume, and he tugged open the door of the rink. From what he could tell, Janine's attitude toward Krista hadn't already spread publicly throughout the whole skating community, so he could still rein her in. If Krista had taken Janine's feedback to heart, she likely felt discouraged. He hated to think of her floundering with her enthusiasm squashed. Maybe he could help her keep the situation in perspective.

Janine had tried to advance her own agenda in the past. All afternoon, while he rammed piles of snow onto a truck and dumped it onto a field at the edge of town, he mulled over the situation. He finally concluded Janine thrived on nitpicking and controversy. Knocking Krista before she had a chance to prove herself was plain unreasonable. Besides, it wasn't exactly easy to recruit a highly qualified coach to a small town like Blue Sky. If Krista didn't work out, then the skating club would struggle along without an instructor for the rest of the season. The best skaters would travel elsewhere for lessons. The rink already teetered on the edge of its budget. Losing valuable figure skating revenue could tip the balance the wrong way.

At the rink, he paused just inside the door, stomping the snow off his boots. He pulled off his hat and mitts and wiped his nose. The arena smell of skates and cold took over from the fresh outside air and pulled him closer to the ice surface. Upbeat music floated over the rink, and as he suspected, he found Krista still working on the ice with a few of the older students.

This late in the evening, not one parent sat watching in the stands.

After a few minutes, Pearl wandered over to greet him.

She must have been curled up snoozing along the boards. "Hey, Pearl." Smiling, he bent and gave her some vigorous pats.

Straightening, he studied the goings-on.

Krista insisted a girl repeat a spiral move over and over. She demonstrated how to extend both arms to form a graceful arc. She shook her head and motioned to continue.

He sensed the grit behind her bare glimmer of a smile. Janine was right about one thing. Krista was tough and held her students to high standards.

As she stroked by, positioning her student's shoulders, she crinkled her brow.

Seeing confusion flit across her face, he felt a wave of uncertainty. He raised a hand and dropped his skates on the floor beside the gate to the ice where they would be handy later. With no one else around, they'd be safe. He hustled along the rubberized flooring toward the storage area, and music echoed down the hallway. When he heard it quit, he'd know she had finished teaching. That would be his cue to hurry back to chat.

Scanning shelves, he scribbled a list of supplies in the musty room just past one end of the rink. Shoving away cleaning supplies, paint cans, and loose pieces of wood, he quickly assessed he could bang together the old sets, then repaint them in the new Mexican theme. He was no artist, but he counted on Hilary to help get the design right. Some of the wood was warped and cracked, so he'd need to repair or replace a few sections. To add to the tropical feel, he could cut plywood into the shape of palm trees and maybe even build a giant sombrero. Goodbye, snowflakes and snowmen. Hello, sand and sun.

The strains of music flowed into a new song, and he glanced at his watch. He better make sure he didn't miss Krista when she left the ice. His work completed for now, he made a few mental notes and headed back toward the entrance to the ice surface. Reaching the opening, he stopped and stared.

Krista glided on the far side of the ice.

In her red jacket, she was a flash of fire flickering over glass. He swept his gaze over the whole surface. She was alone out there. Diving to retrieve his skates, he dropped into a seat, shoved in his feet, and laced them in record time.

Swooping by, she took long, slow strokes, cutting smooth, deep edges. A few yards past him, she swerved to a stop, spraying fine flakes of snow in a circle around her blades. Spreading her feet outward and then pulling them together in a giant lollipop, she backed up. "Hi, Tate. I'm surprised to see you here so late on a Monday evening." She raised her eyebrows.

Her intense gaze through those unforgettable blue eyes made his heart beat faster. "Mind if I join you?" He leapt to his feet and took three long strides onto the ice before she could refuse.

"Do I have a choice?" She laughed.

The tinkling sound smoothed away the sting. "If you prefer to be alone, just say the word." He cleared his throat. He had no reason to assume she'd be happy to see him, but somehow, he had expected to get a better reception. "Are you still designing a skater's program or something?"

"Just unwinding after the day." She sighed. "I like to remember I'm a skater at heart and not just the stern teacher." She spun once in place and raised her arms.

"You don't look grumpy." He grinned. "A little tired maybe but not grouchy."

"And you? What brings you out on a cold night when the girls are tucked in bed?"

"You."

She blinked. "Excuse me?"

"You." He pointed with a fat mitt. "You recruited me to build sets, so I came to scope out the state of the materials."

"Didn't you already do that the night I babysat?"

"I took a preliminary look. But I needed to check some details." A small knot of uncertainty looped in his stomach. She had noticed his excuse didn't fully add up. Maybe as they skated, he'd ease into the real reason for his drop-in visit. "My parents didn't mind staying with the girls for a bit. I grabbed my skates, just in case I had a chance to do a few laps while I was here. Go ahead. Don't let me stop you." He gestured for her to glide ahead.

She shrugged. "Okay. Just don't mow me down with any fancy hockey moves." She laughed and stroked away without looking back.

In four large, fast strides, he passed her and picked up speed.

She carved shapes on clean edges.

He rounded the end of the ice, slicing choppy marks with his blades.

She floated at her own pace behind him, dipping and swirling like a gentle prairie breeze.

Seemingly oblivious to his presence, she curved into a smooth three-turn and picked up speed into backward crossovers, switching direction at center ice to trace a large figure eight.

He sped in circles until his breathing and heart rate increased to the level of moderate exercise. The days of intense hockey training were over, but he never forgot the exhilaration of a tough workout and muscles so taxed he could barely move. He glanced across the ice and watched her reddish hair swish below her black hat as she switched directions, dipped, and soared.

She was the breath of fresh air who could change his life. If her feelings matched his. If they grew close. If she never left. He would always think fondly of the life he had embraced with Whitney. She gave him his two beautiful girls, but he couldn't live in the past and fear the future forever. Did he have the courage to move on? Could he tell Krista how he felt?

He quickened his pace to outskate the thoughts chasing him. His heart tapped hard from the exercise and from something else…a longing for something he couldn't have. Why would she look at him now when she didn't intend to stay? The whole idea was crazy. Focusing on the cut of his blades, he snapped to the present and imitated her graceful moves.

Finally, she noticed and slowed. "I can see why you were a hockey player and not a figure skater." She laughed. "Of course, the skates don't help."

He compared her trim white skates with formidable toe picks to his chunky brown boots with curved blades. They were made for different purposes. "What? You don't think I have talent?" He threw up his hands and widened his eyes, then rotated twice and nearly lost his balance.

She giggled. "You could take a few lessons from Ella and Gracie. I can't judge your hockey talent though."

His heart twanged. Those days were long gone. Now, he saw more ice from the wheel of his truck than he did in an arena.

For an instant, she scanned his face, then bent forward and took off holding an imaginary hockey stick. Grinning, she imitated his technique dodging players and stickhandling a puck toward the end of the rink.

Crackling over the ice with the rush of cold air against his cheekbones, he quickly caught up. He darted ahead, jumped backwards, and faked a maneuver with his own imaginary stick. "Nice try, but you can't beat me at my own game." Puffing lightly, he laughed, flipped forward, and glided alongside her.

"I had you worried." She glanced at his profile and back to the ice ahead.

"Like Janine has you worried?" He abruptly switched topics from fun to serious.

"I saw you with her today." Krista furrowed her forehead.

He couldn't miss her accusatory expression. "Yeah, you did." He took a deep breath. "But only because she came out of the rink first. You were the one I wanted to meet."

"Oh. About the girls or the ice show?" Feet together, she swooped side to side in a snaking pattern.

"Neither one." He paused. "This morning, I didn't come to see you on official rink business." Next to her, he did a couple of crossovers to round the end of the rink.

"I gather you were on official snow-clearing business."

"That too. But I really wanted to find out how your meeting with Janine went and reassure you."

"Reassure me? What does it matter how the meeting went? Janine's the club president. She's my boss and a client who happens to be a fierce skating mom."

Krista's voice was flat.

She pushed harder. "If I value my job, I have to listen to whatever she says."

"Was she tough?" He barely touched her arm with the tip of his mitt, and a surprising warmth shot up his arm. She had a way of sending shockwaves through his whole being.

"Not pleasant." She dropped her arm to her side and grimaced.

"Care to elaborate?" Maybe he shouldn't have reached out, but the meeting must have been as strained as he feared.

"Where should I start?"

"Up to you. Wherever you like." Suddenly, the overly loud soundtrack irritated him like an unwelcome intruder in a sensitive conversation.

"She said a lot, but it all boiled down to three things." Krista raised a hand, but in her mitts, she couldn't use her fingers to count them off for emphasis."

From the gate in the rink boards, Pearl whined.

The dog must sense Krista was upset. "Fire away."

Krista's laugh sounded more like a grunt. "One, she can't stand the idea of a Mexican ice show in

January." She took a deep breath. "Two, she thinks I push Olivia and the other skaters too hard. And three, she didn't say as much, but she hates the fact I'm not Lauren."

"A lot to take in." He kept his tone low and calm. He hoped she could hear his support.

"To say the least."

She clipped her words and dragged a toe pick for emphasis.

He glanced over and caught the frown darkening her pretty face. "I came here tonight to tell you not to worry too much. Janine will always be Janine. She doesn't mind stirring up a bit of trouble. Sure, she's the club president, but she's not the only voice around here. Daisy's on board with the ice show theme. My girls like their lessons okay, and from what I've heard, other parents are happy with your work with their kids too."

He didn't mind Krista's challenging Ella and Gracie. The jury was still out on whether she pushed a little too hard. He glanced over and chuckled. "Despite what she might think, the earth does not revolve around Janine."

Krista slowed and sighed. Her lips lifted slightly at the corners. "Thanks, Tate." She stared up at the stands, then without warning, she swerved and changed direction. "Race you to the gate." With a hop, she took off with quick, powerful strokes.

Caught off guard, he scrambled to catch up and barely passed her before he jumped from the ice onto the rubber floor. "Nice try." He grinned.

"Good effort. Next time, I won't let you win."

He did a double take. She said next time. Next time! He'd make sure he joined her again to skate, for sure.

Krista stepped off the ice behind him and petted Pearl.

The dog batted her tail in a furious greeting.

"Good dog, Pearl girl." She straightened and paused. "Brrr, I'm chilly. Would you like to invite me over for hot chocolate?"

Tate snapped his head toward Krista to read her expression. Surprise jumped like a flying puck into his heart. Did he hear right? "You mean tonight? Right now?"

Chapter 13

Krista swallowed. Now, what had she done?

"Sounds good. Let's walk to my place for hot chocolate." He quickly blinked away his wide-eyed surprise and smiled agreement. "I'll even make you cinnamon toast to go with it."

"Come to think of it, maybe not tonight after all." She backed away and stared at her skates. "I'm pretty tired." Spending extra time with him was definitely not part of her plan. For a brief moment, she had gotten carried away by the exhilaration of cool air rushing past her and freedom from her worries. On ice, she felt at home, like her true self...in her element, where she belonged.

"Sure. Get my hopes up and then change your mind." He plunked onto a bench to remove his skates.

"Sorry to disappoint you, but I don't want to fall asleep on your sofa." She put on her skate guards and turned toward the hallway to her office changeroom.

"The girls might be surprised to find you there in the morning."

She laughed. "Not as surprised as I would be to find myself there." She suddenly felt uncomfortably warm despite the chill in the rink. She had flirted again...with the same guy she couldn't allow to mess with her heart and her plans. She sensed he liked it, but she was right to be wary. What made her think the feelings between them could work?

"Well, if you won't join me at my place, I'll walk you home." Bent over unlacing his skates, he glanced up.

"If you insist. I'll be right back." She hurried to remove her skates and gather her belongings. A few minutes later, she crunched along beside him on the snowy sidewalk. Thoughts tumbling like snowballs, she puffed out her breath in short bursts. She glanced up at his tall, strong presence beside her and dared to dream of what life would be like if she belonged at his side.

Zach had soured her on love after she lost herself in his nastiness and criticism, but was Tate as different—as genuinely nice—as he seemed? Even if he proved he was everything everyone claimed, he still didn't fit into her plans. She didn't belong forever in Blue Sky, and he would never leave.

They passed tidy bungalow homes lit with colorful lights.

One lawn displayed a manger scene with a subdued reminder of the true meaning of Christmas. Another featured Santa and his reindeer. A mix of anticipation and apprehension rippled through her. Christmas was a special time, and she wouldn't skip a visit to her parents' place. But time with Mom always brought its share of strain. "You don't need to walk me all the way home. We'll hit your place first, and I'm just a couple of blocks over. I'll drop you off." She stole a glance at his profile where his cheek and the tips of his nose turned bright red in the biting cold. His rugged good looks snatched her breath away. "I fended for myself in the big city, so I can handle Blue Sky in the dark. Besides, Pearl will protect me."

"Yeah, she's quite the guard dog. If she caught anybody bothering you, she'd lick them to death." He chuckled. "I'm a true gentleman. I'll see you home. Unless I can convince you to turn in here." He swept an arm from the sidewalk up toward his neat light-blue house. Red and white lights twinkled from the eaves, outlined the front window, and splashed across the bushes near the front door.

They had reached his place already. Instead of saying a brisk good night and trudging on, she wavered. The short walk had jolted her wide awake, replenishing her lagging energy. His handsome profile and gallant offer were hard to resist. Bundled up against the cold, he was just as good-looking in his casual clothes as dressed in his formal best man suit at the wedding. Now she'd seen him in action as a dad and as a business owner, and he attracted her even more.

She really could use a cup of hot chocolate to warm her from the inside out. She hadn't eaten since a very early supper, and cinnamon toast sounded very tempting to her rumbling stomach. Sharing a friendly snack as his girls slept seemed harmless enough. She didn't intend to date the guy, but she needed to stay on positive terms for the sake of Ella and Gracie and the ice show. She could use a friend and ally. "Okay. You twisted my frozen arm." She laughed, spun to the right, and faced his neatly shovelled front sidewalk. "I'm in...for just a little while."

"You change your mind more often than I change my underwear." He grinned behind a cloud of fog from his mouth. "C'mon in. My parents will be happy to meet you."

A family visit would take extra energy, but she

couldn't flip-flop yet again. Tate would think she was crazy. Anyway, they were probably nice folks and curious about their granddaughters' new skating coach. "After you." She followed him up the front steps and stomped the snow off her boots.

Pearl circled and batted the house with her thick tail.

Feeling like a teenager about to meet her boyfriend's scrutinizing parents, Krista braced herself for plenty of questions. Stepping inside, she pointed at snow droplets glistening on Pearl's back. "She's going to drip melted snow everywhere. Do you have a towel I can use to dry her and save your floors?"

He shook his head and pulled off his hat in one motion. "Don't worry. The floors have seen worse."

On cue, Pearl shook, spattered wet flecks on the gray walls and charcoal doormat, and romped ahead.

Tate hung Krista's jacket and drew her into the front room. "Mom, Dad, this is Krista Reynolds, the new coach. Krista, these are my parents, Leah and Cole."

"Pleased to meet you." Leah smiled, rose, and extended a hand. "I'm glad you brought your skating talent to Blue Sky."

Vaguely aware of country music strumming overhead, Krista scanned her ash-blonde hair and unlined face. Her gentle blue eyes matched the colors in the room. Tate must have inherited his olive skin and brown eyes from his dad's side of the family. "Thank you. I'm glad to be here, especially when I get to teach promising young skaters like your granddaughters." She was far more comfortable talking about Ella and Gracie.

Leah beamed. "They do have talent, don't they? They obviously got their daddy's skating genes."

"Definitely," said Krista.

"Nice to meet you." Cole rolled his wheelchair closer and held out a hand. He chuckled. "I haven't seen this guy with a woman in years. I was starting to wonder if he smelled bad."

Krista felt the heat creep into her face, and she hoped her skin was already red enough from the cold to camouflage her blush. "I'll keep my distance, just in case." She sidestepped away from Tate. He looked and acted like his dad.

"Don't mind him," Tate jumped in. "Dad's full of stories, and some of them are even true. Don't give the girl a hard time, or she might charge me double for the girls' skating lessons."

"I like that idea." Krista flashed a wide smile.

They all laughed.

She relaxed just a smidgeon. Now she remembered Tate had shared his dad suffered from multiple sclerosis. His disability was the reason Tate left hockey to run the family business.

"Care to join us for hot chocolate?" Tate swept his gaze between his parents. "It's the least I can do to thank you."

"We love to help. That's what family is for, dear. Your father agrees, don't you, Cole?"

"Yep, sure do. You do your share clearing our driveway and walks. You're no freeloader. Hot chocolate does sound tempting, but maybe we should go home and let these two youngsters alone on their date." He winked at Tate.

"Oh, Cole, you're so silly." Leah batted a hand in

his direction. "But I agree we should go home so I can get my beauty sleep."

"You've always been a beauty."

Cole's tone hovered somewhere between sincere and teasing.

Leah smiled and threw him a soft look.

Clearly, she loved her husband and son. Krista's heart panged at the obvious affection and easy banter among them. Of course, Mom loved her, but she never looked at her with a soft, kind expression.

Driven for the best for Krista, she pushed and never let up, even now. Blue Sky didn't meet her standards.

Cole and Leah gracefully bowed out of the snack, bundled up, and left for home.

Right away, Tate got busy in the kitchen.

Krista followed and sank onto a wooden chair painted a bluish gray and leaned an elbow on the white table. With the kettle whistling and the smell of bread toasting, the room felt cozy and welcoming. Placemats sat neatly stacked in the center of the table, and two dolls perched side by side on a chair opposite her spot. She felt strangely at home here in this warm family environment. "You have a cute place."

"Cute. Yeah, that's my goal." He faced her and smirked.

"Okay, what description do you prefer? Nice? Pleasant?"

"Sure, whatever you say." He shrugged. "This place is home. It works for the girls and me. Let's grab a comfortable chair." Carrying a tray, he led her into the living room and set it on the coffee table. He waved her toward a chair and switched on gentle jazz music.

His music tastes ran beyond country. She helped herself to a mug of steaming hot chocolate and a plate with two pieces of toast doused in butter and cinnamon. The sweet scents mingled and made her mouth water. Settled in a comfy leather armchair with a navy-blue blanket slung over the back, she took a deep breath and drank in the homey surroundings. They were the ideal backdrop for the nicest guy she'd met in a long time—a guy who just happened to have the most enticing brown eyes, wide cheekbones, and full lips, not to mention his trim, muscular build. For a few seconds, she felt an odd, off-balance sensation swirl so fast in her stomach she might not be able to even nibble at her toast.

Pearl flopped at her feet and groaned but kept her gaze trained on the toast.

Krista blinked, and just as quickly, she regained her composure. She didn't need to feel nervous. This was Tate, the entertaining best man she had laughed and celebrated and danced the night away with at Amy's wedding...the devoted dad of two of her skating students...the willing ice show helper. Unwinding together after a busy day was okay. "Delicious." She inhaled the sweet steam and let the rich taste trickle down her throat.

"Tell me more about yourself."

"That's a rather broad question." She could feel his genuine interest in the tone of his voice, and it scared her in a way. The more she shared, the closer they'd grow, and she had already decided it wasn't a wise idea at all.

"Okay, I'll be more specific."

He asked about her parents, her brother, her friendship with Amy, and what she liked to do in her spare time. He bantered and made her laugh, just like at the wedding. They could be friends during her months in Blue Sky. Why not? He made time together easy. Somehow, she could talk with him with no fear of being laughed at or criticized. He was nothing like Zach, with an endless supply of cutting words. He made her feel respected and safe.

"If you're not comfortable, you don't have to answer…"

His tone slipped halfway between teasing and serious. Was he heading toward personal territory?

"Are you divorced? Or did you leave a brokenhearted guy behind?"

"Neither." She swallowed and stared off at a watercolor picture of birch trees on one wall. She loved birch trees too—in one way, so stark black-and-white but in another, radiating the peace of nature. Then she examined another piece of artwork on the wall above the sofa. The painting was an impressionistic view of hockey skates showing just the lower part of the player's legs speeding over the ice. Krista's and Tate's dreams had been tied to skating, but for different reasons, they had shattered like pieces of ice dropped on a hard surface. Wistfulness ached in her throat.

Waiting, he just slowly sipped his drink and munched on a bite of toast.

"Where should I begin?" How much should she share? Were they kindred spirits who knew the pain of broken dreams and lost relationships? Somehow, she felt safe letting him know more. She cleared her throat. "All my life, I've carried the weight of my mother's aspirations. Now, looking back, I realize moving to train with a top coach in Toronto was as much a way to escape her grip as it was to shoot for a national medal. Things were exciting at first...but then..." She had disappointed herself and, most of all, Mom.

He nodded.

"My skating didn't get better. It got worse. The next season, I didn't even make the top five." But that wasn't the worst part. She set down her mug and plate on the table beside her chair and reached into her pocket. Grabbing a tissue, she squeezed it hard. She would not cry.

He blinked and studied her expression.

"After I bombed at the championship, I received devastating feedback. A top skating judge named Zach told me I lacked the artistry to ever win a national medal. I don't know who was more crushed, my mom or me. I retired from competitive skating and started coaching." She shrugged.

"Then—don't ask me how—Zach charmed me into a relationship. At that point, my confidence level was so low I fell for any positive attention. Eventually, we even got engaged, but the whole thing was a disaster. The fact he was a judge says it all. He was smooth and charming on the surface...but not underneath...behind closed doors..." She shook her head. His cutting words couldn't hurt her anymore, but they were hard to totally forget. Any hint of criticism made her want to flee to safety.

"Tough." He shook his head.

"I felt so insulted and demeaned I could hardly make a simple decision like what color shoes to wear." Why was she spilling so much of her painful past to Tate? Amy had been her confidante all along and the person who taught her how to truly believe in herself.

Without Amy's strong push from afar, she might still be squashed under Zach's thumb. Few people knew she'd quit coaching to avoid any contact at all, and he was the reason she'd run away to perform on cruise ships. But now…she'd given Tate a glimpse of the Krista beneath the surface.

She sighed and absorbed the soothing piano and guitar sounds floating in the background. "I still have an iceberg inside, and it hasn't completely thawed yet. Maybe someday…" Regret squeezed in her throat at the contrasting paths their lives had travelled. Tate became a good, solid dad while she floundered under the criticism of Mom and Zach. Would her hardened and hurting heart ever recover?

He raised his eyebrows and widened his eyes. "That's a lot. Thanks for—"

The pad of little feet down the hallway interrupted, and Gracie appeared in the doorway. Eyes half closed and hair rumpled, she sniffled and launched herself onto Tate's lap. "Daddy, I had a bad dream."

Tate wrapped his arms around Gracie and set his chin on the top of her tousled head. "It's okay, darlin. Don't worry. I'll keep you safe."

Krista imagined how comforted his words would make her feel, but they were for his beloved daughter.

Gracie snuggled against his chest, opened her eyes, and stared. "Why is *she* here?"

The little girl had a good point. Why *was* she here?

****

Tate glanced at Krista. "I'll be right back. Don't move." After soothing Gracie for a few minutes, he ushered her back to her bed. A few minutes later, he found Krista had ignored his instructions.

She had gathered their dishes and delivered them to the kitchen. With Pearl wagging beside her, she stood in the front entrance dressed in her red jacket and black hat.

Thanks to Gracie, the intimate mood was broken. Just when he had started to build Krista's trust and unearth her closely held secrets, he hit a wall. A wave of disappointment washed over him, surprising him with its intensity. "You don't need to run away."

"Oh, but I do. It's late, and Pearl and I need to get home to bed. Thank you for the snack and the chat."

"Can we do this again sometime?"

"May...be." She shrugged.

He liked hearing her sound teasing and amused. "Can we skate together again?"

"May...be." She offered a half smile.

"Can I have one of Pearl's puppies?"

Krista inhaled a sharp breath and grimaced. "Was I the last person in town to find out Pearl is pregnant?"

"May...be." He imitated her lilting way of answering his questions.

She huffed and crinkled her brow under her fuzzy hat. Twisting, she reached for the doorknob and then faced him again. "I just thought she was a little overweight and needed more exercise. Melanie at the gift store tipped me off. I feel like a fool for not realizing sooner."

"I just thought you loved dogs and were a little bit crazy." He grinned and looped a finger in a circle near his ear.

"Gee, thanks. You're right I love dogs, and I'll take a little crazy over plain dumb." She rolled her eyes. "In answer to your question, why stop at only one? You can have eight puppies if you like. Why not give them to your whole family for Christmas?"

"Hey, the girls would love a puppy." He hadn't been serious when he first tossed out his joking request. He was more interested in getting a reaction out of Krista than in actually adopting one of his own. He had quite enough responsibility to juggle already. Still, he could picture Ella's and Gracie's faces shining like Christmas lights and hear their delighted shrieks to receive their own puppy to love. Seeing Pearl was a highlight of their skating lessons. "But I don't need one more thing to do."

"Well, think about it. Because I'm going to have a lot of puppies to place in good homes." She rolled her eyes.

He couldn't miss the stress in her tone. "When are they due?" She had her hands full enough already.

"Good question. Stay tuned." She snapped on Pearl's leash. "I made a vet appointment, and I have a lot of questions. So far, all I know is the gestation period is around sixty-three days, give or take. Depending how far along she is, she might or might not give birth before Christmas." Krista threw up a hand. "I've already started to schedule extra practice sessions for the ice show, so I hardly have time to run a dog nursery."

"I take it you'll stay close by for Christmas." He watched dismay darken her light-blue eyes.

She cringed. "I promised my parents I'd drive to Saskatoon on Christmas Eve and stay until December twenty-sixth. It's the highlight of the year for Mom, so I can't back out now. I'll find out if Pearl can travel or if I need to find a dog sitter."

At the sound of her name, Pearl looked up and gave a low woof.

"Good girl." Krista petted her smooth head. "Thanks for reminding me of my predicament."

She coated her words with light sarcasm but softened them with an almost smile. At least, he hadn't offended her too badly.

"Now I really better go." She turned the doorknob.

"Okay, but I have one more question." He kept a straight face and held back a chuckle at her fleeting glare. "Don't worry. Not about Pearl."

She stiffened her shoulders under her parka. "All right. What this time?"

"Did you know the rink is a public building?"

"Of course. Why do you ask?" She crinkled her forehead and pulled her hat lower, nearly to her eyebrows.

"Anyone can use the rink." He suppressed a chuckle. She had no idea where he was headed with his line of questioning.

"Yes. And?" Sighing, she released the doorknob and jammed a hand on her hip.

"I might feel like another late-evening skate." He raised his eyebrows and plastered his face with what he hoped was a totally innocent look. "Whether or not I get an invitation."

Chapter 14

The next morning, Krista marched next door to Daisy's place and rapped three times.

At her heels, Pearl wagged and panted, despite the cold.

Now that she had digested Melanie's surprise announcement about Pearl and found out Tate knew too, she needed to confront Daisy head-on. The news had rolled her stomach into a lump the size of a dog dish, and it hadn't shrunk much.

She still couldn't believe what all happened last evening when she found herself skating with none other than Tate Harris. She had stayed after lessons to absorb the freeing feeling of gliding over the ice in swooping patterns, stretching her arms and legs, and letting her stress and tiredness fly away through her fingers and toes.

At the sight of Tate, she tensed at first and then forced herself back into the moment, enjoying his erratic hockey moves and weak attempts at figure skating. She had no idea what prompted her to challenge him to a race or to hint she'd like to be his guest for hot chocolate. A cold wind gust swept over her, and she shivered as she heard Daisy's footsteps thumping toward the door before it swung open. She didn't look forward to a confrontation.

Daisy's breath puffed out in a cloud. "Well, come

in, girls. What brings you here on this frosty morning?" She ushered them into the entranceway and held out a hand for Krista's jacket.

Krista savored the blast of warmth and took a couple of deep breaths to keep her irritation in check. Already, she couldn't imagine life without Pearl. But she never dreamed of a busy life with Pearl and eight miniature versions.

"Let me pour you a hot drink." Daisy backed up and motioned for Krista to follow.

Pearl didn't wait for a second invitation. Toenails clicking on the wooden floor, she dropped pellets of snow and bumped her nose against Daisy's leg for a pat.

"I only planned to stop for a minute." Krista wanted to deliver her message and escape, but she also didn't want to appear rude to her neighbor and Janine's mother.

"Never mind a minute. Let's sit and chat. What else would you rather do on such a cold morning? I insist. Go and sit in the living room, and I'll be right back." Daisy bustled to the kitchen and returned with steaming cups of tea.

Krista sank into a mulberry velour sofa opposite Daisy on the matching chair. Sounds of instrumental Christmas carols floated over the room. Judging by the burgundy and rose décor, Daisy loved any shade of pink. Outside the large front window, Krista traced snow sifting over the front lawn and street. With Christmas season here, the weather was no surprise. She breathed the scent of her hot apple-cinnamon tea and gathered her courage to confront Daisy.

Pearl made herself at home and, with a groan,

flopped on the patterned area rug in the center of the room, then rolled over to expose her round belly.

She was sure to leave tufts of her golden fur behind.

"There. We can relax now and get down to a good visit." Daisy raised her mug with both hands and peered over the rim.

She wore stretchy wine pants and a long sweater the color of cherries like she dressed to blend with the rest of the room. Her wiry gray hair spiked in different directions with a mind of its own, just like Daisy. "I met Melanie in her shop yesterday." Krista sipped her tea and forced a calm tone.

"She has a lovely little store, doesn't she? It's my favorite place to shop for treasures you won't find anywhere else."

Krista nodded. Under different circumstance, she would have thoroughly enjoyed exploring the shop and selecting a unique gift for Mom. Reeling from the news of Pearl's condition, she stayed only a few minutes, promising to think over options and return another time. "Melanie told me something that surprised me…a lot." Her throat clenched like Pearl's jaw when she tugged a toy.

"Oh?"

Daisy either didn't guess or feigned innocence. Krista wasn't sure which.

"With all the people in and out of her store, Melanie is a hub of information." Daisy nodded and chuckled, shaking her plump middle. "She might even know more than me about what's going on in town. And that's saying something."

"So I gathered. She even knew something about

Pearl that I didn't." She watched Daisy's face for any glimmer of discomfort but didn't detect even a hint. "Melanie announced she might adopt one of Pearl's puppies. I almost fell over because I didn't even know she was pregnant."

"Isn't that exciting?" Daisy's eyes lit, and she set down her mug and dove forward to rub her hand along Pearl's side.

"But why didn't you warn me?" Krista fought to keep her tone gentle. She couldn't afford to alienate anybody in town, especially Janine's mother. "I love Pearl, but if I had known, I might not have welcomed her." She crinkled her forehead.

Daisy laughed. "Of course, you wouldn't. But don't hold it against me. Honestly, I suspected but didn't know for sure. I thought I owed it to Pearl not to spread rumors." She shifted back in her chair.

Scanning Daisy's wide face and the laugh lines radiating from her eyes, Krista decided the woman's heart was in the right place. She had wanted to find a good home for Pearl, and she succeeded. Maybe she deserved forgiveness. Krista took a deep breath and sipped her tea, savoring the flavor. "I wish you had shared your suspicions. I'm not really equipped to take care of a litter of puppies. How will I find eight or more good homes?"

Daisy crinkled her eyes. "There's always a way. I'm right next door and willing to help. Off the top of my head, I can already think of a few good prospects to adopt one or two. Don't worry. Things will all work out. They always do."

Pearl thumped her bushy tail on the carpet.

Was the dog reassuring Krista? Would everything

turn out okay? She raised her eyebrows. "I'm not as sure as you, but I can't imagine giving up Pearl now." Her presence made Krista's rented house feel cozy like home.

Pearl rolled to her feet and nudged her muzzle into Krista's lap.

Krista stroked her smooth head. The dog swished her tail and brushed the sofa cushions. "Don't worry. I won't desert you now, girl." She made eye contact with Daisy. "Be ready. I'll hold you to your word. I'll take her to the vet, but with a little online research, I guess the puppies will arrive close to Christmas."

"The ideal gift." Daisy clapped her hands. "But seriously, I'll be happy to dog sit and even help deliver puppies."

"You better promise." Krista forced a quiet noise she hoped sounded like mild amusement. On the inside, she felt like puppies only added to the snowstorm blowing through her life.

"You can count on me." She set down her mug and heaved herself out of her chair. "More tea?"

"No, thank you. Pearl and I need a walk to get our exercise before I start afternoon lessons. Some of the school kids are coming for a beginner session today." Krista stood.

Pearl wagged and stared at her face.

"Okay, whatever you say." Daisy followed Krista to the entranceway and slipped her jacket off the hook by the door.

Krista bent, pulled on her boots, and wiped Pearl's sloppy lick off her forehead.

"You're not upset, are you? Imagine how much fun eight little Pearls will be." Daisy grinned, then narrowed her eyes and examined Krista's expression.

Stretching upright, Krista couldn't help smiling. Daisy's enthusiasm was contagious. "Put it this way. I'm calmer about the idea now, thanks to you soothing me with herbal tea and offering to help." She forced a small laugh that almost felt genuine. The lump of annoyance inside her stomach shrank a little. "Thanks for the tea. See you soon." She turned to leave.

"Next time, we can talk a little about my precious daughter."

When she heard the lilting words behind her, Krista froze. Maybe she shouldn't leave after all. She spun and waited for Daisy to say more.

"Never mind. Janine is a topic for another day." Daisy shook her head. "All I'll say for now is I love my daughter dearly, but…"

"But?" Krista inhaled, her senses tingling. Would she gain an insight to help her deal with Janine's demands?

"I shouldn't say a word." Daisy folded her arms across her ample chest. "Maybe some other time."

For Krista, the right time couldn't come soon enough. Would Daisy become the ally she needed?

****

Every day for the rest of the week, Tate pictured himself skating with Krista. He picked up Ella and Gracie from their lesson on Saturday and was disappointed she was busy on the ice. He didn't even get a chance to wave. By then, he couldn't stand to wait any longer to see her, so he arranged a sleepover for the girls at his parents' place. After dinner, he would drop them off, and then he'd do some work on the ice show sets. With any luck, he'd find her at the rink.

"Look how I can twirl, Daddy." Gracie pirouetted to the table for supper.

"Impressive." Tate paused, holding a pot of pasta. The delicious spicy aroma of simmering meat sauce filled the kitchen. He didn't mind cooking, and spaghetti was one of his specialities, loaded with tangy tomato sauce seasoned with garlic and oregano. "Now you can twirl your noodles."

Both girls scrambled onto their chairs at the small round table, just the right size for three. He always looked forward to their dinnertime chatter. He never knew what he might learn. "Tuck in your napkins, please." Sniffing the rich aroma, Tate served pasta, sauce, bread, and salad. "Did you have a fun day?" He looked at Ella first.

"Sort of." Ella rolled her eyes.

After their morning skating lesson, she and Gracie played with dolls and puzzles all afternoon. Except for the occasional sister squabble, they had chatted and giggled like best friends.

Meanwhile, he had whisked around with the vacuum and dust cloth, threw in laundry, and then worked on billings for his business. "Oh? Not so great?" Tate studied her face. Did something upset his happy little Ella? She was usually easy to please.

She shook her head.

"Krista isn't very nice anymore." Gracie jumped in, crinkling her nose.

Ella nodded.

Tate gripped his fork and stopped halfway through swirling a bite of pasta. "What do you mean? Why don't you like her?" At first, they had loved their new teacher, so what had changed their minds? Once or twice, he heard them mention she was grouchy, but he assumed they misinterpreted her strictness for a bad mood.

"She's sort of mean." Ella's eyes welled as she stuck a bite of spaghetti in her mouth, leaving a long strand dangling down to her chin.

"She stares and hardly ever smiles." Gracie clenched her fork with the tines pointing up. "When we fall, she just says 'get up and try again.' She doesn't even ask if we're hurt."

"She wants to help you learn to be really good skaters. Maybe she thinks if she smiles and laughs, she won't be in charge. Kids will fool around too much." A ripple of concern travelled up Tate's back. The frowns on both girls' faces were very unusual. They weren't complainers, and he couldn't stand to hear they felt uncomfortable and sad. He had thought Janine and Olivia exaggerated their concerns and didn't give Krista a fair chance. He had even defended her, but now, his own girls echoed the same feelings.

Could Janine possibly have a point? "Tell me more about what happened." He finished loading his fork, filled his mouth, and chewed. He couldn't stand to hear problems with Krista, but he needed to protect Gracie and Ella.

"She made me practice my crossovers and bend my knees really far." Ella stabbed a piece of lettuce. "I told her my legs hurt, but she didn't listen."

"I showed her my new mittens, and she didn't care." Gracie blinked and chomped on a big bite of bread. "She just said 'Sorry, I'm busy teaching. I'll look at them later. Right now, you need to practice skating fast backwards.'" She stabbed her fork into her pasta. "I was happy when skating was over. I didn't try to show her my mittens again."

"Why didn't you tell me sooner?" He should have known. Where was his head? His little darlins were his first priority. He should never ever get too distracted to notice how they felt.

"Well, you like her."

Ella's comment was a punch in the gut. His perceptive and considerate little girl didn't want to offend him.

"Aww, darlin." He reached over and squeezed her forearm. "You can tell me anything. Make sure you let me know whenever you're worried or sad about something. Promise?"

Both girls nodded.

Ella blinked and gave a small smile.

The thought of Krista hurting their feelings and pushing them too hard—even if she didn't intend any harm—made him feel like a terrible dad. His stomach twisted and squeezed with concern. Was Krista too hardnosed? Maybe she was trying too hard to produce champions. Did she want to prove she was tougher than her demanding mother and nasty ex believed?

How could he help his sweet girls without creating tension with Krista? He rubbed the back of his neck. He needed to do something. But how and when best to handle things? He didn't look forward to a tough conversation, but he'd do anything for Ella and Gracie. "How about if you see how your skating lesson goes on Tuesday? Then tell me if you have fun or if you have any problems. Okay? I know Krista wants to do a good job, and she wouldn't want you to be sad."

"Okey dokey, Daddy." Gracie tapped her fork on

her plate. "It's a deal."

Tate smiled at her words, and his heart melted a little. Sometimes, she sounded so mature for her age.

"You too, Ella?" He looked at the quieter twin.

She nodded and took a big swig of her milk.

The serious moments passed, but Tate finished his meal with not quite as much of an appetite. Some of the luster of the evening ahead had dulled. How could he get excited about spending more time with Krista under the circumstances? He hated to think Janine might be right. "Christmas is coming soon." He searched for a happy topic to finish off their meal. "What do you hope Santa brings?"

Ella widened her eyes.

Gracie grinned.

They were his precious treasures and the most important people in his life. Nobody else could come close.

"I want a puppy." Gracie burst out. "Pleeeeease, Daddy. I love puppies."

"I would love a puppy more than anything in the whole wide world." Ella stretched her arms wide and flung a piece of spaghetti across the room.

He couldn't possibly scold her for her innocent mistake. Her enthusiasm would carry her a long way.

"Ella, you're not supposed to throw food." Gracie giggled.

The space from her missing front teeth added to her cute expression.

"Oops." Ella scrunched her face and hopped off her chair to retrieve it. "I promise Gracie and I will feed her and walk her and brush her. I want a girl puppy like Pearl, and she can sleep between our beds."

"I'm not so sure Santa brings puppies." A picture of Pearl's gentle face and growing belly lodged in his mind. Could he handle a dog on top of everything else? "Maybe you should think of some other ideas, just in case."

The rest of dinner passed in a flurry of conversation about Christmas and the special traditions their family celebrated, and even though he shouldn't, he wondered how Krista would celebrate the special day. After supper, he loaded the dishwasher, swept the floor, and sent the girls to pack their overnight bags. They loved a sleepover at Grandma and Grandpa's place, so he didn't feel a bit guilty for leaving them in his parents' care until morning.

He glanced at the clock above the table. The timing should work out just fine. He'd drop off the girls, get to the rink in time to cut out some palm trees, and put on his skates right when Krista's last students left the ice. "Let's go, Ella. Come on, Gracie." They all bundled up and got ready to trudge down the street to the house where he grew up. No point starting the truck on a cold night for such a short hop down the block.

"I'm freezing, Daddy." Gracie's voice muffled behind her face warmer.

"Me too," Ella piped in.

"We're almost there." He drank in the frosty air and watched his breath form clouds. The Christmas lights on his neighbors' homes twinkled below a starry sky. "Hey, let's see how fast we can walk." Traipsing along, he tried to calm his heart, speeding much faster than it should for the pace he walked.

If he couldn't contain his feelings, maybe he could smooth Krista's tough outer crust. Was she actually as bad as Janine believed? But she wasn't the only one. Krista had offended his little darlins, and nobody was allowed to hurt them. Maybe his plan to meet her tonight was all a big mistake. "Here we are." He followed Ella and Gracie up the steps to his parents' front door.

Inside, welcoming warmth encircled them all, and the faint aroma of apple crisp floated to greet them. His mouth watered, and he was tempted to stop for a helping.

"I hope you girls have room for dessert." Mom swept them into a three-way hug. "Brrr. You feel like giant ice cubes." She gathered their jackets and hats. "Go give Grandpa a big cold hug." She turned to Tate. "Will you stay for a while?"

"Thanks, but I better run."

"Big plans?" She raised her eyebrows.

"Just some work on the ice show sets." His shrugged, and the anticipation in his stomach flipped like a hockey puck. "Other than that, I'm not sure." He wasn't about to admit the real reason for time at the rink. Mom could wonder all she liked. The last thing he needed was her teasing him about Krista.

Chapter 15

"You mean she'll deliver her puppies before Christmas? That's only a few weeks away." Krista practically choked out the words."

In one of the two examination rooms at the Blue Sky Animal Clinic, Dr. Bryden nodded without rustling her stubby gray ponytail.

She had kind brown eyes, and Krista could tell she genuinely loved animals. The sign on the wall showed she had been serving the community for over thirty years. Her lab coated covered in assorted animals brought a down-to-earth humor to her image. Krista took a deep breath. The small clinic smelled like a mixture of strong antiseptic and musky animal fur.

"She has all the signs of a dog moving quite far along in her pregnancy." Petting Pearl, Dr. Bryden smiled.

Her eyes crinkled at the corners with a combination of amusement and empathy. Krista immediately trusted her for advice.

"I take it you were surprised."

"Shocked is more like it." Krista hadn't quite recovered from the news that she would soon be responsible for a large litter of puppies. "Will she really have eight?"

"On average, golden retrievers have eight, but the number can vary from four to twelve." She peered at

Krista's face.

Krista felt her cheeks flush. Dr. Bryden had just confirmed what her online research showed. She was about to have her hands very full. Suddenly, her annoyance with Daisy rushed back. She did not need this on top of everything else. Daisy might be an ally against her unreasonable daughter, but she had sure caused some trouble of her own. "What do I need to do to prepare?" Krista heard the slight tremor in her own voice. She didn't know a thing about delivering and looking after puppies.

"Your part of the job is pretty easy." Dr. Bryden patted Krista's arm, then bent to stroke Pearl and rub behind her soft, smooth ears. "She does all the serious work, don't you, girl? Don't worry, Krista. You can handle things."

Krista took a deep breath and reached for Pearl's reassurance.

The dog gave her a big, wet lick on the hand.

"You'll need to build a whelping box to give her a comfortable place to give birth. You'll need newspapers and towels to line the box and clean up the puppies and the rest of the mess."

She spoke slowly and clearly, giving information in a calm and reassuring way.

"I'll give you a pamphlet to read, and you can call me anytime you have questions. I've even been known to come and check on progress during the delivery." She winked. "Helping animals deliver their babies is one of the fun parts of my job."

"Thank you. I feel a little better. Not much, but a little." Krista forced a laugh.

"Let's stay in touch." Dr. Bryden smiled and

straightened. "If I hear of anyone who wants a puppy, I'll send them your way." She gave Pearl a final pet and exited the room, leaving Krista to follow.

Walking home, Krista scanned the businesses along Main Street, and the colorful display of window decorations buoyed her mood. She could handle this situation, and when she pictured happy people snuggling brand-new puppies, she couldn't help smiling too. Waving at a passing driver, even though she didn't know him, she imagined calmly assisting Pearl and soothing a squealing, hungry litter. She shuddered but caught herself. *Relax, Krista.* She taught skaters to visualize themselves successfully completing jumps and spins, and she could apply her own advice. Krista's Kennel was kind of catchy. The thought almost made her laugh out loud.

Hunching her shoulders against the cold, she picked up her pace. Striding along, she scuffed her toes and puffed up little clouds of snow. With Christmas approaching and the ice show only two weeks later, she had a lot of work ahead to help her students perfect their performances. She was completely happy with the choreography, but the skating moves still needed more polishing. Already she devoted a part of each lesson to the ice show, getting the skaters to practice their programs to music. Over the Christmas school holidays, she'd schedule extra practices and make sure every detail was ready for the big show.

Today she'd check in with Hilary on costumes. They had already selected fabric together in tropical shades of pink, orange, green, and yellow with sparkly sequins and glittery accessories to catch the lights of the stadium. She felt a little surge of excitement at the way everything was coming together. Performing for an audience would be the icing on the cake—a delicious reward for her and the skaters for the hours of tiring practice and hard work.

Rounding the corner toward home, she spotted a woman shovelling snow about two blocks up. Even from a distance, her purple ski jacket was a splotch of color like paint on a white canvas. As she got closer, she recognized the woman. If she was timid, she could wave, turn left at the next corner, and avoid another encounter. If she was brave, she would pull back her shoulders, stop, and smile. Calmly and maturely, she'd approach with a friendly greeting and gauge whether Janine was receptive to a casual chat.

A gust of wind propelled her along with Pearl trotting by her side. She wanted to turn another corner and get to work, but she also knew she'd feel better if she spoke with Janine away from the rink in a more relaxed setting. With every footstep, she felt her heart rate pick up. She would face Janine for the first time since their tense meeting a week ago. The woman was her boss. Even though she might be a challenge, she was somebody Krista needed to impress. According to Tate, Janine would never change her opinionated ways, but she could be managed, and Krista would do the job.

Janine tossed a shovelful of snow, glanced up, and paused. From halfway down the block, Krista couldn't see the details of her facial expression, but she suspected Janine narrowed her eyes and pressed her lips together in a firm line. Now, she couldn't turn and run. Keeping her pace steady, she approached.

Pearl trotted ahead, tugging on the end of her leash. "Good morning, Janine. How are you this cold morning?"

Janine rustled and tossed a scoop of snow, then stopped and leaned on her shovel. "Good morning." She backed a few steps away from Pearl. "She's cute, but remember, I'm allergic."

Krista couldn't read Janine's expression between the black scarf wrapped up to her chin and the matching hat pulled low over her forehead. She shifted and struggled to think of the right thing to say. She needed to stay on good terms with this woman, no matter what.

Behind Janine, a neat path led to the front steps of her peach stuccoed house. The piles of snow on either side were almost symmetrical. Except for the odd dip where the wind gusted, the snowbanks stood straight as a short cement wall. Tate was right. Janine made sure everything was in order, just the way she liked. Her single-mindedness wasn't necessarily a bad quality as long as Krista measured up. "I wanted to thank you for your feedback last week."

Janine widened her eyes.

She clearly hadn't expected an impromptu visit this morning or Krista's grateful, humble tone. Maybe this conversation could help smooth the situation.

"Oh. You didn't look happy at the time." Janine jostled her shovel.

"I was sorry to hear you have concerns." Krista smiled and gathered her strength to charm Janine. Maybe they could eventually become allies, if not friends. "I really want things to work out well here. I like the skating club. I see potential in the skaters. And I want to build a strong relationship with the board."

"Well, I'm extremely glad to hear you know what's important. I'll support you as long as you promise not to put me in an awkward position." Janine narrowed her eyes.

Krista inhaled a sharp blast of air and felt the chill right to her lungs. "What do you mean? I would never want to make things awkward for you...or for anyone."

"What I mean is this." Janine straightened, stood her shovel upright, and tapped it on the bare sidewalk. "I have a reputation for running a strong board. If you head off in your own direction, you make me look weak. If you won't ease up on Olivia and the other kids, you leave me with an unhappy teen and complaints from other parents. If you present a disappointing ice show, you cause fallout from a disgruntled club. They are all problems I need to deal with. See what I mean."

"I understand." Krista nodded and squeezed her hands into fists. She understood but didn't have to like the situation. The sting in her chest felt all too familiar. Criticism hurt. Images of her tough-to-please mom and impossible-to-please ex prickled in her memories, and she wanted to run.

She breathed in a mouthful of cold air. "I think we can help each other. If I don't succeed with the skating club, I'll consider it a major personal failure." She spoke the truth. She'd laid it out for Janine. After the negativity and letdowns in her past, she absolutely couldn't handle one more failure. She shivered. "Please, Janine. Let's find a win-win solution."

"I can't guarantee anything. But I like the fact you listened and want to make changes." Janine hunched her shoulders. "Brr. The wind is picking up, and I'm just about done here. Would you like to come in for a hot drink? I baked muffins earlier this morning. Pearl can wait in the veranda, so she doesn't stir up my allergies."

"Uh…" Krista felt the lump of ice inside her melt just a little. She had work to do, but she couldn't refuse Janine's peace offering. "Thank you. I can stop for a few minutes before I get down to work."

"Come." Janine headed up the front walk and motioned for Krista to follow. "How are the show details coming along anyway? I still can't picture Mexico in January."

"I'll give you a full update." Inside the porch, she paused. "Stay, Pearl. Lie down." She'd reassure Janine that preparations continued right on schedule, but a nervous twinge ran down her arms and tingled in her fingertips. Janine was still skeptical. But Krista had a glimmer of hope, and at least, she had Tate's full support.

****

"Go ahead." Tate brushed snow off his shoulders and ushered Ella and Gracie into the house. They had just returned from their annual expedition to find the perfect Christmas tree, and they all agreed it was the best yet. Tate made sure he always supported the local tree lot because it was operated by volunteers, and all proceeds went to the local animal rescue service.

Behind them, he squeezed the massive tree through the door, sending a shower of snow droplets and evergreen needles onto the floor. The smell of pine wafted up and filled his head with Christmas memories.

"I love it." Ella clapped and sprinkled sparkly crystals of snow off her mittens.

"It's ginormous!" Gracie threw her arms wide and stared up. "Can we decorate it right now?" She jumped and spun in a circle.

"As soon as we eat dinner. Hang your jackets and set the table, please." The heat in their cozy home hugged him, and before he even removed his parka, he plunked the tree into the stand waiting in the living room. Soon the tree would glow in the center of the front window with multi-colored lights and a mishmash of decorations—some old, some new, and some handmade by the girls. All were special in their own way. He swallowed a small lump in his throat. The haphazard bells made from egg cartons and tied with red ribbons were his favorite.

The beef stew simmering in the slow cooker smelled rich and savory and swirled around them with a warm and comforting aroma. His stomach rumbled, more than ready for a hot meal.

"Can Grandma and Grandpa come over and help decorate?" After setting plates and cutlery on the table, Ella searched his face for a *yes*.

"Good idea. You call and invite them, and I'll serve dinner." He added buns and napkins to the table. Setting the large pot in the middle, he ladled piping-hot servings of meat and vegetables coated in thick gravy. The aroma of onion, basil, and thyme wafted upward, and he inhaled deeply. His cooking was basic but usually tasted pretty good. Considering the weather and the time of year, the hearty meal was the perfect start to a Christmassy evening.

By the time he supervised their decorating project, he might not have time to go skating. But if his parents were here anyway, maybe they'd stay long enough to let him slip out for a while. Even though he asked for their help often, he never got the feeling they minded. The more time with their beloved granddaughters, the better. Their support meant the world. Maybe someday he'd have a wife to share the load, but for now, he did his best with frequent help from Mom, Dad, and Carly.

Ella grabbed the cordless landline and scooted off to her bedroom, with Gracie right behind, to make the call.

A few minutes later, they reappeared side by side, both grinning.

"They're coming after supper," announced Gracie.

Their company would make the tree trimming tradition even more special. His heart tapped an extra beat. Seeing Krista would top off the evening.

Three times in the past week, he'd caught up with her when lessons ended for the day. Three times, he'd connected with her in a personal way, but he still hadn't found the right words to tell her she might be a little too tough on the skaters. The closest he had come was to ask how she was handling Janine's feedback.

"You told me I could take her demands with a grain of salt." Krista had huffed and skated faster like she wanted to escape.

He caught up within seconds. "My mistake. I meant Janine can be harsh and annoying. But nobody can totally discount the club president's opinions."

"Obviously."

She had shot him a look with a murky mix of hurt and confusion in her blue eyes. He hated to admit Janine could be right, but Gracie's and Ella's feelings mattered. Maybe tonight he would summon the courage to be more direct. He noticed that after work hours, she softened a little and might be open to his feedback if he kept it gentle enough.

He thought of Krista multiple times during the day,

and he daydreamed of the next time he might see her. He'd already spent more hours on the ice show decorations than were really needed, but he wanted to make them perfect and live up to her high expectations. More than anything, he wanted to see her again.

After a quick supper, he played Christmas music and hauled out boxes of lights and decorations. The girls' faces lit with excitement.

Ella and Gracie practically bounced through the room like a pair of rubber balls. When the doorbell rang, they raced to the front door to greet Grandma and Grandpa.

A gust of chilly wind blew in with them, carrying a faint hint of smoke from a neighbor's fireplace. Mom's and Dad's cheeks shone rosy red with the bite of the air, even though they were bundled in down jackets, wool hats, and heavy scarves.

"I'm going to hang the green and silver balls, and Ella's going to put on the red and gold ones." Gracie didn't even wait for Grandma and Grandpa to take off their coats before blurting the plan.

Mom would be pleased to see the girls both wore the blue sweaters with snowmen on the front she had given them.

"How fun!" She handed Tate her jacket and clapped at Gracie's report.

"Daddy will string the lights and add the angel on top," said Gracie.

"You and Grandpa can unwrap the ornaments and hand them to us." Ella nodded as she delivered the instructions.

Her eyes glowed with the wonder of Christmas. Tate savored every moment of his sweet daughters' excitement.

"Marvellous idea." Mom beamed and pulled the twins into a group hug.

"Hey, what about me?" Dad stuck out his bottom lip in a fake show of dismay.

The girls tore themselves away and plopped on his lap, one on each knee.

"Hang on." He spun his chair.

They shrieked at the ride.

An hour and a half later, the tree glowed bright, and thanks to Mom and Dad, the tissue and cardboard from the storage containers were mostly gathered and organized.

"Bea…u…ti…ful!" Gracie joined hands with Ella, jumped, and grinned as she admired the results of their decorating job.

"It's gorgeous," Mom agreed. She crinkled her eyes and blinked away tears.

"Good work, girls. It's one of the prettiest trees I've ever seen." Dad gave them a big thumbs-up.

His parents were model grandparents, and he admired Dad for not letting a disability slow him down. Tate stood back, rubbed his hands together, and smiled. The ornaments were concentrated mainly at Ella's and Gracie's height and lower, but he agreed the overall effect was pretty nice.

Drinking in the sight of his parents and girls celebrating the moment, he felt a surge of love and peace squeezing his throat so tight he couldn't speak right then, even if he tried. The evening was just about perfect, but still, he couldn't ignore the restless tug inside him—the secret place in his daydreams Krista increasingly occupied. He'd love to see her reaction to the shimmering tree.

"I could use a mug of hot chocolate and a cookie after all my work. What do you think, girls?" Dad winked.

Tate knew the snack was more for the benefit of Ella and Gracie than the adults.

"Yes, please. Yes, please." The girls chorused, but Gracie rubbed her eyes.

Bedtime was not far off, and Tate felt a twinge of guilt. He glanced at his watch. He still had time to meet Krista at the rink.

Mom caught him checking the time, and she smiled and quirked an eyebrow. "Why don't Grandpa and I spend some special time with these sweethearts? You should probably go to the rink and work on those sets."

"Okay with you, Ella? Gracie?" He called after them as they dashed to the kitchen. He chuckled. "I don't think they'll miss me."

"Have fun at the rink, dear." Mom giggled and raised a hand in a half wave. "With the amount of time you're spending on those backdrops, you must be creating a masterpiece. I can't wait to see."

Her teasing tone told him she knew exactly his reason for spending so much time at the arena.

"Do what you need to do, son." Dad echoed Mom's joking manner, spun, and wheeled into the kitchen.

As much as a quiet evening and snacks tempted him, the woman at the rink tempted him more. After quick hugs, Tate threw on his warm clothes and twisted the doorknob.

The chatter drifted from the kitchen on a chocolate-scented cloud. When he heard Gracie's little voice rise above the others, he froze.

"He likes Krista, but I don't."

Her words hit him like a hockey puck in the gut. Gracie and Ella needed his help. He couldn't delay any longer. He better broach the subject with Krista tonight.

Chapter 16

Krista wanted nothing more than to sink into a hot bubble bath, but a few minutes of private ice time would ease her tense shoulder muscles and help her process the trying week. She stroked hard and picked up speed, inhaling the arena scents of exhaust from the ice resurfacing machine, popcorn, rubber, and leather. She breathed deeply and absorbed the pleasurable sensation of swooping and bending her knees until her thigh muscles ached.

Much as she craved time alone, she also kept an eye on the perimeter of the ice surface in case Tate arrived. He had joined her three times this week already, and sharing the ice was as comfortable as slipping into her well-worn skates but, at the same time, as exhilarating as landing a triple jump. Sometimes, they were quiet except for the crackling sound of their blades cutting the ice, and sometimes, they chatted easily about his girls, town gossip, and Christmas plans.

So far, she had mostly avoided the topic of Janine, not wanting to sound like a complainer or someone too weak to handle her own problems. She didn't need Tate or anybody else to fight her battles. The evening he advised her not to totally discount Janine's feedback, she felt betrayed. His words had felt as prickly as the toe picks on her skates. But tonight was a clean slate. As though visualizing Tate made him appear, there he was in the flesh. She almost glided by and then stopped sharply, throwing a fine spray of snow ahead in his direction.

"Nice move. I hoped you'd still be here." He studied her expression.

She loved the fact he didn't even pretend he came to work. The sets were progressing nicely, and he would easily finish them in time. "I'm here all right." Her voice held the hint of a quaver. "For now." She sighed and thumped her thick mitts against her thighs.

"What do you mean?"

He answered quickly like he didn't want to believe the possibility she might leave sooner than expected. Did he really care that much? "Come and join me, and I'll explain." Not waiting for him to answer, she planted a toe pick, hopped, and jetted away. He was an ally, and she needed all the support she could get to survive in this skating club.

She pushed harder and harder, curved, and cut a sharp edge into smooth forward crossovers. Changing directions at center ice, she carved a giant eight over the entire surface. Flipping backwards, she switched to back crossovers, leaning in until her thighs burned. Then she stepped forward, leapt, and rotated into an axel jump. Her landing was sure and solid just like always. Turning and gliding forward, she tilted at her waist, spread her arms, and raised her right leg into a graceful spiral. After the uncertainty plaguing her, the familiarity of favorite basic figure skating moves was a comforting distraction.

Within minutes, Tate jumped onto the ice and soon caught up as she rounded the far end. His blades scratched, and the scuffed surface left from Krista's students crackled as he approached. "Good evening, señorita."

"Hi, señor." She mustered what she hoped sounded like an upbeat tone. Anticipation crowded into her chest as she locked on his eyes. They shone as dark and delicious as chocolate. She couldn't resist chocolate, even though too much of it definitely wasn't healthy. He had stripped off his heavy gray parka and wore a thick sweater, a shade of brown lighter than his eyes. His blue jeans showed off his muscular build. He left on his knit black hat, but she could imagine his close-cropped dark hair underneath. Skating together felt warm and familiar and pulled her in a direction far too tempting for comfort.

"Care to dance?" He glided on one foot and extended a hand. His eyes crinkled with amusement. "Come on. I won't bite."

She brought her hands together in front and then slowly straightened one arm toward him. If her thick mitt wasn't on her hand, she might not have accepted his invitation. Skin on skin would awaken feelings she wasn't prepared to handle. Against her better judgment, she allowed him to grasp her hand like they were ice dancers who had skated together forever.

She'd always loved the idea of ice dancing but never found a suitable partner, so she had focussed on singles skating instead. "Try this." She couldn't resist enjoying the moment and forcing away all the uncertainty and unpleasantness caused by Janine. She pushed into long strokes and then curved into arcing rolls.

He kept up without a pause, glanced at her, and grinned. "Nothing to it. Now what?"

"A chasse."

"Not the car part?"

She laughed. "Hardly. Watch." She demonstrated a deep edge and switched feet using a small step motion.

Still holding hands, he studied her movement and then imitated it in slow motion. "Simple. Now what?"

"Try faster." She sped up and curved into long rolls.

He kept up and completed the move like a pro.

"Not bad."

"Not bad?" He winced. "I'd say pretty darn good."

They circled the rink, repeated the sequence, and soared faster and smoother with each round.

"With a little practice, we can perform together at the ice show." Chuckling, he glanced over.

Her breath quickened, and excitement twirled in her stomach. "Uh, probably not." Slipping her hand out of his, she laughed. "I want to set a good example for the kids. Do you mean we could do a comedy number?"

"Hey, don't write us off too soon."

The amusement in his tone warmed her insides, and she slowed beside his left elbow, feeling his strength. Could she trust he was everything he seemed? He was always fun and interesting, the perfect gentleman, and so far, he'd been her biggest supporter. But should she know more? Even now, his steady presence melted her feelings into a messy pool, which did not help anything.

Should she trust him enough to confide in him? "I…uh…" She'd already called and consulted Amy. Who better to ask for advice than her best friend? If only she lived close enough for a heart-to-heart in person. Over a video call, Amy had given her a glowing reference on Tate's character and had agreed Janine sounded horrible. But not knowing the difficult woman personally, she said Tate would be a far better sounding board on how to win her over.

"What's going on?" He glanced over.

"Janine." She sighed and launched into two-footed swerving motions, swaying like her emotions in the face of open criticism." She glanced at Tate. The music floated above at a fast pace. She had selected it to energize and motivate skaters, but now, it felt like a jarring interruption to a thoughtful conversation.

Krista took a deep breath. "I already told you Janine and I chatted last week. At first, I was optimistic I could become her partner in making the skaters and the club stronger. By the time I finished my tea at her kitchen table, I knew the only way to get along was to deliver on every demand she made."

Krista pictured Janine's pristine white kitchen accented with Christmassy red-and-green tea towels and a snowman cookie jar on display. They had sipped steaming, apple-cinnamon tea from mugs decorated with poinsettias. Even during a short visit, she observed everything was precise and perfect, just the way Janine liked it. In her home and in her community work, she showed no sign of flexibility.

Tate imitated Krista's swerving manoeuvers. "Why am I not surprised?" He clamped his jaw.

"She won't let up until I lower my standards and let Olivia and her friends socialize instead of practice. She also informed me she expects to meet weekly and give me feedback and suggestions. I'll never hear the end of her views on the ice show theme."

"Sounds like typical Janine...but maybe you could

give a little."

What did he mean? Tate was supposed to be her biggest supporter. Now he sounded like he didn't think Janine was all wrong. His words cut dangerously close to criticism. "Lower my standards? No, thank you." She would stand firm. She came to Blue Sky to rebuild her confidence. Giving in would be plain weak. They rounded the end of the rink at a quick pace. The cool air brushed her cheekbones, but they still burned with indignation. This evening wasn't what she had expected at all.

"Kids do better when they're having fun."

"Kids do better when they listen to their coach." Sure, Tate was a dad—a very good dad from all she had seen—but clearly, parents could be biased and overly protective. She had a lot of experience teaching kids, and she wasn't naïve.

"Hey, don't get so defensive." He tapped her forearm.

"I have every reason." She caught an edge and nearly pitched forward but caught herself just in time. "I have principles. I came to Blue Sky understanding I would run the skating school, not become anybody's puppet. Janine knows how to judge and criticize. She reminds me of my mother and Zach." Tension throbbed in her temples.

Now, Tate was getting all opinionated too. "I just don't need the headaches and the pressure." She sighed. "I've already dealt with enough criticism to last a lifetime. Maybe I should just resign and move to somewhere I'm appreciated. Mom and Zach walked all over me for far too long. I refuse to give anyone else the chance."

Gliding on two feet, Tate reached out, snatched Krista's puffy mitt off her hand.

This time, he enveloped her cool fingers with his warm hand. The delicious sensation sizzled down her back right to her toes.

Slowing, he eased to a full stop. He turned to face her, pulled off her other mitt, and dropped both on either side of their skates. Searching deep into her eyes, he clasped her hands and squeezed. "You can't give up."

His face threatened to crumble any second. She wanted to look away but couldn't.

"I won't let you leave. I nee—" He stopped short of finishing the word *need*. "The club would miss you. I would miss you."

She opened and closed her mouth, overwhelmed by his intensity. Was she dreaming?

He raised her hands and kissed each fingertip. Leaning forward, he kissed the tip of her nose, her cheeks, and then pressed his soft and warm lips onto hers. He lingered for a few seconds.

Her breath caught in her throat. Intense heat radiated throughout her body. She no longer stood in a chilly arena. She basked in a scorching sauna, and the ice beneath her skates could melt any moment. What was happening? She couldn't let it continue. Breathless, she placed her hands on his broad chest and inched back. "You can't mean what you said."

"I mean every word." Tate squatted, retrieved her mitts, and held them while she pushed her hands into their warmth. "Please, don't leave. Promise you won't disappear."

Krista's thoughts dipped and whirled like a sit spin.

Tate almost said he needed her. He must have gotten swept away in the moment. Was he really ready to risk his heart? Was she ready to trust his words wouldn't cut her to the core? Could she let go of her pride and her plans and do everything possible to build a life in Blue Sky? They were all tough questions, and she didn't know the answers.

Her knees felt slightly shaky like the first time she set foot on this ice surface. But romance couldn't change everything. Love couldn't erase an unhappy work situation or fix a critical partner. She couldn't let her attraction to Tate influence decisions about her future. The more she allowed her feelings to grow, the worse her heart would hurt when she left the club and moved away. The more she trusted, the worse she'd suffer if he wasn't as nice on the inside as on the surface. Even if she stayed until the end of her contract, she would still leave in just a few months. If she backed away now, she could minimize the pain for both of them for so many reasons.

The facts stared her in the face. Janine would not change. She was sure. And now, even Tate questioned her coaching style. As cold reality hit, she shivered. She couldn't promise she would stay and torture herself much longer. Where she would go, she didn't know, but Blue Sky wasn't the only skating club in western Canada. "I...I'll see. But Tate, I think we should stop seeing each other like this."

Absorbing the bewilderment and pain etched across his face, she almost crumpled. But she wouldn't make a promise she might not keep. Now was the time to convince him—and herself—to quash their feelings for good. They could remain close friends but nothing more. "It's getting late." Krista wobbled, feeling like her knees might give out if she tried to skate away, and she straightened and shifted her weight to test them. "We should go." She would love to stay forever and dance in his strong arms, but the situation was already complicated enough.

"I understand, but if you think you're getting rid of me this easily, don't count on it." Following her, he stroked to the sideline and tromped onto the rubber flooring.

She glanced at his lips folded together into a sad, straight line. "I'm sorry." She blinked.

Pearl batted him with her tail.

She had no reason to cry when she was the one resisting the idea of romance. "I'll go to my office to take off my skates. Please, go ahead." She couldn't stand to look at his expression crushed into a picture of pain. The magnitude of what she had just done stabbed her in the chest, and she barely contained a flood of emotion.

He plunked onto a bench and bent to untie his skates. "Nah, I'll wait."

As she scooted away down the hallway, she heard the disappointment strangle his voice. She couldn't answer, or her own voice would waver and crack. Unlacing her skates in the security of her own space, she couldn't stop her hands from shaking. She dared to imagine what would happen if she resigned before Christmas and slipped quietly away from Blue Sky. She wasn't a quitter, but she also knew how to take action when she had made a mistake.

****

"Christmas is my favorite time of the year."

Walking Krista home, Tate swung his arms and didn't reach out to hold her hand, even though he ached to feel her close. He pointed out light displays on homes of people she might recognize.

"I like that blue-and-white combination. It's so peaceful." She gestured across the street.

She spoke to the sky as though she was alone and Tate wasn't right beside her. Scuffing through ribbons of snow winding along the edges of the sidewalk, he scanned the stars and absorbed the vastness of the universe. Love felt the same never-ending way. He sucked in a huge mouthful of nighttime air, inhaled the clean scent of snow, and glanced over at Krista.

She stared ahead.

The reflection from a streetlight glittered in her eyes. Was there moisture there too? Despite what she had said at the rink, she couldn't possibly refuse to see him anymore. Not when their kiss had sent him to places he had only imagined. Not when he sensed she felt the same.

She couldn't possibly pack up and leave Blue Sky without even completing an entire winter season. He wanted her to assure him she would stay and work through her differences with Janine, but now was not the time. He tightened his jaw around the secret of how his girls felt about Krista and their skating lessons. He needed to set aside his attraction and admit Janine wasn't alone in her concerns. He would initiate the tough conversation, but not tonight. Right now, he couldn't load on more worries to end her day. "Will Pearl give birth before Christmas?" When he caught her wince, he could have kicked himself. Pearl's pregnancy still upset her.

"I hope not."

He chuckled. "You don't want Santa to bring puppies?"

"Santa's supposed to bring us what we wish for." She bit her lip. "I didn't put *that* on my list. Seriously, the puppies better wait until after Christmas. Lessons finish on December twenty-third, and I'll leave early on Christmas Eve to join my parents in Saskatoon."

"Will Pearl make the trip?"

"I hope Daisy will dog sit. She dragged me into this mess in the first place."

"No rush to make arrangements," Tate teased. He'd do anything to make her smile. "It's well over a week away."

"I can hardly believe Christmas will be here so soon." She stopped.

Pearl circled, batting their legs and panting.

Her belly seemed to expand by the hour. He didn't blame Krista for being concerned.

"Well, here we are." She looked at Pearl, then at the sidewalk and the house. Under the front window, a sprinkling of multi-colored lights lit up a couple of small bushes.

He drank in her pink cheeks and blue eyes. They were as pretty as a dusky December sky. The faint lines at the outer corners suggested she'd had a long and tiring day. Anybody would be exhausted teaching kids of all ages and preparing for a major ice show. He wanted to kiss her again so much he couldn't resist any longer. Tilting forward, he reached for her shoulders.

Avoiding his touch, she dipped and backed away. "I want to kiss you again, but I can't. We can't do this, Tate."

Her eyes burned like blue flames. He refused to believe she meant what she said.

She dropped her gaze from his face to his feet.

"I know what I hope Santa brings me." His feelings hit him like a prairie blizzard. More time with her and a hint of her love would be the biggest gift she could offer. Hope quivered in his chest.

"Dare I ask what?" She took another step back and shivered.

Like she could read his mind, she looked to the front door as her escape. How could he convince her to stay?

"Never mind. Your wish can be a secret between you and Santa." She backed away. "I really should go in before we both turn into ice sculptures."

The words were on the tip of his tongue. He wanted her in his life more than anything. Never mind any issues with her coaching. He could help her understand and soften her ways with the skaters. He'd be gentle but honest, supporting his precious daughters. "Krista, wait." But she was already halfway up the front walk with Pearl at her heels. Either the wind blew away his words, or she pretended not to hear.

He stared at the twinkling colored lights until she closed the front door. She didn't even glance back, and her abrupt end to the evening stung. Instead of being a welcoming reminder of the season, the wreath on the front door hung like a stop sign he couldn't pass. Reluctantly, he turned and headed toward home.

All the way, he kicked snowbanks until he heard the hiss of scattering snow. The force made his big toes hurt inside his chunky winter boots. She was the woman for him. He crunched along, reliving the magical moment when he kissed her on the ice. Beneath the bite of winter on his lips, he tingled with the warmth of her touch. He could convince her to stay and help her succeed. He'd find a way.

Arriving at his front path, he felt his nagging inner voice elbow its way to the surface. Gracie and Ella were his very first priority, and they didn't like Krista anymore. How and when could he offer the feedback she needed? Would she even listen? He paused, and the squeak of his boots on the packed snow faded to silence.

Struck by the magic of the season, he drank in the festive appearance of his home decked out with red and white lights like a candy cane. His chest expanded full of love for his girls, satisfaction from his business, and surprisingly, an irresistible longing to unite with Krista. He'd find a balance, showing his girls how to persevere through challenging situations and, at the same time, encouraging Krista to make small changes that would make a big difference. He would do whatever he could to keep his girls happy and win Krista's heart.

Chapter 17

"Arms out, straight backs, and point the tips of your fingers so you float like a bird." Krista watched her beginner class wobble and concentrate on following her instructions. They had come a long way in a few weeks, and they would be adorable little dancers in the Mexican fiesta on ice. With only ten more days until Christmas, she needed to drill all the skaters in their programs for the ice show.

"Now, let's skate in a circle, stop, twirl, and clap three times." She wore a firm expression so even the youngest skaters knew she meant business. No slacking off allowed. "Good, but now let's see you make your pushes fast and smooth."

"Can't we have free time now? I'm tired." Gracie groaned and scrunched her face. Her pink mittens sparkled with ice shavings from her last fall, and she stood with her hands on her hips and her right toe pick planted.

Around her, the other skaters scratched in a circle, stretching themselves to do what Krista expected.

"Soon. We have to practice until you're almost perfect. When we finish, Hilary will help you try on your costumes. They're beautiful and colorful and sparkly." She flashed a brief half smile and sighed. "Just a few more minutes, and then you'll be done for today."

The last week had been a giddy mix of work and dreaming of Tate. Over and over, intense memories transported her back to that special moment on the ice last Saturday evening. She still marvelled that the heat from their embrace didn't melt the ice into a shiny pool around their skates.

"Please try again, Gracie." The energetic sounds of loud mariachi music—guitars, violins, and trumpets— swirled over the ice surface. Gracie's expression turned stormy, but Krista pretended not to notice. Usually, she was a lively little skater, so she must be really tired today to reach her limit. She'd get a break soon enough.

"Okay." Gracie sighed and pressed her lips together. "I guess I will." She glided and rejoined the circle.

Krista clapped in time to the music so the kids would follow the beat. Gracie's crumpled expression looked just like Tate's when Krista had pushed him away. It made her insides feel even heavier than pregnant Pearl. Did Krista really need to demand so much of a little girl and all the skaters? Yes! The kids would benefit in the long run, and she would prove she was stronger than her mother and Zach knew. How else would she show no one could push her around?

She had bristled at Tate's suggestion she make changes to please Janine. Any hint of criticism hurt and reminded her too much of her past—another good reason to avoid him. Even so, all week long, she struggled to control her feelings, but they still fluttered like snowflakes in the wind. Realistically, she couldn't tempt them both with romance when she was on the verge of leaving Blue Sky, maybe even earlier than planned. Falling in love wouldn't be fair to either of them.

But—a big *but*—if she was willing to stay in spite of Janine, maybe she could open her heart a crack. She couldn't wait to see his reaction when she let him know the answer was *maybe*. Shoving away the image of Tate's handsome face, she scanned the ice to make sure all the skaters stayed focused on their jumps and spins and didn't drift to the sidelines to chat with their friends.

"Krista. Krista."

At first, she barely heard the cry, but at the sound of several skaters calling her name, she spun and glided toward the commotion.

"Gracie hurt herself." Arms flailing and purple skirt rippling, Ella sped toward Krista.

"I'm coming, Gracie." Krista's heart picked up, and in four long strokes, she reached Gracie's side.

The little girl sprawled in a heap on the ice. She rubbed her left ankle and sobbed.

Her cry was loud enough to compete with the music in the rink. Falls were common, but usually, kids bounced up ready to try again. Most times, any tears by the youngest skaters were easy to soothe.

The rest of the group circled round and stared, frowning and wrinkling their foreheads.

Krista squatted and placed a hand on Gracie's back. "Did you have a bad fall?"

"I…broke…my…ankle." Gracie's voice shook, and huge tears dripped down her cheeks onto the snowflake pattern on her pink sweater. "It hurts sooo much. I want my daddy."

"Aww, sometimes a fall hurts a lot. It'll feel better soon." Krista took a deep breath and gently straightened

Gracie's leg. She glanced toward the sidelines to see if Tate stood nearby. She didn't spot him, but she couldn't miss Janine peering over the boards, frowning.

"I…need…to go…now to…the hospital." Gracie shrieked and writhed.

Ella squatted beside Gracie. "Don't worry." She blinked back tears.

"Someone, call Tate." Janine shouted over her shoulder and continued to glare at the scene on the ice.

"Let me see." Krista's stomach clenched. Of all the skaters to get hurt…and under her watch… Accidents happened, but she was responsible for the kids' safety on the ice. The situation would only fuel Janine's concerns, but she'd deal with the fallout later. Right now, she only cared about Gracie. "Take a deep breath. I know it hurts a lot, but I don't think it's broken." She hoped her reassuring words were true. The boot of Gracie's skate offered strong support, and serious injuries in a beginner group were rare, so she probably didn't break anything.

Gracie inhaled a long shaky breath, and her sobs subsided to whimpers.

"I'll help you stand and see how it feels." Straightening, Krista felt the stares of the skaters and their parents close in. "Okay, everyone. You can have some free time." She dismissed her students. "But keep practicing until I say you can stop."

All the kids except Ella skated away.

"I'm staying to look after my sister." Ella stuck her chin forward and set a hand on Gracie's shoulder.

Krista bent, tucked her hands under Gracie's arms, and lifted. "See if you can stand on both feet." The weight of Krista's guilt was much heavier than the weight of the little girl. Gracie had complained of being too tired to practice anymore, but Krista insisted she continue. Was the accident her fault? Maybe she should have listened.

"Ouch, ouch, ouch." Gracie put a little weight on her sore ankle and winced. Her brown eyes pooled and threatened to overflow again. "I want Daddy."

"Somebody called him. I'm sure your dad will be here soon." Concern churned inside Krista, but even in the midst of an alarming emergency, she felt a jump of anticipation at the chance to see him again. She glanced toward the gate. Strong, calm Tate would arrive any minute in all-out dad mode. He'd soothe Gracie, and she'd soon be just fine. As a former athlete, he would understand that injuries were sometimes unavoidable. "I'll help you glide to the edge, and you can sit and wait." Krista kept her voice quiet and soothing.

Gracie sniffed, braced her sore foot against the other, and let Krista guide her to the edge. On the rubber mat, she hopped a couple of times to reach a seat.

Ella crinkled her face and squeezed into the seat beside Gracie.

"I'll carefully unlace your skate and take it off so we can see your ankle." Krista glanced toward the door. Surely Tate would arrive soon.

A few feet away, Janine tutted and shook her head.

Krista tried to ignore her. She didn't need more guilt loaded onto the heavy lump already weighing her down.

"It's going to hurt." Gracie whimpered.

"I'll be gentle." If her ankle really was broken, the best thing to do would be to leave the skate in place and let the hospital cut it off. But she doubted the injury was as serious as Gracie thought.

"Leave it." Tate rushed to Gracie's side.

His tone was sharper than a skate blade.

"Let me."

"Of course." Krista jolted back like she had been shoved. She'd never seen him this way, and even though she understood, she cringed at his reprimand.

"Daddy!" At the sight of Tate, Gracie burst into tears again. "I...broke...my ankle." She stared at her foot. "Daddy, it...really...really...really...hurts." Her little shoulders shook, and her bottom lip quivered. She gulped air and forced out her words between sobs.

"It's okay, darlin. I'm here. I'll look after you." He focused on Gracie.

"I'm so sorry, Tate. I turned my back for a few seconds, so I didn't see how she fell." Krista wanted to shrink right into the floor. His usual soft and open expression was stiff, and it was all her fault. Why hadn't she allowed Gracie to take a break when she announced she was too tired to continue?

"Deep breath, Gracie." Tate knelt, hugged her, and then backed away so he could reach her foot. "Bend it a little for me." He gently guided her toe upward and then from side to side, stopping when she winced.

"No, no, no. Please stop." Gracie sniffled and shook her head. "I want to go to the doctor."

"Tell you what. Ella, go to the dressing room, take off your skates, put on your jacket, and bring your sister's jacket and boots here." He clasped both of Gracie's hands. "Very carefully, I'll loosen your skates, slip on your boots, and carry you to the truck. We'll get you all fixed up in no time."

Krista stood next to them, shifting awkwardly and squeezing and releasing her fists. She offered Gracie a reassuring smile.

Gracie only blinked and lowered her gaze back to her foot.

She couldn't think of a thing to do except apologize. "I'm sorry this had to happen, Gracie. I'm sorry, Tate."

Tate grunted an answer she couldn't decipher. Despite his gentle, calming tone toward his distraught daughter, his stiff back left little doubt he was upset, concerned, and not interested in chatting.

"How is she?" Janine's feet tapped along the mat, and she peered over Tate's shoulder. "Maybe she got pushed a little too hard."

Krista blinked, focused on Gracie, and steadied herself against the rink boards. She would not allow Janine to shatter her confidence the way her mother and Zach always did. She would stand up for what she knew was right. Nobody would make her crumble.

"She'll be just fine, Janine. Don't worry." Tate discouraged any further discussion.

Krista silently thanked him. He might be upset, but he didn't appear to side with Janine, at least, not right now. Krista dared a glance at Janine and bit back waves of annoyance. Injuries happened in sports all the time. Janine didn't need to point a finger at her when she was just doing her job.

"Good. Well, everyone knows I don't like to hear of unnecessary accidents in our club." Janine scuttled away, hugging her arms around the middle of her purple jacket.

"I better go and dismiss the other skaters." Krista

paused. "Please, call later and let me know how she's doing."

Tate glanced up and nodded, his lips set in a firm, straight line.

She'd never seen that expression darken his face, and her knees quaked at his obvious disapproval. She wouldn't rest easy until she heard Gracie was okay and Tate smiled again. What a mess she had made! Anxiety filled her insides and rotated painfully, faster than a corkscrew spin. She hated to see an injured little girl and an unhappy dad—the very same guy who also invaded her daydreams and disrupted her sleep. "Bye, Gracie. You're a brave girl. I hope you feel better soon." Krista turned and glided back onto the ice surface. The music blared so loudly it was irritating. She motioned for the beginner group of skaters to cluster round.

They scratched their toe picks as they approached and stopped.

She smiled reassurance and made eye contact with each one. "Gracie will be okay. Your lesson is over for today. I'll see you next time." After waving goodbye, she skirted the ice and called encouragement to the older skaters working on their jumps and spins. She felt sick. She had hurt Tate emotionally, and now his daughter was hurt physically. He hadn't wanted to shut down the possibility of romance before, but now, he probably wanted nothing to do with her anymore, even if she changed her mind. How could she have messed up everything so badly?

****

"She'll be fine." Tate got straight to the point over a phone call with Krista. "It's just a sprain." He knew he sounded clipped, but he didn't care. His emotions wound tight to his temples and gave him a nagging headache. The strain of dealing with a whiny child was taking its toll. The realization he might have prevented the accident upset him even more.

Balancing the phone on one shoulder, he removed a tray of roasted vegetables from the oven and sniffed the rich, savory scent. With two hungry girls waiting and his stomach growling, he had no time or energy to flirt. Besides, he was too mad at Krista for demanding so much from every skater and at himself for not speaking up sooner. At the very least, if he'd been at the rink, he could have backed Gracie. Now, it was too late to prevent an injury but not too late to make sure the same thing didn't happen again.

"Oh, I'm so relieved to hear her injury is not more serious." Krista took a deep breath and exhaled in a whoosh.

"She's sitting with her leg up and an ice bag on her ankle. She'll survive this one." He cleared his throat but couldn't force any small talk. He was still too upset. Janine was right. Krista pushed the kids too hard. When he first overheard Gracie saying she didn't like Krista, he should have taken her feelings seriously. He kicked himself for not acting sooner.

All things considered, he wasn't in a talkative mood, and he didn't know what else to say. "I need to get a late supper on the table, so I better let you go." He sniffed the fragrant chicken sizzling on the stove and switched off the burner. Then he paced to the living room to check on the girls. Maybe the motion would chase away the anger and concern simmering ever since he received the emergency call.

"Sometimes Krista's nice, but sometimes she's mean," Gracie had commented as he gently buckled her into her booster seat in the truck next to Ella.

Hearing Gracie's assessment, he had steeled his chest. He would do anything to protect his little darlins. Behind the wheel, he checked the backseat in the rearview mirror.

"I'm mad at Krista."

Gracie's frown overtook her cute little face. "I know your ankle hurts. Why are you mad at Krista?" He had a pretty good idea, and he didn't blame her. The back of his neck prickled. He was mad too.

"I told her I was too tired, but she wouldn't let me quit."

Mean was probably overstating, but he agreed Krista's coaching style was too rigid and demanding. If she had listened, she might have prevented the accident. Athletes pushed themselves hard and occasionally suffered injuries, but beginner figure skaters weren't headed to a national competition. He had taken Gracie straight from the rink to the medical clinic and got her checked in record time.

Brett—Dr. Riley to Gracie—examined her and sent them away assured the injury was only tissue damage and not a fracture.

Now, cozy at home, he drank in the touching scene in his living room.

Snuggled next to Gracie with a pink fleece blanket tucked over their legs, Ella whispered encouragement and gently stroked her sister's arm.

He turned away and snapped his attention back to the phone call.

"I understand you're busy."

Krista's voice wavered. She must feel bad, but he didn't attempt to soothe her feelings. She *should* feel concerned and sorry for the situation. A child got injured under her supervision. He couldn't bring himself to say everything was okay because it wasn't. Now, his emotions were all a jumble. He'd made a big mistake. His heart shouldn't pound at the thought of her, and he shouldn't long for her far into the night.

Thinking back over the past few weeks, he had been wrong to focus on seeing her at the expense of time spent with his daughters. Defending Krista against Janine, he shouldn't have ignored his recent nagging feelings about her approach as a coach. Hinting about the need for change wasn't enough. He had let intense attraction cloud his judgment. Although Janine could be harsh, she wasn't totally off base. He had no choice but to have a serious talk with Krista and let her know where he stood. "I'll be busy until I tuck in the girls, but what are you doing later?" He kept his tone cordial yet firm, not wanting to send a misleading message. He in no way anticipated a romantic evening. Far from it.

"Uh, I planned to listen to music and design some choreography for one of the skaters. Hang out with Pearl. Nothing too major."

She sounded open to the possibility. She must have taken his question as an encouraging sign he wasn't angry.

"Why do you ask?"

Her reply held a hint of amusement, and a twinge of guilt pinched his temples. She might even think he was paving the way for another kiss. Under other circumstances, he might hope but not now. Maybe never.

He smiled at the girls, strode back to the kitchen, and lifted a carton of milk from the fridge. "Would you like to drop by later this evening after Gracie and Ella are asleep?" Until bedtime, he'd give them his undivided attention. That silent promise was the least he could do to comfort Gracie and settle them both. He rotated his stiff shoulders to loosen the tension in his neck and back. He knew Krista had been right all along. Romance between them was wrong, and now he needed to insist she soften her tough teaching style. The whole situation felt plain awkward.

"I…guess I could. What time?"

He stirred the chicken. She had no idea about the purpose of the get-together. She probably thought it was a private party for two, picking up where they left off. "I'll see you around eight-thirty." He dropped the phone back on its holder with a *thunk*. Normally, he'd fill with anticipation at the prospect of an evening visit with Krista, but now, he couldn't muster the same enthusiasm. He had a serious issue to confront.

For the next hour and a half, he would concentrate on only his daughters. He carried Gracie to the table, helped Ella adjust her chair, and served three plates of chicken, potatoes, carrots, and broccoli.

After dinner and five stories, Gracie was back to her animated self with a running commentary and endless questions. Her wide, innocent eyes searched his face for answers.

"I want to be in the ice show, Daddy." Gracie stretched her leg gingerly under the fluffy pink duvet on her bed. She tilted up her face. "Krista won't be happy if I miss it. She says we have to practice and practice and can't stop. Will my ankle get better in time? Will it,

221

Daddy?"

"I hope so, darlin." He bent and kissed her on the forehead.

She closed her eyes.

In the background, soothing lullaby music filled the room. "You're a strong girl, so you'll get better soon. We won't worry about what Krista thinks right now."

"Ella, you have to teach me everything you learn in skating lessons." Gracie popped her eyes open.

"Of course, I will," promised Ella.

Tate bent and kissed Ella's forehead. "You're kind sisters, but you can talk more tomorrow. Time for dreamland, girls." He straightened and switched off the overhead light, leaving only a muted nightlight glowing near the doorway. "I love you." He backed up, and just as he was closing the bedroom door, he heard a tap at the front door.

Both girls bolted upright.

"Who's here? Who is it? Can we see?" They chorused together. "Is it Grandma and Grandpa?"

The questions peppered him so fast Tate didn't know which eager girl said what. He groaned inwardly and clenched his jaw. This was not supposed to happen. He had timed things almost perfectly so his world with Gracie and Ella didn't collide with his meeting with Krista. He sighed. Honesty was the best policy. No sense trying to fool the girls when they were now wide awake and curious. "Krista's here."

"Why?" Gracie's mouth flickered between a smile and a frown.

"We have some important things to discuss. Now, good night."

"What things? My leg?" Gracie plopped both hands on the covers and grinned.

His dear little Gracie liked the idea she might be the topic of conversation.

"Maybe she's sorry she was mean," Gracie continued.

"I want to see her too." Ella nodded and rustled her bouncy hair.

"If I ask Krista to come and say good night, will you promise to lie quietly and go to sleep?"

"I promise," said Gracie.

"We promise," said Ella.

"I'll be right back." He hurried to the front door and swung it open.

With Pearl next to her, Krista waited on the front step. She wore her black hat pulled low over her forehead and a black jacket zipped high around her neck. Holding the handrail, she braced herself against the wind.

The biting cold air leapt around her and into his entranceway and instantly chilled him. He forced a pleasant expression and beat back a jolt of attraction. "Come in. I have two little girls waiting to say good night."

She brushed snow off her sleeves and Pearl's back. "Is Gracie upset with me?"

He shrugged. "Not too upset to want to see you or get better in time for the ice show."

"How does her dad feel?" Krista tipped her face up toward him.

Her eyelashes glistened with melted snowflakes. Heart pounding, he glanced from her questioning eyes to her full lips and back. "We need to talk."

Chapter 18

"Hi, Ella. Hi, Gracie. You're awake pretty late."
Next to Tate, Krista peeked into the bedroom. She
lowered her voice to just above a whisper to keep the
atmosphere calm for their bedtime.

"Hi, Krista," the girls chorused.

Ella smiled wide enough to show the space from
her missing front teeth.

Gracie hugged her covers, narrowed her eyes, and
smiled with her mouth pinched shut.

Obviously, Gracie still held a small grudge for
being pushed beyond her limit. Krista only demanded
more because she saw the girl's potential, but she
should have noticed Gracie was exhausted and allowed
her a rest break. A knot of regret had twisted in Krista's
stomach ever since the accident. "How's your ankle?"

Tears welled in Gracie's eyes, and she wiped them
with her sheet. "I almost broke it, and it still hurts."

"Oh, ouch. I'm sorry you got hurt." Was the
accident Krista's fault? Did she expect too much?
"You're a very strong and brave girl. I know you'll get
better soon." She wanted to rush in and hug Gracie, but
she settled for a reassuring smile. "You're a very good
skater. You and Ella both learn quickly."

"Do you really think so?" Gracie blinked and sat
straighter.

From her own bed, Ella grinned.

"Of course. You have a lot of talent, and you both might be skating champions someday." She paused and watched Gracie's eyes widen and the gaps in her teeth peek out. "Champions work really hard, so that's why I make skaters practice and never give up."

"Oh." Gracie nodded. She wrinkled her forehead.

Did she understand now why Krista was strict about practice?

Ella stared and nodded.

Krista had tensed at the sight of Gracie crumpled and crying on the ice. To make the bad situation even worse, Janine witnessed the whole thing and glared in a disapproving, almost threatening way. Then Tate had barely acknowledged her before he whisked Gracie away to the medical clinic. Would they all forgive her? Forcing her attention back to the girls, she gripped the doorframe and smiled.

"When I was younger, I twisted my knee doing a jump, and I had to wear a brace for quite a few weeks until it got better. Another time, I accidentally cut my leg with the end of my skate blade, and I had to get five stitches here in the side of my calf." She pointed down toward the spot. "I wasn't happy, but I knew that sometimes skaters get hurt."

"Oh." Gracie stared.

Krista didn't need to justify her actions to a pair of seven-year-olds, but she wanted Tate to hear too. She needed him to know she never intended to come across as harsh. She just meant to challenge every skater.

"Okay, girls. Enough visiting for tonight. Time for lights out." Tate brushed by Krista into the room.

She felt the breath squish out of her lungs at his closeness and his delicious scent of outdoors mixed with the scantest hint of pine. She couldn't explain the effect he had—only that it was full, deep, and rich and nothing she had ever felt.

"Aww." Ella groaned.

"I'm not ready to go to sleep." Gracie scrunched her whole face into a frown.

"Yes, you are, little darlins." Tate pulled the covers up to their chins and gave them both a kiss on the forehead. "Good night, Ella. Good night, Gracie."

Krista's heart tugged at the warmth and love filling the room, and she backed away. "Good night, girls. I'll see you soon." She gave a little wave and nearly blew two kisses but stopped herself before she did something too presumptuous. She was their teacher after all.

Treading lightly back along the hallway, she heard the faint rustle of Tate's jeans and glanced over her shoulder to see he was close behind. With his nearness, she felt her heartbeat tap in her throat. Over the last few days, she had argued with herself about whether to follow her head or her heart. Could she possibly invite Tate into her life?

He had gotten swept away in the moment on Saturday evening—they both had—and he must have mistaken strong attraction for genuine feelings. How could he trust her when she didn't even know if she could trust herself not to leave? If things didn't work out well at the skating club, she wouldn't stay in Blue Sky. His roots here were so deep no amount of tugging would ever pull him free.

In the end, her options were pretty straightforward. She could list all the reasons why she shouldn't build a relationship with Tate, or she could rip the mental list to shreds and listen to her thudding heart. After another broken sleep last night, she had decided what she must do. She would make her job here in Blue Sky work if it killed her. She would find a way to charm Janine if she had to do back flips. She would give in to her feelings and let Tate know they had a fighting chance. If the chemistry at the rink on Saturday evening was any indication, then he would be happy to hear the news…as long as Gracie's ankle injury hadn't changed everything.

"Have a seat in the living room. I'll make herbal tea." Tate veered right to the kitchen and left Krista and Pearl to wait. Krista selected a chunky gray armchair facing the Christmas tree and nestled her toes into the plush navy-and-gray area rug.

Pearl groaned and flopped beside her.

Krista inhaled deep breaths and rolled the right words around her tongue. Instead of feeling calmer, she buzzed with anticipation and uncertainty. She couldn't stand the commotion in her brain any longer. She would tell him how much she cared.

Tate must have switched on music because Christmas carols surrounded her with festive cheer and a strange sense of melancholy. Another year had passed—a year of change and new beginnings. Through the months of self-reflection, she had grown stronger and more confident. What did the New Year hold in store?

"I'm back." Tate carried a tray of steaming mugs of tea and a plate of gingerbread cookies. "Before you compliment me, you should know my mom baked them." He chuckled.

The merriment didn't radiate up to his eyes. He didn't look like the usual fun-loving Tate. His cheeks were stiff and flushed, and his eyes were dull and guarded. "Thank you." She reached for a mug and a cookie. "You could have fooled me into thinking baking was one of your many talents." Krista set her mug on the table beside her and caught the scent of orange spice wafting. She nibbled a bite of the sweet molasses cookie, and the taste of ginger transported her back to her childhood and her grandmother's kitchen, which was always a comforting place. Shifting in the chair, she balanced the cookie on a napkin on her lap and cradled her mug. She needed both hands to steady it.

Tate moved a toss cushion and sank onto the sofa.

Even with music strumming in the background, a thick silence filled the space between them. He must be preoccupied with Gracie's injury, so why did he invite her here this evening? "I feel sorry for Gracie, but fortunately, kids usually make a quick recovery." She swallowed and peered at Tate over the rim of her mug. Even sipping tea, her mouth felt strangely dry.

He stared at the lights on the Christmas tree and furrowed his brow. "Yeah, I hope so. She already talked about getting back to skating in time for the ice show. A good sign."

"Oh, I'm glad." His strained expression wasn't typical at all. She set the mug on the table next to her chair. Her hands still felt shaky like her breath and her insides. She couldn't stand her nervousness much longer. "Tate, I—"

"Krista, I—" He tugged his gaze from the tree and focused on her face.

Suddenly, she felt as uncomfortably warm as sitting too close to a fireplace. He had something to say too, and his firm demeanour suggested it might be something serious. Maybe he was about to beg her to reconsider a relationship. The nervous twinge in the pit of her stomach jumped and twirled like a skater. He would be surprised when she agreed with the crazy idea. "You go first." She rubbed one foot along Pearl's furry back. Magic danced in the air as she waited to hear Tate say the romantic words first. The moment would be better than a gift under the Christmas tree.

"Are you sure?" He made direct eye contact.

"Definitely. Gentleman first." She nearly laughed, but something about his sombre face made her hold it inside.

"Okay, here goes." He swallowed. "Krista, I don't blame you for Gracie's injury. Accidents happen in sports all the time."

He wanted to talk about Gracie? Not about their relationship or a future together? The delicious heat she felt only moments ago seeped from her middle along her limbs and drained from her fingers and toes. Gracie would be fine. The injury wasn't Krista's fault.

"But many accidents can also be prevented." Tate glanced at the tree and back to her face.

He had said he didn't blame her, but he clearly did. She swallowed and waited for him to continue. She couldn't argue with his point, but where was he headed? Bending forward, she stroked Pearl and slowed her breathing.

"I want to give you some feedback." He clenched his jaw. "I should have been more direct much sooner."

"Yes?" She studied his stiff expression. Wariness closed around her chest to protect her heart. His message might hurt...a lot.

"I try not to be too overprotective, and I encourage Ella and Gracie to always do their best. Not to give up, even if something is hard. But I also listen and honor their true feelings. Gracie's a determined and outspoken little girl. If she says she's too tired to do something, she's too tired."

Krista nodded. Her eyes burned, but she would not allow them to fill with tears. Tate was pointing the finger, and his implied criticism stung.

He stared at his mug and then back at her. Rubbing his forehead, he bowed his head for a moment before he faced her.

A faint glow from the blue tree lights shadowed his face but didn't cover the hard lines of his cheeks and jaw.

"You're a strong coach. No doubt. Are you too tough on kids? Probably."

"Oh?" She swallowed and waited. He disapproved of her methods. He judged her…just like her mother and Zach and Janine. They were all the same. On the surface, they might appear nice enough, but they couldn't contain their negative opinions.

"You can't build champions overnight." He inhaled a large breath. "If kids get pushed too hard too early, they will never last in the sport."

She avoided his gaze and the way it spilled with concern. She picked up her mug and cradled it. The fragrant steam did nothing to soothe her shock and betrayal. Tate was supposed to watch her back, no matter what. She needed him to keep her heart safe and never batter it with criticism.

"I support you as a coach, Krista. I want you to succeed here." He planted his hands on his thighs, pressing until the tips of his fingers whitened. "But ease up a bit. Let the kids have some fun. Give them a break once in a while. Show you care about them as people, not just as skaters."

She couldn't blame him for wanting to protect his daughter. But still... With Janine's words echoing in her head, Krista flashed back to the group of gossipy girls led by Olivia who were more interested in socializing than practicing. She couldn't tolerate laziness and mediocrity. Janine wanted results, but she also wanted skating to be pure fun for Olivia and her friends. How were both possible?

Clenching her jaw so tight her teeth hurt, she focused on the tree decorations. The Christmas season should be filled with love and peace, not the hurt and anger rising in her chest. Tate had been her number one supporter in Blue Sky. He had acted like he truly cared. He was more than a little interested in romance. Or so she had believed. Now, the cold truth struck her in the face. Nothing was what it seemed. "You sound like Janine." A chill crept into her and spread until her insides turned to ice. She shivered. "You can't resist coaching the coach. I hear you loud and clear. Change or else."

He sighed. "I'm telling you this as a concerned parent and a true friend. I want to protect you from Janine. You have coaching talent. You can succeed here. Just loosen up a little."

Thank goodness she had urged Tate to speak first. If she had bared her soul and then received his reprimand, she would have died of embarrassment. A relationship would never work. The shine was quickly fading from life in Blue Sky. She set aside her cookie and tea and leaned forward. She needed to escape before her emotions burst out.

"One more thing, Krista."

"What?" With her voice choking in her throat, she almost whispered.

"The situation with Gracie and the advice I just offered don't change a thing. I still know you're the woman I want in my life. Don't run away."

"Maybe nothing has changed for you, Tate, but everything has changed for me." She choked back a sob. To think she had nearly confessed her feelings. "Like I told you Saturday, I can't be your partner. Ever." She stood, strode to the door, and reached into the front closet for her jacket.

"Krista, wait." Tate followed and touched her arm.

Pearl circled and batted them with her tail.

"You had something you wanted to say before you made me go first."

"Forget it." How could he possibly think he could take Janine's side, criticize her style of coaching, and still woo her like nothing at all was wrong? "It's not important anymore."

"Come on. Tell me. Please." He shoved his hands into his jeans front pockets.

"I thought we might have a chance, but I see we don't." She shook her head and pressed her lips together. Tate was no different than Janine, expecting her to lower her standards and bow to the skaters' and parents' wishes. She came to Blue Sky with a mandate to produce results, and she intended to live up to her promise. She felt bad about Gracie's accident. Maybe she should have allowed the girl a quick break. But Tate shouldn't criticize her overall coaching approach.

Growing champions meant hard work for everyone, starting at an early age.

"Oh, Krista…"

She watched Tate's face crumple into a frown.

"Try to understand…" He lowered his voice. "I care about you."

His anguished plea didn't change anything. "I know exactly where we stand." The ice chips inside her splintered into shards like broken glass. "Thank you for the snack. I'll consider your comments and decide where to go from here." Tate was just like any other skating parent now. She'd keep her distance except when she needed to discuss his girls' progress or logistics for the ice show. *If* she lasted until then. She threw on her jacket, pulled her hat low, and grabbed the doorknob. "Come, Pearl. Let's go."

****

The next morning, Krista stared into the bathroom mirror at the faint dark shadows underlining her eyes. She looked as crushed as she felt. All night, a painful mix of hurt and desire had churned inside her and ruined any chance of sleep. She had plenty of work to do with choreography and billings, but she'd never be able to concentrate when she was so drained. She couldn't stand a day of torturing herself with what-ifs and a deep sense of loss.

After breakfast, she knocked on Daisy's door. Jovial, motherly Daisy would likely welcome her and might even offer comfort. She had already hinted she was an ally against her own daughter, so she might side with Krista over Tate too.

"What a nice surprise." Holding a roll of gold foil wrapping paper, Daisy promptly swung open the door and flashed a wide grin.

The sweet scents of butter and caramel whooshed out, but Krista didn't feel tempted in the least. She didn't feel like eating one bit.

"Come in. I have cookies in the oven, and I'm ready to take a break from wrapping gifts."

Pearl didn't need an invitation, and she nudged ahead and rubbed against Daisy's leg.

Krista followed her into the entrance, took one look at Daisy's wide, open expression, and burst into tears.

****

A week later, Tate set up a gift-wrapping station at the kitchen table with assorted boxes, colorful paper, and shiny bows. "I'll help you cut the paper." He reached for the scissors.

Gracie wrinkled her forehead and put out a hand to stop him. "I can do it. I'm not a baby."

"I know. You're getting bigger every day." He smiled and handed over the scissors. "Ella too."

He watched as the girls scrunched and taped festive wrapping paper around their handmade gifts. Gracie had drawn pictures for Grandma and Grandpa, and Tate helped her frame them. Ella made a tissue flower collection for Grandma and colored a small rock as a paperweight for Grandpa.

Tate hadn't slept much since Krista left his place in a huff last week. As he came and went for Ella's lessons with a limping Gracie in tow, he glimpsed her on the ice, and he still felt a surge of longing. A couple of evenings, when he headed to the workroom to put the finishing touches on the show sets, he raised a hand to wave at Krista, but he didn't get a reaction. Either she was too engrossed in her students to notice, or she deliberately ignored him. From a distance, he couldn't read her expression, but he definitely felt a chill beyond the temperature of the rink.

Gracie's ankle improved a little every day, so he wasn't worried about her recovery. After Christmas, she'd get back on the ice, rehearsing her performance for the ice show. Missing lessons and hearing Ella's reports bugged her and spurred her on to test weight on her ankle, which was a good sign. He had also talked with Gracie about Krista's reasons for being tough and how he had asked her not to push too hard. He assured both girls they could bring him their problems, no matter what. He was happy to hear Gracie had decided Krista was okay after all.

"She's just strict so I can be a champion," said Gracie.

Ella nodded. "Yeah, I don't mind. Sometimes, she smiles and says nice things."

"I like her very much," Tate spoke gently. "I'm glad you do too because I want us all to spend more time together." The way both girls had stared with wide eyes and smiled knowingly suggested they understood well beyond their years.

Gracie's injury didn't keep him awake at night. Missing Krista did. He had thought she trusted him and would accept his gentle advice as caring and constructive input. Instead, she grimaced and bolted to the door, leaving him stunned and begging her to stay. He coaxed, but she refused to divulge what she started to share. She had clearly slammed the brakes on any chance of romance. The ache in his chest squeezed so tight every drop of joy and hope dried up. All the hurts of the past rushed back. For days, he had suffered with a sense of loss—different than the grief of Whitney's passing or the disappointment of quitting hockey but painful just the same.

A week later, Tate switched his truck windshield wipers to high and crawled to the grocery store to buy a few last-minute items for Christmas Eve tonight and Christmas dinner tomorrow. His parents would host the family gatherings as usual, but he would contribute an appetizer for this afternoon and his popular Caesar salad for tomorrow's special dinner. Gracie and Ella were already at Grandma and Grandpa's place in a frenzy of excitement, baking shortbread cookies for Santa's snack. He pictured their flushed little faces as they measured ingredients and stirred the batter.

The wind whipped thick snowflakes into such a fury he could barely see the road. Trust prairie weather to blow in a blizzard just in time to mess up holiday travel plans. Turning up the radio, he caught the end of a broadcast with an alarmist announcer recapping the weather report.

"Visibility is near zero on the highways, and roads are covered with ice and snow. Travel is not advised in most areas of the province."

Plowing through a drift, he steered into a parking space in front of the store and jammed the gear into Park. No way could Krista travel to Saskatoon to spend Christmas with her parents in a snowstorm, and she probably had nobody but Pearl for company. He hit his padded mitts on the steering wheel, braced himself for the freezing blast, and dashed inside.

Inside, the store was warm and bright, and Christmas carols floated overhead. The air smelled like cinnamon and oranges. Yanni and his staff wore gaudy

Christmas sweaters.

"Merry Christmas, Tate. Glad to see you this morning. We'll be closing early today."

"Merry Christmas! Looks like I'm one of the few brave souls out shopping."

The store was small but well stocked with basics. Zipping up and down aisles, he grabbed cream cheese, green onion, canned shrimp, and chopped walnuts for a cheeseball and a fresh bunch of romaine lettuce and croutons for salad. Pausing, he selected a large box of chocolate-covered nuts and two candy canes from a festive display at the end of one aisle. Approaching the checkout, he glimpsed a sheet of white obscuring the view out the front window, and a pinch of concern expanded in his stomach. He needed to call Krista.

He paid for his purchases, then dashed back to the truck, turned the ignition, and idled in place. He'd have plenty of snow to clear later. The wind whooshed, hissed, and pelted the windows with ice crystals. In the few seconds outside, his hat and jacket were coated, and he brushed off the snow before it melted. Retrieving his phone from his jacket pocket, he pressed Krista's number and held his breath as it rang.

He sat practically buried in snow and couldn't get her off his mind. After five rings, her phone jumped to her recorded voice instructing him to leave a message. Instead, he pressed End and then redialed. Again, her phone sent him to voice mail. He huffed and hung up. She couldn't possibly be driving, but she might ignore his calls. One last time, he punched in her number.

This time, she answered on the third ring. "Yes, Tate?"

Obviously, she had caller ID and dispensed with

any niceties. Her voice stretched taut like a skate lace about to snap. He almost smiled. She was feisty, and he didn't mind. He could be just as direct. "You can't travel. Come to my parents' place for Christmas Eve and Christmas dinner. They love company."

"Daisy already invited me to Janine's, and I declined. Pearl isn't welcome there. We'll be just fine on our own."

Her tone mellowed from her greeting, but he still heard the waver in her voice. "C'mon, Krista. Nobody wants to spend Christmas alone. I'm on my way to pick up you and Pearl. We can spend the afternoon playing games with my family." She probably would rather spend Christmas on her own than with Janine. But his family was different.

"Thank you for the invitation, but no."

"You can't celebrate by yourself."

"Shouldn't you be out clearing snow?"

"Minding my business?" Still parked, he switched his wipers to high and saw nothing but white.

"Maybe. I learned from you."

Did he deserve the gentle jab? He snorted. "Nice shot. No point wasting my time until the storm blows over." He waited and imagined her pursing her lips and stretching them to the side, weighing her options. Silence meandered in the space between them. Finally, he couldn't stand the suspense any longer. "Get ready. You'll have fun."

"Thanks, but I don't think so…"

He sensed her weakening. "See you in about five minutes," he insisted. "Pearl too."

She blew out a deep breath. "Give me fifteen."

Chapter 19

"Hi, everybody. Thank you for including me…and Pearl." Krista smiled at Tate's parents, Ella, and Gracie, all clustered around the doorway to greet her. The delicious buttery scent of shortbread swirled in the warm air, and Christmas music whispered in the background. Energy and excitement radiated from the whole family, and Krista almost felt like she belonged. The nervous twitch in her stomach relaxed just a smidgeon.

The last week had been miserable. When Krista burst into tears with no warning at Daisy's place, she was mortified.

Daisy encircled her in a big, warm hug, which only made things worse.

Finally, Krista calmed enough to join her at the kitchen table. Through shaky breaths, she spilled her hurt and shame over Gracie's injury and Tate's reaction. "I thought he supported me, but he's just as critical as the others." She couldn't mention Janine by name, but she assumed Daisy knew who she meant.

"Dear, one thing I know for sure is Tate is in love with you." Daisy smiled and patted Krista's hand. "Anybody can see it a mile away."

"Really?" Wonder flipped in Krista's stomach. She knew he was attracted to her, but were his feelings true love? Could they both have discovered love at first sight?

"Absolutely. Don't you ever forget."

Krista just blinked and wiped her nose with a tissue. Shouldn't true love mean he accepted her, no matter what? Routine disagreements maybe. But no criticism. No disapproval.

"Tate is one of the most kind and honest guys I know. His comments and any advice he offered had the best of intentions. I know it in my bones." Daisy boiled the kettle and set two burgundy mugs on the table. "You can brush off my daughter and her snippy comments—I can say that because I'm her mother—but don't block out Tate. He cares."

"I trusted him to have my back." Krista heard the wobble in her own voice.

"He *does* have your back." Daisy leaned over and squeezed Krista's hand. "You can still trust him...and love him. As a coach, you know everybody can improve, and you're no different."

Should she listen to Daisy? Her advice sounded a lot like Amy's pep talks over the phone. Could her best friend and her neighbor both be right?

Krista snapped her attention to Daisy's wrinkled face where wisdom hid in the lines. She felt hot and cold at the same time. How did Daisy know Tate filled her heart? But Daisy couldn't know the feeling of betrayal twisting her into an aching mess. "I'll think about what you said." After a soothing cup of tea, she had left more confused and tormented than ever.

Later last week, when Tate had tromped along the sidelines at the rink, she felt her heart pound uncontrollably, and she had flushed with a murky combination of longing, regret, anger, and loneliness.

She didn't want to escape his cozy world, but she had no choice. He wasn't the totally accepting man she had counted on...unless she listened to Daisy. Siding with Janine, he was a traitor—not the man filling her heart. Or did Daisy know better? His criticism hit hard like a prairie storm. But Daisy saw things differently. Did he have her best interests at heart? Was he respectfully coaching the coach?

She somehow survived the week. Then to add to her misery, the blizzard struck and stranded her in Blue Sky. But Tate cared how the storm affected her. As she finally answered his call, she felt her hand shake, and she had fought to steady her voice. Now, she found herself at his parents' home, crashing his family celebration.

"We're happy you're here." Leah put an arm around both her granddaughters.

She wore a forest-green sweater decorated with a red-nosed reindeer, and the girls wore matching red sweaters covered in candy canes and snowmen. Krista was glad she too wore a festive sweater, featuring a whimsical collection of sparkly Christmas balls on a snowy white background.

Pearl burst forward, wriggling her fat body and licking the girls' cheeks.

They giggled and wiped off the dog slobber.

"Nobody should have to spend Christmas alone. Everybody is welcome in our home. Even Pearl." Cole wheeled back his chair to make space for Krista to step farther inside. She peeled off her jacket and handed it to Tate.

Scanning the room, she breathed the evergreen scent of the Christmas tree, glowing in the front window. The neutral shades of beige in the furnishings, carpet, and artwork of the living room helped calm her jumpy heartbeats. "How's your ankle, Gracie?" Krista could see she favored it slightly, but she took solace from the smile back on the little girl's face.

"Pretty good, I guess." Gracie nodded. "It'll be better in time for the ice show."

"I'm really glad." Krista flashed her a big smile.

"Do you want one of our cookies?" Grinning, Gracie clasped her hands.

"Yeah, we baked with Grandma." Ella bounced on her toes and waved Krista toward the kitchen.

"I'd love a cookie." Krista breathed a little easier. Neither girl appeared to hold a grudge. She glanced from Tate to Leah to gauge their reactions.

Both smiled fondly at the girls' spontaneous show of hospitality.

"Make sure you leave some for me." Cole chortled and tickled Ella's armpit, making her wriggle and giggle.

"Come right in and make yourself at home." Leah leaned forward and hugged Krista.

Mom would never welcome a newcomer with such genuine warmth. Krista liked the feel of Leah's soft, motherly arms encircling her. A wash of gentle comfort flooded her, but just as quickly, a flicker of guilt questioned why she could appreciate Tate's mother more than her own.

Mom cared, maybe too much. Her life had always been bound up in Krista's goals and accomplishments. She wanted her dreams to become Krista's dreams. Figure skating medals had meant more to her than to Krista. When the awful weather forecast threatened to interfere with Christmas plans, Mom had cried on the phone. This morning, at the news Krista definitely couldn't travel, Mom cried again. Sometimes, so much love was a little overwhelming.

"I'm sorry." Krista had choked back her own tears. "I wish I could be there." She pictured Mom's firm jaw and watery blue eyes. "I love you, and I miss you and Dad. I'll make sure we see each other soon." When she ended the call, she hugged Pearl and let her tears flow onto the dog's thick coat. She hated to disappoint her parents and miss Christmas together, but at the same time, she felt relief like a warm blanket hugging her shoulders. Time with Mom was never smooth and always guaranteed to add pressure to everything. Mom expected her to be best, first, and almost perfect.

Letting Pearl lick tears from her cheeks, Krista had decided to make the best of a tough situation. Christmas on her own would be different and lonely, but she wouldn't let it crush the joy of the season.

Now, she sat in the midst of Tate's warm family celebration, still a little stunned at how everything had happened. She hadn't intended to ever see him again socially, and after her less-than-graceful exit from his place, she suspected he had finally gotten the message. She accepted his Christmas invitation as a friend and nothing more.

"Let me get you a cup of apple cider to go with your cookies." Following the girls, Leah led her into the spacious kitchen. Little white lights twinkled along the tops of the cupboards, pine boughs nestled along a deep window ledge, and a clear glass vase filled with red and silver beads decorated the island. "Come and take a seat here." She patted the back of a wooden chair at a table covered in a red-and-green-plaid tablecloth.

"Beside me," said Ella.

"No, beside me," insisted Gracie.

"How about I sit in the middle?" Krista neatly prevented a sister squabble. The aroma of apple and cinnamon wafted from the stove and mingled with sweet scents of chocolate and peppermint from goodies placed next to shortbread on a platter.

"Carly, Will, and Sam, along with Leah's sister, Lorraine, will join us too. When you meet them all at once, you won't know what hit you." Cole laughed and wheeled behind them. "Enjoy the peace while you can."

"Don't scare her away, Dad." Tate strolled to the stove and ladled cups of steaming cider. "She wasn't easy to convince."

"Oh, don't worry, I don't scare easily." Were her words true? First, Janine's ongoing concerns and now Tate's tough feedback made Blue Sky an unsettling place. Right now, her fight-or-flight instinct leaned heavily toward flight.

Settling into her spot at the table, Krista glanced at Tate and felt her breath catch in her throat. His hair was the same shade as the dark chocolate treats, and it curled at the edges, still tousled from when he pulled off his knit hat. His cream cable-knit sweater skimmed to the hips of faded jeans accentuating his long, muscular legs. She imagined running her fingers along the nubby surface of his sweater to the coarse texture of his jeans. Before her daydream took over, she snapped her gaze away to the welcome distraction of Leah bustling to set plates and napkins next to the tray of cookies.

The surroundings were the perfect blend of tasteful

and lived-in—a place a family could relax and enjoy each other's company. She might be the outsider here, but she felt like she belonged. Only she didn't or couldn't truly belong this close to Tate, could she? She'd visit and giggle with the girls and make small talk with Cole and Leah. At the same time, she'd avoid Tate as much as possible without appearing rude.

No one knew that inside she craved another kiss. Inhaling a shaky breath, she pictured their embrace on the ice and made her heartbeats trip. If only he hadn't criticized her and triggered bad memories of Mom's harsh demands and Zach's nasty tongue. If only Tate didn't sound like Janine, he could still be her dream guy. She could nestle into his strong chest, run her hands along his firm sides, and wrap her arms around his lower back. "Thank you." She accepted a fragrant cup and set it down before her quivering hands spilled a drop.

"After snacks, do you want to help us finish our snowman puzzle?" Ella tapped Krista's arm. As she spoke, she bobbed her ponytail and bounced in her chair.

"Ooh, I like puzzles." Krista nodded. If she kept busy with the girls, she wouldn't have to work so hard to avoid fixating on Tate. Across the table, she caught him staring at her, and she felt a hot flush creep to her cheekbones. She raised her mug to conceal it, and when she glanced up, she caught his smile.

"No, let's play a good card game." Gracie brushed cookie crumbs off her lips and waved away her sister's suggestion.

Krista laughed. "How about if we do both? We have all afternoon together."

"Daddy can play too." Gracie grinned across the table at Tate.

"You bet I will, darlin. But Krista better watch out because I usually win." Tate crinkled his eyes and scanned around the table.

Of course, he couldn't resist teasing. With a pang, she realized how much she would miss him.

"Daddy."

Gracie sounded totally disgusted with his bragging.

"You don't always win." Ella shook her finger at Tate.

Leah and Cole groaned.

Tate was totally unfazed and lapped up all their attention. He laughed and widened his eyes, clearly having fun provoking everybody.

"Oh, Tate." Leah rolled her eyes. "Always causing trouble."

Joking aside, Leah had no idea of the truth for Krista. He had teased her heart, then squashed her like a bug. So why did she agree to come, and why wouldn't her ridiculous longing quit? Sure, he was every bit as handsome as her first impression. He was a great dad. He ran a successful business. He had made her feel like a princess—for a while. He'd even made her believe everything would work out and she could make Blue Sky her permanent home. But could she trust him to support her, no matter what? If she couldn't, how could she dream of a future together?

A snowball of confusion rolled through her middle, and she shivered. This Christmas would be like no other. The holiday wouldn't be lonely like she had feared, but it might be even worse—a huge test of her willpower and patience. If she wasn't stranded by the howling blizzard outside, she wouldn't even entertain the thought of spending two hours in his unsettling company, let alone two days.

****

Tate pretended to care he lost the card games, but he didn't mind at all. He gave a big, exaggerated huff of disappointment and slumped his shoulders. "Way to go, Ella. You did well too, Gracie. Congratulations, Krista. Must be your lucky day." He couldn't resist teasing the winners, and he grinned at the trio sitting next to each other and celebrating across the dining room table.

"Not luck, *skill*." Krista gathered the cards and straightened them into a neat pile.

She had laughed easily throughout the game, and her face melted into soft lines. She was gorgeous. Any tension in the air floated away, and his shoulders felt lighter. Her soft heart peeked out from behind her protective shell, and he wanted to sweep her into his arms and kiss her. The sparkly blue decorations on her sweater deepened the color of her eyes into a pool of water he wanted to soak in forever.

He had felt her gaze as he gently coached both girls in strategic moves. He hadn't consciously demonstrated a lesson in how to engage kids in a positive way, but maybe she noticed and would learn from his style.

Ella and Gracie threw up their arms in a victory cheer.

He gave them both a big thumbs-up. They took great pleasure in beating him. For a moment, he paused and drank in the cozy scene and the nostalgic sound of a classic Christmas song filling the background. A lump formed in his throat. His life, surrounded by family, was nearly perfect. The picture only lacked one thing. If

Krista had a permanent place at the table, she would fill his heart, and life would be complete.

"Good work, girls. All of you." Wiping her hands on a kitchen towel, Mom peeked through the archway from the kitchen.

Before his deep wistfulness overshadowed the light atmosphere, he leapt up and motioned for Ella and Gracie to follow. "Want to put presents under the tree?" Leading them away, he overheard Krista offering to help Mom in the kitchen.

Before long, Carly, Will, Sam, and Aunt Lorraine arrived in a blast of cold air and thick snowflakes.

As Dad predicted from experience, the noise level immediately escalated with a hallway full of voices and laughter nearly drowning out the sound of jingling bells from the carols.

Wagging her tail, Pearl joined everyone at the door.

She moved much slower these days, her belly heavy with puppies.

Carly bent to pet the dog. "Well, you're a nice special guest. Looks like you're going to be a mommy any minute."

She switched her voice to the extra-sweet tone people often used with little kids and house pets.

Dad wheeled to greet everybody.

Tate gathered jackets. He hoped all the hubbub wouldn't be overwhelming for Krista.

Shivering from the cold, the rest of the family gathered 'round.

Soon, Sam scuttled away to play downstairs with his cousins.

Meanwhile, Krista hung back in the center of the

living room, out of the way of the onslaught of noisy traffic. She wore a modest, half-smiling expression.

Tate dropped the jackets into the spare room, circled, and approached Krista from behind. Along with her fuzzy sweater, she wore blue jeans with thick red socks bunched at the narrow ankles of her pants. His heart pumped an extra beat. Casually dressed for the cold, she curved in all the right places.

He touched her elbow to guide her to meet the newcomers and felt her flinch. Her sudden stiff reaction stomped on his hope once again. Whenever he watched her relaxed and laughing, he felt like she invited him to love her more. Right now, she sent the clear message he should keep his distance. He took a deep breath and stepped aside. Could he still hope his Christmas wish would come true? "Carly, Will, Sam, Aunt Lorraine, this is Krista."

"I'm very pleased to meet you all." She shook Carly's and Will's hands and extended a hand toward Aunt Lorraine.

"I've heard so much about you." Aunt Lorraine tossed her ash blond waves, stretched out her arms, and pulled Krista into a hug. "Merry Christmas!" She backed up. "Don't be alarmed. I'm a hugger all the time—not just at Christmas." She laughed in a throaty burst. "You're just what this town needs. My nephew too, after all he's been through. Right, Tate?" She flashed a giant wink.

Tate stiffened. Aunt Lorraine was a tornado of hot air, not exactly known for her tactfulness. He glanced at Krista and hoped she didn't mind the teasing too much. He couldn't miss the slight tension in her cheeks and the way her eyes darkened to ocean blue. He wished he could slip an arm around her waist to show his support.

"Oh, I think Tate is doing a fine job taking care of himself and his girls." She backed up a step. "He was very kind to rescue me from spending Christmas alone."

"How nice! Anyway, you two look like the perfect couple." Aunt Lorraine patted Krista's upper arm.

"Okay, Aunt Lorraine. Enough matchmaking." Rolling her eyes, Carly jumped in. "You better give the poor girl a break before you chase her right out of the house."

"I agree. You better behave, Lorraine, or I'll banish you right to the kitchen." Mom laughed and tapped her sister's shoulder.

"Oh, leave me alone, and quit the boring lecture." Lorraine flicked both hands and turned away.

She wasn't one bit fazed. The family resemblance with Mom was unmistakable with their light coloring, but their personalities were nothing alike. Tate was very thankful. "Better go sit in the living room before you get yourself into more trouble, Aunt Lorraine." He gestured toward the brushed tan furnishings.

"I just lit a fire. All we need are some chestnuts to roast." Cole laughed. "Only kidding. Maybe we'll just listen to the song."

For the rest of the afternoon, Tate kept a close watch over Krista, in case he needed to stickhandle any more awkward comments by Aunt Lorraine. But he wasn't surprised at how well Krista handled herself.

"You can't fool me the way you look at each other. When did you two start dating?" Later at dinner, Aunt Lorraine passed the mashed potatoes, leaned toward Krista, and whispered so loudly no one could miss her teasing.

At the same moment, every conversation stopped, and even the kids quit giggling. The last notes of "Jingle Bells" faded, and silence descended on the gathering.

"We didn't start. I mean, we aren't dating." Krista raised her eyebrows, shook her head, and accepted the potatoes. She glanced around the table, then focused on the bowl in her hands.

"*Yet*, Aunt Lorraine. We aren't dating *yet*." Tate kept his tone light. He might as well signal to Krista his feelings hadn't changed. She was the woman he needed, and maybe his gift tomorrow would convince her. He had chosen it at Melanie's gift shop just days before everything soured. "We'll see what she says when I propose on Christmas morning."

"Propose what?" Krista shrugged.

He chuckled at her quip and wide-eyed expression.

The rest of the adults laughed.

"Atta boy. My son always was determined." Dad grinned and helped himself to meatballs.

The rich gravy scent trailed over the table. Good basic food and the perfect company. Tate knew Krista belonged right here in these homey surroundings. Did she know it too? Her eyes reflected light from the candles on the table. Her expression was relaxed.

"He thinks he's funny." She scanned around the table and got a sympathetic nod from Mom.

With the corners of her lips tipped up, she didn't look as exasperated as she sounded. He'd swear she even tried to conceal a hint of amusement.

"I love weddings." Aunt Lorraine set down her fork and clapped.

"Daddy, are you going to marry Krista?" Gracie narrowed her eyes.

He should know better than to tease when little ears were nearby, but he couldn't resist.

"Are you, Daddy?" Ella bounced forward in her chair.

"Not until after Christmas." Laughing, he slathered butter on a crusty bun. He winked. His girls knew he wasn't serious.

"Daddy." Both girls groaned.

"You know your daddy is always teasing. What do you think Santa will bring?"

Carly neatly diverted the conversation to another topic. He couldn't ask for a better sister. She was always fun, helpful, and protective. She would probably like to see him married too, but at least, she was more subtle in her matchmaking attempts.

After dinner, the men cleaned up the kitchen while the kids played and the women visited in the living room.

"Easy, son," said Dad, "If you don't want her to run away to safety."

Tate kept his hands in the dishwater, scrubbing pots with lemony soap bubbles. He glanced over his shoulder at Dad's wide grin. "Nothing ventured, nothing gained."

"Go for it." Will shook out a tea towel and sent flicks of tepid water onto the back of Tate's neck. "Carly played hard to get, and look at us now."

"Never a dull moment." Tate drained the sink and dried his hands. He appreciated the easy camaraderie with Dad and Will. They wanted the best for him.

"You said it." Will hung the damp towel on a hook

next to the sink.

Dad chortled. "Good luck."

After dinner on Christmas Eve, the whole family usually bundled up for a drive around town to admire all the Christmas lights. This year, the blizzard outside blew away the tradition. Instead, everyone gathered in the living room to visit and sing carols.

Pearl curled up for a nap.

"I can't wait for Santa." Gracie squealed. "Let's sing 'Here Comes Santa Claus.'" She jumped right in.

The rest of the group joined her in the classic song and, for the next hour, continued singing the kids' picks and other family favorites,

"What's your favorite carol, Krista?" Dad gave her the final choice.

Tilting her head, Krista smiled. "I do love 'Silent Night.'"

Tate gave a slight nod. He somehow knew what she'd choose, and he soaked up the peaceful music and lyrics. His neck tingled at the sound of Krista's sweet soprano voice mixed with the others.

"What a perfect last song!" Mom smiled, stretched out her arms, and waved her grandchildren close for a hug.

"Aww." Gracie and Ella groaned at her signal the singsong was over for the night.

"Hey, don't you want to go home and make Santa's snack?" Tate stood and stretched.

"Okay!" Gracie answered for her twin.

All three of the kids jumped and clapped.

"Thank you, everyone, for a wonderful afternoon and evening." Krista rose and swiveled to show her appreciation to each member of the family. "Pearl and I better head home and wait for Santa."

"We'll see you in the morning for presents and brunch." Mom rested a hand on Krista's arm.

"We insist," said Carly.

"Of course, you'll come," said Aunt Lorraine.

"Come. Come." Ella and Gracie chorused.

"You can see what Santa brings." Ella bounced on the spot.

"Yeah," said Gracie. "We'll have lots of presents to show you."

"She'll be here." Tate spoke with authority. When he'd invited Krista, he included the whole celebration and was sure she'd agreed. They would spend another entire day together. Storms with buckets of snow kept him in business, but he never dreamed an old-fashioned blizzard could make Christmas even better.

"I like Krista," Carly whispered into Tate's ear.

Throwing on his coat, he nodded, and anticipation jumped in his heart. Family support was nice, and he trusted Carly's instincts, but he didn't need anybody's assurance Krista was special.

"Okay, you convinced me. Thank you, all. See you tomorrow." Smiling, Krista swooped her hand in a wave like a windshield wiper, bundled into her warmest jacket, and hustled into the storm with Pearl close behind.

By the time Tate, Krista, and the girls trudged out front to Tate's truck, they were coated in snow, and their cheeks shone red. Drifts mounted along the sidewalks and road. "It's worse than I thought," he murmured to himself. He couldn't let the roads in town get so clogged that emergency vehicles got stuck. A heavy lump of regret settled in his chest. He should be at home playing Santa, but first, he needed to plow the key routes around town. "I'll take you and Pearl home and then ask my parents to stay with the girls."

Silence fell over the front seat. A single dad's life was never easy. He glanced at Krista. Together, they would be a formidable team. The single-minded determination that got her into trouble as a coach might test his patience at times, but she would be a caring and strong role model for Ella and Gracie.

"Don't call your parents." She held up a hand.

What did she mean? Glancing over, he caught her gaze.

Shivering, she hugged her arms around her middle. "I'll wait at your place and babysit."

"I might work late." Her generous offer made his pulse jump. Did she just want to return the favor of inviting her to share his family Christmas? Or did she especially want to help him?

"Take as long as you need. If I get too tired, I'll nap on the couch."

The image of her curled under a blanket in his living room, hair spilling onto a toss cushion as she rested her head, almost sent him into a snowbank. "Are you sure? When I finish, I'll let you borrow my truck to drive home."

"Of course, I'm sure." She peered out the front passenger window, but frost blocked the view. "On one condition."

"What? You want your sidewalks cleared?" He joked but wouldn't mind a bit.

"I'll spare you the trouble, but I need you to swing by my place so I can pick up a few things."

"Your pajamas?" He glanced over and took great

pleasure in seeing her jolt back and contain a smile.

"Tate." She spit out his name but not so loud Gracie and Ella would hear.

"Kidding." Squinting at the road, he chuckled.

"You better be." Her tone turned playful.

What could she possibly need from home right now? "I know. My gift." He braked in front of her house, and the truck fishtailed and skidded to a stop.

"I'll be right back…with your lump of coal."

She knew how to make him chuckle better than anyone. After he finished work, maybe he could even convince her to stay longer and spend time together without his whole family around.

Chapter 20

"Stay, Pearl. I'll be right back." Krista leaned on the truck door to wedge it open against the fierce wind gusts. Snow blasted through tree branches and drifted up to her knees, and she waded to the front door. Tate was so kind to everyone, she couldn't possibly hate him, especially when he continually made her smile, even against her will.

Inside, she kicked off her boots, brushed snow off her jacket, and sped around the house, throwing ingredients and supplies into an oversize tote bag so she could make gifts while Tate worked. She couldn't crash the Harris family Christmas and arrive empty-handed, so she'd borrow Tate's kitchen and get to work. For a moment, she hesitated. Should she, or shouldn't she? Before she had time to reconsider, she grabbed the token gift she'd previously bought from Melanie's shop before their recent upheaval.

The scents of pine, peppermint, and cinnamon from candles and decorations hung in every room, awakening poignant Christmas memories. She never dreamed this year's memories would include Tate and his family.

Five minutes later, she traipsed back to the truck, her head down and tipped forward against the wind. "Ready." She slammed the door shut and flicked snow at Tate. Dropping her hands to her lap, she stared ahead. Why did she flirt with the guy and tease them both?

"Hey." He chuckled. "I could get even, you know. Better watch out." Glancing at the size of the bag she plopped on the floor of the truck, he did a double take. "You didn't need to get me a gift that big."

"Don't worry. I didn't." She laughed, and her affection for him came tumbling back like an avalanche. Overwhelming warmth and an odd nervousness rippled from her stomach to her chest. Tate made everything more fun, and his lips were so kissable she could hardly resist.

Parked at his place after the short drive, he hustled the girls inside.

She followed, bracing herself against the wind and wincing at the sting of snow on her cheeks.

Pearl straggled behind until she joined them and slapped everyone's legs with her thick tail. Even after everyone petted her, she still panted and paced.

Sudden dread crept into Krista's stomach. Was this the start of labor? Why now, on Christmas Eve of all times, when the vet clinic was closed? She stroked Pearl from head to tail to calm her and watched for other signs. "Please, not now," she whispered. She shrank out of the way to give Tate and the girls space and privacy for their Christmas Eve preparations. Sitting beside Pearl on the living room floor, she listened to Gracie and Ella bubbling with excitement as they served Santa's snack.

Tate switched on soothing Christmas carols and guided the girls to put on their red fleece pajamas patterned with snowflakes.

Krista would have relaxed in the cozy atmosphere filled with festive piano music, if not for Pearl's restlessness. The whole time, her stomach fluttered like it did on Christmas Eve when she was a girl and knew something very special would soon appear under the tree. She sighed. Christmas was the season for surprises and memories, mostly good but some more difficult. Later, she'd brace herself and call her parents again.

"Do you think Santa will like his milk and lots of cookies?" Ella scooted across the living room to Krista and held out a plate at a slight angle.

Krista stood to examine it. "Awesome." Just in time, she helped steady it before three cookies slid off.

Gracie followed, clasping a glass of milk and flashing a note in haphazard printing.

Dear Santa,

We were good this year. Thank you for bringing us presents.

Love, Gracie and Ella

"I know he'll love his snack and letter." Smiling, she drank in the adorable sight and Tate's soft expression. Suddenly, the image blurred, and she blinked away tears.

The girls set the snack on the coffee table and placed the note beside.

"Will you watch to make sure Pearl doesn't eat the cookies?" Ella crinkled her forehead.

"Of course. Now, the sooner you get to sleep, the sooner Santa can come. Sweet dreams."

A few minutes later, Tate reappeared. "I tucked them in, so I'll head out now."

Fine ice crystals scratched like sandpaper across the front window, and Krista shivered.

He bundled up, turned the doorknob, paused, and glanced over his shoulder.

His gaze burned a pathway to her face, and she felt heat in her cheeks. "I'm taking over your kitchen for a while." She didn't ask permission. She knew his answer would be to go ahead.

"Oh." He shrugged. "Feel free to whip up a few dinners for the freezer. Lasagna's my favorite."

"Don't get your hopes up." Her quip croaked out through her throat, thick with longing. She wanted to know everything about him. Was his favorite dessert chocolate cake with vanilla ice cream? Did he like his eggs scrambled and his toast buttery? Did he like action movies as much as country music? She already knew, aside from when he was the best man at a wedding, he rarely wore anything but blue jeans with a casual shirt or sweater. He was unfailingly polite and considerate with everyone he met.

"Why not? It's Christmas. I've been very well behaved." Chuckling, he ducked out the door.

Even though she hadn't known him for very long, she found their casual banter as familiar and comfortable as an old pair of jeans. All joking aside, she made a mental note of his favorite dinner. Maybe someday, she'd treat him to homemade lasagna. "It's okay, Pearl." She squatted to eye level. "Don't have your babies yet. Just hang on another week. Please."

Pearl just panted and paced.

Krista's insides felt just as unsettled. From the moment she met Tate, she knew he had integrity and was honest to the core, just like Amy and Daisy insisted. Was it possible his feedback was well intentioned? Should she listen to his advice? Would his guidance help her become a more effective coach? If she conceded he was right, did she need to admit Janine was right too? His criticism, although gentle, still burned in her chest.

Krista gathered her supplies and whisked into the kitchen. She had a lot of work ahead to make gifts for Tate and his whole family. The space was clean and compact with an efficient layout, and she set out flour, oil, cream of tartar, chocolate, and butter. Measuring and stirring, she let her mind drift, and she dared imagine this was her kitchen. The girls fast asleep in their room were her stepdaughters. She shook her head, ran a glass of cold water, and gulped large mouthfuls. What was she even thinking? The magic of Christmas played tricks on her mind and sent her daydreams into a dizzying spin.

She squirted food coloring into three lumps of warm white dough and kneaded until the color dispersed throughout. "Don't worry, Pearl. I'll pet you again soon." She tried to soothe her restless dog with reassuring words. Working quickly, she packaged the finished play dough—pink for Ella, purple for Gracie, and blue for Sam—and then tied the cellophane with gold ribbon. Setting the presents aside, she pictured the way Tate's wide smile and crinkled eyes would light while watching his girls tear into their gifts.

Her throat closed around a lump as big as a snowball. Tate's family was the warm and loving kind she'd always envied. Without a doubt, he would never hurt her on purpose. He had probably thought long and hard before he even said a thing after Gracie's accident. She couldn't argue with Daisy's assessment of Tate's integrity and respect for others. But love? Was Daisy right he was in love with her? Was she in love with him?

Next, she started on a large batch of creamy fudge as a treat for the adults. Stirring together melted butter and chocolate chips, she breathed the sweet, rich scent and let her thoughts float back to Tate. Deep inside, she wanted to belong in his arms, but could she actually follow her heart? Could she unlock enough acceptance and forgiveness and courage to give him—them—a true chance?

She added condensed milk and chopped walnuts, beat together the mixture, and poured it into a pan to set. Licking a finger, she tasted the creamy chocolate concoction. Hopefully, Tate and the others enjoyed sweets. Once the mixture set, she carefully cut uniform squares and arranged them in four cellophane bags for Tate, his parents, Carly and Will, and Aunt Lorraine. Adding gold ribbon as the finishing touch, she stood back and admired her work. Then she hid everything in her tote bag, ready to place under Leah and Cole's Christmas tree tomorrow morning. If the mood felt right, she might add the extra novelty item she had selected days before Gracie's injury, just in case she wanted to give Tate something special.

The whole time, Pearl paced and panted.

Based on what Krista had learned from Dr. Bryden and Internet searches, she recognized the early signs of labor. She could no longer deny the obvious. Santa might deliver a litter of puppies tonight. She glanced at her watch, strode to the living room, and peered out through the snow. How long would Tate need to work? The sooner he returned, the sooner she could settle Pearl at home. With a whelping dog on her hands, she sure wouldn't be spending Christmas with Tate's family after all. "You'll be okay." Krista ran her hands along Pearl's sides and hustled back to the kitchen. She washed pots and utensils, wiped the countertops, and surveyed the room. She would leave it as tidy as she found it. Glancing at her watch again, she judged it wasn't too late to make two calls.

Dr. Bryden answered on the first ring. "Merry Christmas."

"I'm sorry to bother you on Christmas Eve." Krista hesitated to interrupt Dr. Bryden's celebrations. She was probably absorbed in family activities and didn't need to hear from an anxious dog owner.

"You're no bother. I'm always on call." Her voice held a smile. "How's Pearl? Do you have a concern?"

Krista paced from Tate's kitchen to the living room and stared at the multi-colored lights on the tree. The aroma of fresh pine enveloped her in one of her favorite scents of the season. "I think she's in labor." Krista heard the tremor in her own voice. "What should I do?"

"Don't worry."

Dr. Bryden's voice was as smooth as eggnog.

"Pearl knows exactly what to do. Just lead her to her whelping box, and she'll do the rest. If you need moral support, don't hesitate to call."

A hundred questions marched through Krista's mind, but she took a calming breath. "Thank you. I hope I don't have to call again." She paused. "Merry Christmas." She pressed End and dove to hug Pearl. "Everything will be okay." She needed reassurance as much as her dog. Not knowing what else to do, she paced from room to room and keyed in another number. Soon, she might need to bother Tate at work, but for now, she'd wait a little longer. "Merry Christmas, Mom."

"Krista! I was just about to call you."

A note of concern rang around her words.

"Your dad and I are worried about you on your own. Where are you? How are you spending your Christmas Eve alone?"

"I'm not alone, Mom."

"You're not?"

Mom's voice rose in surprise coated with relief. "I was invited to spend Christmas Eve and Christmas day with a family." The Harrises were hardly just any family. "Remember, I mentioned Tate was the best man at Amy's wedding. He told me about the coaching job in Blue Sky."

"Oh, him. The guy who dragged you away from starring in ice shows to coaching beginners in that teeny-tiny place."

Mom still hadn't gotten over the fact she chose small-town life over performing on cruise ships in glamorous places. "Yes, him. I teach his cute little twin daughters." She wouldn't bother explaining the babysitting part. "Tate, Gracie, and Ella are celebrating with his parents and his sister's family, and they included me."

"Oh?"

Mom stretched out the word as though deciding whether she liked the idea or not. She never held back her views on anything, and Krista hoped she would skip any judgment, which was unlikely.

She sighed. "If you can't be here with your dad and me, then I'm glad you have someone to keep you company."

"They're very warm and welcoming, but I think plans are about to change again I'm sorry to say." Mom would disapprove of this bit of news for sure. "Unfortunately, Pearl appears to be in the early stages of labor. I'll probably have to help take care of a new litter of puppies. Don't worry. I'll be too busy to be lonely." She braced herself for another onslaught of opinions. Mom wouldn't care today was Christmas Eve and a time for peaceful celebration.

"Oh, Krista. The last thing you needed was a dog, let alone a crop of puppies." Mom tsked.

"I know. I know." Krista held back a huff. She wouldn't get drawn into any kind of unpleasantness on Christmas Eve.

"Well, I suppose you've always loved dogs. Now, tell me about this Tate fellow and his family. If he has children, is he divorced?"

"He's widowed."

"Oh, how sad."

Mom lowered her voice respectfully.

"Is he an eligible bachelor?"

"I suppose." Sudden hope lifted Krista's insides as light and high as a floating waltz jump. Not only was he eligible, he was interested. She couldn't confide the feeling was mutual until she was one hundred percent certain. Amy and Daisy both believed she and Tate belonged together. She thought about him day and night. Recent tensions aside, what held her back?

"Lovely. All that garbage with Zach is behind you. Maybe Tate is a man who deserves a wonderful person like you."

Mom's voice wavered with emotion. Krista had seldom heard her sound this way.

"You never know what could happen. Christmas is for surprises, and it's a very romantic time of year.

Have a nice time with Pearl and the puppies...and Tate."

"Thanks, Mom." Krista's throat squeezed. Mom just called her *wonderful*, the kind of praise hard to come by all her life. Swallowing, she paused to steady her voice. She couldn't say any more without having her words catch in her throat. Mom loved her and, in spite of her demands, meant well.

Krista stared at the Christmas tree again and admired the varied ornaments. This was indeed a season of surprises. She never would have guessed Tate had the power to crush her spirit with a few words...or a blizzard would wipe out her Christmas plans with Mom and Dad...or Tate would include her in his family celebration...or Pearl would go into labor on Christmas Eve...or Mom would nudge her toward Tate.

"You will come home when the roads clear, won't you?"

Mom's question was more of a command. She flipped back to her take-charge self. Of course, she always felt better when she was in control. Krista held no illusions she'd ever totally change and show her softer side.

"Christmas without you will not be the same."

"I'll try, Mom. I will do my best, but I can't miss too much teaching time with the ice show coming up.

Mom sniffed. "You sure have your hands full. Well, I guess we'll have to make the best of things, won't we?"

With a slight edge to her voice, she didn't sound pleased, but she didn't argue either. Hearing Pearl whine in the background, Krista needed to end the call right away. "Merry Christmas. I love you, Mom. Tell

Dad I love him too, and I'll talk with you both for sure tomorrow." She tucked her cell phone into the back pocket of her jeans. Now what?

Squatting, she enveloped Pearl in a hug, then stood and peered out the living room window. She crossed her arms and shivered in the draft. The wind howled and threw scratchy crystals at the glass. The song "We Wish You a Merry Christmas" floated above and faded, and then the festive playlist launched into the brassy sounds of "Joy to the World." Tate had his work cut out for him in this nasty weather, but she had worries of her own.

Panting, Pearl pawed at Krista's leg.

Krista petted the dog's head. "Okay, pup. I'll take care of you." She paced from living room to the kitchen and back to the sounds of continuous carols.

Pearl trundled away and dug at the carpet in the front entranceway.

Krista couldn't wait any longer to summon Tate. If she didn't take Pearl home soon, she might greet him with a litter of puppies in the middle of his hallway. "Look what Santa brought" would be quite a greeting.

Now she'd be forced to spend Christmas alone after all, except for the company of Pearl and tiny newborn puppies. She tapped his number into her phone and held her breath. Heaviness squeezed into her chest and mingled with sparks of anticipation and…it couldn't really be love, could it?

****

As Tate turned the corner and pulled up in front of his house, he heard his phone ring. Jamming the car into Park, he picked up the call. "Krista?" Just saying her name revved his heartbeats into overdrive. He could have worked continuously all night to keep the roads anywhere near clear, but he had made a pass through the main streets and would continue the work tomorrow between gift opening and dinnertime. He couldn't wait to see Krista again. She cared for his sleeping children like she belonged in his home. "I'm right here out front." Through the white squall, he spotted a shadowy outline in the front window. She was watching him. "Are the girls okay? I'll be right in." He battled the wind and snow all the way to the front door and rushed inside. "Whew. Crazy weather out there."

"The girls are fine. I haven't heard a peep." Standing in the hallway, she shivered at the cold blast and wrung her hands. "I think Pearl's in labor."

"What? You're kidding, right?" Peeling off his parka, he widened his eyes and surveyed the whole scene. "The Twelve Days of Christmas" played in the background. Krista's sweater glittered blue, silver, green, and red with her slightest movement, and her wrinkled forehead and half smile showed a curious combination of concern and excitement. He gathered all his willpower not to sweep her into a never-ending hug and cover her face with tender kisses.

Around her, Pearl panted and paced.

"I wish I was kidding. Look at her." Krista pointed. "I need to take her home to the whelping box right away."

He chuckled. "Thanks a lot, Pearl." He hung his jacket, tossed mitts and hat into the closet, and faced Krista. "Trust a dog to interrupt my romantic plans."

"Tate, I…" She shook her head.

In two long strides, he reached her, close enough to inhale her subtle scent, a delicious hint of orange, vanilla, and other good things he couldn't quite name. "Merry Christmas, Krista. Don't hate me for giving you feedback." He squeezed her hands, and his heart hammered in his ears. He had so much to tell her about the depth of his feelings—for not the skating coach but the woman who awakened a need so strong he forgot to fear he could lose her.

For a second, she melted into him, then backed away. "I can't...not right now. Pearl needs me."

"More than me?" He smirked.

"Are you about to give birth?" She grimaced.

He shouldn't tease at a time like this. "Just kidding. I see what you mean. Go ahead. Right away." He grabbed her coat from the front closet and held it out.

Pearl groaned and flopped onto the floor. She lay on her side, panting.

He thrust his truck keys at her, then grabbed them back. "It's too late." He pointed at Pearl.

The dog huffed and strained.

"But her whelping box." Krista raised her hands to her cheeks.

"I have spare lumber from the ice show sets in the basement. Stay here and watch her. I'll go bang a box together and throw in some newspapers and old towels. Within minutes, he had constructed a shallow box with edges in place just high enough to keep puppies from wandering.

Back upstairs, he helped Krista coax Pearl to her feet and guide her down the stairs to her own private space. He had positioned the box on a plastic sheet in a cozy corner next to the furnace room.

Glancing around, he visualized the room through Krista's eyes. Numerous framed pieces of the girls' artwork brightened the neutral gray walls. In the main area, she would be comfortable enough, if she had to spend the night on the sectional couch. The durable brushed fabric made a soft makeshift bed. Shades of gray and blue followed the same color scheme as the living room upstairs. Inside, he smirked. As if he knew a thing about décor. Carly deserved all the credit. "There. She's all set." Tate watched the tension slip from Krista's face. She was beautiful, even when she was agitated, but now she glowed with relief.

"I can't thank you enough. Dr. Bryden says Pearl will know what to do." She peered at the makeshift setup.

"I hope so because I sure don't." He laughed.

"I'll wait and watch." She glanced around for a chair. "You better go play Santa and then get some sleep."

"Help yourself to the sofa. We'll take shifts. I'll check back in a couple of hours." He paused and edged closer. "It's midnight, so let me be the first to wish you Merry Christmas." He wanted to draw her into his arms so much he ached. He wanted to share a kiss so much his lips burned. Searching her face, he looked for any sign she felt the same.

She glanced at Pearl and back at him. "Merry Christmas, Tate."

Her smile made him feel like he was the only man in the world. Her voice sounded slightly husky and a little unsure. He would assure her they belonged together. He would show her how much he cared. But for now, his desire would have to wait for a litter of puppies to arrive. This Christmas would be a day like no other, guaranteed.

Chapter 21

At seven o'clock on Christmas morning, Krista heard the patter of little feet upstairs, then delighted squeals from Gracie and Ella.

"Merry Christmas, darlins!" Tate's deep voice reverberated down the stairwell. "Looks like Santa came."

Krista smiled and hugged a knitted gray blanket over her shoulders from the pile Tate left folded at one end of the sofa. He was such a dedicated dad, so caring and enthusiastic. Like Daisy said, he was a plain good man. As promised, he had checked on her and Pearl around three a.m. She appreciated his late-night caring but insisted he go back to bed. She couldn't leave Pearl in the midst of whelping. With his thick, sleepy voice, he didn't argue.

Now, wriggling in front of her was her biggest Christmas surprise. At least, she doubted anything could top this one. Like Dr. Bryden promised, Pearl knew exactly what to do, and she now lay nursing eight puppies.

As Krista had witnessed each puppy emerge and start to breathe on its own, she inhaled her own shaky breath. She was tired but relieved. The ordeal was over. All she had to do was help Pearl take care of them for the next eight weeks and find eight good homes. No small feat, especially when she faced one of the busiest times of the year at work.

For today, she lectured herself not to worry. She'd find a way. Even though she had wanted to flee Blue Sky, she knew she had to stay. Pearl and eight puppies needed her. The skaters and the ice show depended on her. Best of all, Tate didn't want her to leave. Could they possibly belong together?

Moving slowly, she left the blanket on the chair and crept toward the whelping box. She had already discarded the soiled paper and towels and replaced them from a clean supply Tate left. Pearl glanced up but showed no sign of distress. Krista stood and drank in the wonder of new life and soft whimpers.

About thirty minutes later, she heard Tate's footsteps tap down the stairs toward her. "Merry Christmas again. How are they?"

"Merry Christmas. Doing well from what I can tell." Krista caught her breath at the sight of Tate with his hair damp from a shower, red plaid flannel shirt, and faded jeans. He embodied the outdoorsy, rugged kind of handsome she couldn't resist.

From a distance, he peeked at Pearl's new family. "I haven't told the girls about the puppies yet. I figured you and Pearl could use a little peace. We're heading to Mom and Dad's place now. Will you come?"

She felt torn in two. Would Pearl and the puppies be okay if she left them so soon? Should she skip the family celebration? "How's the weather now? I'll stay here a little longer and make sure they're fine. I need to go home, shower, and change before I'm presentable. I'll catch up with you later."

"Promise?"

"Promise." She nodded. "I think I'll join you." He

really wanted to spend the day together, and so did she.

"I hate to think of you out alone in the storm." He frowned.

"I can walk a couple of blocks. A little blizzard won't stop me."

He raised his eyebrows. "If you're sure. See you soon. I'll leave a house key on the kitchen counter so you can lock up." He spun and thumped upstairs.

She'd count the minutes until she could see him again. The clatter of excited voices and rustle of wrapping paper echoed down the stairwell. Grabbing her mobile phone from a pocket, she called Dr. Bryden to report in.

"Merry Christmas, Krista. Are congratulations in order? Are you the proud human mom of a litter of puppies?"

"Merry Christmas! I sure am. Will they be okay if I leave them for a couple of hours later?"

"I'm sure they'll be just fine."

Dr. Bryden's reassuring smile travelled through the airwaves and soothed Krista like a hug.

"But tell you what. I'll fight the storm and check on them on my way to my daughter's place. Give me your address."

"Uh, are you sure?" Krista's face flushed. How would she explain the puppies were here? "It's a bit of a long story, but the puppies and I are not at home. We're at Tate Harris's house."

"No problem."

Her tone was warm and matter-of-fact with no hint of innuendo. She gave no signal of anything unusual and was purely professional in her response, which made Krista like and trust her even more.

"I know where he lives."

"I can't thank you enough." Relief washed over Krista, but it couldn't quite erase the nervous quiver in her stomach. She might be free to join Tate's family for dinner.

"You're very welcome. I never tire of puppies."

Krista ended the call and gave Pearl a reassuring pet on the head. An hour later, she gratefully welcomed Dr. Bryden.

The vet's gray hair swung in a neat bob. She slipped a white lab coat over a beige sweater with reindeer prancing across the middle. After a quick examination on her hands and knees, she straightened and smiled. "Pearl is very healthy, and all the puppies are doing well. I suggest you keep an eye on them for the next few hours to make sure nothing changes, and then don't worry at all about leaving them for a couple of hours. You'll remember this Christmas!"

"You're right," said Krista. "I can't thank you enough. I hope I didn't interrupt your day too much."

Dr. Bryden smiled and shook her head. "I love puppies." Smiling, she replaced her lab coat with her navy-blue jacket, climbed the stairs, and swung open the front door to an icy blast. "Have a wonderful day!"

"I will." The frigid air couldn't cool her burning anticipation. Today would be memorable and not just because of Pearl's new family. The moment Dr. Bryden left, Krista sent a text to Tate.

—*I'll have to miss the morning fun but will join you for dinner.*—

His response was quick.

—*Miss you. Get some rest. I'll save your gift for later unless I get reports from Santa you're on the naughty list.*—

He missed her! She laughed and keyed a quick reply to his joking threat.

—*Never! Nice all the way.*—

Every time she felt a little sorry for herself for spending Christmas day alone, she admired Pearl's litter. The tiny, wriggling bundle of newborns would warm anyone's heart. She savored the irresistible, sweet puppy smell, and after an uneventful few hours, she updated Tate.

—*See you around five. Popping home to freshen up. I'll check back here and then join you at your parents' place.*—

She left her tote bag of homemade gifts ready to pick up before dinner, then headed outside, leaning into the driving wind and squinting against the prickly snowflakes. She hoped the small gift for Tate wouldn't draw too much attention or teasing from his family. It was a sort of peace offering now that her anger had cooled and she couldn't deny her feelings any longer.

The storm showed no signs of letting up. She trudged home, showered, changed into fitted black jeans and a cozy red sweater. Then, bundled up so just her eyes peeked out between her hat and face warmer, she traipsed back to Tate's place for a pre-dinner check on Pearl and the puppies. She arrived coated in snow with her eyelashes frozen into mini icicles. As she unlocked and swung open the door, she heard chattering voices and the cheery sounds of "Frosty the Snowman" blasting. What was going on? Wasn't she supposed to meet Tate's family at his parents' place? Wind whipping behind her, she froze in the doorway.

"Welcome back, Krista." Cole wheeled toward the

entrance to greet her. "Merry Christmas! I hear Santa brought you quite a surprise."

"He sure did! Uh, wasn't I supposed to join you at your place?" She struggled to digest the scene. In the hour she had been gone, Tate's quiet house had been transformed into a full-fledged Christmas party. Quickly, she closed the door before more cold air blew inside.

Suddenly, Tate and the rest of the family gathered round like a choir, shouting "Merry Christmas" and urging her to take off her jacket and soak up the warmth. Holiday songs accompanied by piano music filled the background, and she breathed in the delicious aroma of turkey, sage, and sweet potatoes.

"You're just in time for dinner." Carly smiled and waved her in.

Aunt Lorraine beamed and winked. "Nice you lovebirds can share Christmas dinner together."

Krista followed Carly into the living room and slipped her gifts under the tree for later. She felt like a true guest of honor with the rest of the group clustered around. "What surprise did Santa bring?"

Barely limping, Gracie squeezed through the group to face Krista and find out more about Grandpa's comment. She cradled a bald baby doll dressed in mauve.

"Santa brought me this doll." Ella held it up. It was identical to Gracie's except for its yellow outfit. "What did he bring you?"

Krista glanced at Tate.

He gave a slight nod.

His eyes shone as irresistibly bright as the lights on the tree. "The surprise is…Pearl had her puppies." She laughed at the girls' wide eyes and open mouths. They looked as shocked as she had felt when reality set in.

"Can we see them?" Ella and Grace joined hands and bounced on the spot. Dolls forgotten for a moment, they peppered Krista with questions. "When can we see them? How many? Daddy, can we get one? Are they at Krista's house? Where are they?"

Sam stared with his mouth open.

"Guess where they are?" Tate raised his eyebrows and looked from Ella to Gracie.

He showed the softest, kindest expression she had ever seen. How could she not love a man who was such a devoted dad? Why did she ever doubt his kind heart and wise advice?

"Where?" Ella and Gracie chorused, tugging at his sleeves.

"In our basement." He pointed at the floor.

"Here at our house?" Ella crinkled her forehead.

"Right now?" Gracie squealed.

"Right now." Grinning, Tate glanced back and forth at both girls. "Guess how many?"

"Six," said Ella.

"Seven," blurted Gracie.

"Close." Tate paused until both girls grabbed his arms. "Eight."

"Why are they at our house?" questioned Gracie.

"Do we get to keep them?" Ella shouted.

They danced in a circle.

Tate could explain everything later. Krista would love to give all three of the kids their own puppy, but Tate, Carly, and Will might not be convinced. For now, she shoved away the worry of how she would find the right eight homes.

"Mother dogs are very protective of their babies, so we have to make sure we don't upset Pearl," said Krista. "After dinner, I'll take you down one at a time to see them." Fortunately, with all the excitement of new toys, Ella and Gracie gracefully accepted the delay. "Right now, I'll peek in on them and come right back." Returning from the basement, she reported Pearl and the puppies were resting quietly, and now she could settle in and enjoy dinner.

Tate pointed everyone in the direction of the dining room table covered in a green-and-gold tablecloth.

She followed and swept her gaze from the back of his dark hair down the full length of his broad back clothed in red-and-navy-plaid shirt, to the close fit of his blue jeans, and right to his fur-trimmed moccasin slippers. In the flurry of activity with everyone finding seats, she leaned close and whispered, "Thank you." Breathing his subtle, outdoorsy scent she felt slightly off balance. How could she hold back any longer? He was the man who completed her—the man she wanted to breathe in forever.

He brushed her elbow and ushered her to a spot between Gracie and Ella before they insisted.

Leah and Tate bustled in and out of the kitchen with a platter of savory turkey and bowls of mashed potatoes, moist stuffing, rich gravy, and baked vegetables.

The conversation ricocheted around the table like a hockey puck, and mostly, she followed it like an interested spectator. Dinner at home with her parents was never this relaxed and lively. She savored a bite of creamy mashed potatoes and helped pour more gravy for Ella and Gracie. The tart, fruity scent of cranberry sauce tempted her, and she added a dollop to her turkey meat. Preoccupied with the food, she let her mind drift from the table conversation for a moment. Suddenly, she heard her name and snapped her attention to Leah.

"We knew you couldn't leave the puppies for too long, so Tate decided we should move the party here." Leah paused in cutting her meat and glanced around the table.

Krista drank in Tate's beaming grin and Leah's equally wide smile.

"He'd do anything for you." Aunt Lorraine pointed her fork at Tate, then Krista.

"Now, you can check on the puppies, and you don't have to rush away from dinner with the family." Leah set down her cutlery, reached in front of Ella, and squeezed Krista's hand. "If you're distracted, you can't really enjoy the moment. You deserve to enjoy the day to the fullest."

"Thank you so much. You're wonderful! I didn't need to inconvenience you all." Tate had convinced his family to move their celebration just to include her. Joy and wonder fluttered in her chest. How could she not love a man who enlisted his whole family to show how much he cared?

"I know we didn't have to move Christmas." Tate paused eating and focused on Krista alone.

She raised her napkin to her lips and hoped it covered her sudden blush.

"But my family understands my Christmas Day fun wouldn't be complete without you."

"They do? Really?" The chatter of voices, clatter of cutlery, and strumming carols all faded away, and she hung suspended in a precious moment alone with Tate.

Krista placed a hand over her heart and pressed hard to keep her intense feelings from jumping out in front of everyone.

"Of course, we understand," said Leah. "If Tate's happy, we're happy."

"Tate was the spoiled one. He always liked to get his own way." Carly teased as only a sister could.

"Since he's the host, he can do the dishes."

"Good thing we like you, Krista." Cole chuckled. "Or we might not have been so agreeable."

Krista swallowed and blinked to keep sudden moisture at bay. "You're all so kind." She glanced at Tate and nearly melted like a candle under his hot gaze.

"Daddy *really* likes Krista. He told us." Gracie giggled and looked to her sister for confirmation. They both nodded, ponytails bobbing.

Sam stared and smirked.

The adults all laughed.

"I think he's pretty nice too." Krista gripped her napkin and could have crawled under the table with embarrassment but faced the teasing head-on. "Most of the time."

Her quip brought another round of laughter, and she joined in. The family might as well know the truth. Tate was her guy. The rest of the meal passed with light conversation, and she basked in the Harrises' warmth.

"Can I help with dishes?" Krista slid back her chair.

"Leave the mess to Carly." Tate smirked.

Sighing, Carly rolled her eyes. "He never quits."

"Seriously, everyone leave the mess in the kitchen for now. Let's go into the living room to finish opening gifts."

The kids didn't need any coaxing.

"My gifts aren't much, but I wanted to let you all know how much I appreciate your amazing welcome and hospitality." Krista rubbed her hands along the soft surface of her armchair.

"I'll never say *no* to a present." Cole wheeled his chair around to face her.

"Don't get your hopes up too high or you might be disappointed." Krista sprang out of her chair, retrieved several colorful gift bags from under the tree, and passed them to everyone.

"Oh goody. More presents." Ella clapped her hands.

The kids all flopped in a cluster in the center of the room and flung tissue paper over their shoulders.

"Play dough!" Gracie shouted first.

Ella and Sam jumped in, comparing notes on colors.

"It's the best! Hey," said Ella, "We can break it into pieces and share so we'll all have some of each color."

"I love chocolate fudge. How did you know it's one of my favorites?" Cole dipped into his and Leah's package.

"Thank you! I can't resist fudge." Leah motioned for Cole to pass it over. She patted her hips. "Forget about a diet at this time of year."

"What a treat!" Carly glanced at Will.

"I hope I get some too, or I might have to steal." Tate chuckled and lunged at Carly's bag.

She swung it out of reach and would have hit Will in the nose if he hadn't ducked. "Brothers." She heaved an exaggerated huff. "See the trouble he causes. Are you sure you don't want to avoid him, Krista?"

"Thanks for warning me." She backed up to her chair and pointed at Tate. "Your turn." She was having fun, but she needed to check on the puppies again. "Dig in."

Tate rooted in his bag and unwrapped his own bag of fudge. "Glad you don't play favorites. Or is my bag a little bigger?"

"Krista doesn't like you *that* much." Carly scrunched her nose.

"Oh yeah? Did she give you two things? I got something else." Tate reached into the bag and pulled out a small package wrapped in tissue.

Krista hadn't known whether to save Tate's gift for a private moment or bring it here, but she decided it wasn't too personal to share in front of his family. "It's nothing really." Suddenly, she felt hot again and hoped no one noticed her flushed face.

****

While he unwrapped the tissue, Tate couldn't slow his racing heartbeats. Krista cared enough to give him something extra besides the homemade treat everyone else received. Maybe she wouldn't mind when she learned he had a special gift for her too. The package contained something small and hard, and when he uncovered it, he knew instantly she honored his past and cared for the important things in his life. Inside was a tree decoration—a hockey player outfitted in the blue uniform of his former top team. The player's blades gleamed silver, and his jersey number was twenty-two like Tate always wore.

"Aww, look at that. A cute miniature Tate." Carly dove forward for a closer look.

"Thanks, Krista." He paused and swallowed. His

chest squeezed with a mixture of regret over his broken dreams and hopes for the future. He would remember the exhilaration of his hockey years but take pride in taking over the family business. He would forever treasure the happy years with Whitney and their precious twin daughters. But he would fully embrace the renewed joy and excitement Krista brought into his life.

He held up the ornament, and it rotated on its ribbon like a slow skating move. She had chosen something to remind him of Christmastime and happy memories and a passion they shared for the ice. His chest felt so full it might burst. "I don't know if he looks as good in his uniform as I did," he joked, "But he'll look great on our tree."

Krista wiggled forward in her chair. "I'm glad you like it. Now, I need to check on the puppies."

"Wait, wait, wait." Cole held up a hand like a stop sign. "Not so fast. You can't skip out without your gifts."

Leah and Carly placed parcels on her lap, and she widened her eyes and smiled. "Thank you, but...you really shouldn't have—"

"We wanted to make your day special." Leah smiled and patted her shoulder. "When you share our Christmas, you're like family. Now go ahead and open them."

When they heard the news Krista would join their celebrations, somebody had done some quick last-minute shopping. She tore into her gifts and admired a set of lavender bath gel and body lotion.

"For a long, hot soak after a day at the rink," said Carly.

"Lovely!" Krista twisted off the lid and sniffed. "Thank you very much."

From Leah and Cole, Krista received cream-colored oven mitts covered in black pawprints and the phrase *Love is a Four-Legged Word*. Krista laughed and tried them on. "Perfect. You know how attached I am to Pearl, and now I have eight more to love. Well, I really must—"

"Not yet. One more." Tate jumped up, rooted at the base of the tree, and presented her with a small silver box tied with a royal-blue ribbon.

"What is it?" Gracie crawled to a spot in front of Krista.

"Let us see." Ella scooted beside her sister.

Krista glanced at Tate, widened her eyes, and bowed her head to examine the gift.

The conversation tapered off, and the group fell silent, leaving only the quiet, timeless melody of "All I Want for Christmas is You."

He didn't hold back in his message on the card.

Krista, you're the one and only for me. Tell me you feel the same. Tate

"Oh, my goodness." Krista read the card, paused, and placed a hand on her heart.

He felt her gaze like they were the only two people in the room.

Smiling, she gave a slight nod.

Her signal was so subtle only he caught it. His heart thundered so hard a hockey breakaway was nowhere close.

"I know for sure they're in love." Gracie laughed and clapped.

In the caring circle of his family, he heard his

daughter, but his attention never wavered from Krista's lovely face. He had chosen her gift carefully and cautiously. What he really wanted to give, he couldn't. Not yet. He needed to wait until he knew she was one hundred percent ready, but he sensed that thrilling day would not be far off.

Slowly, Krista tore away the paper, lifted the lid, and gasped. "It's beautiful." She held up a sparkling silver necklace. On a delicate chain dangled a tiny pair of shiny silver skates, swaying slightly because of the tremor in her hand. "Thank you, Tate." She blinked, and her voice wavered. "I love it."

"Yup, I can tell they're in love." Ella jumped up and clapped.

Leah nodded and laughed. "I think you're right."

"I told you so." Grinning, Aunt Lorraine winked.

Cole and Will exchanged glances and rolled their eyes.

"Pretty good taste for a guy." Carly flashed Tate a thumbs-up.

"Sometimes, I even surprise myself." He chuckled, and the whole family joined in. "Here, let me." He pulled Krista to her feet, raised the necklace to her neck, and fastened the clasp. Leaning forward, he brushed her cheek with his lips and murmured into her ear, "I can't wait to kiss you for real."

For an instant, the family faded into the background, and they were alone, focused only on each other. Backing away, he searched Krista's expression, and he knew. Her eyes shone as bright as the future they would share.

Who would have ever guessed a friend's wedding, an ice show, and a prairie blizzard would all lead to one of the very best days of his life and this heartfelt moment?

She placed a hand on her heart and collapsed into her chair. "I'll never forget *this* Christmas!"

Epilogue

Two months later, on Valentine's Day, Krista circled the ice, dipping and twirling as she waited for Tate. He would take her to a special restaurant for a romantic dinner on the weekend, but tonight, they would celebrate with a private skate. Time together was the only gift she needed.

Her heartbeats still quickened at the memory of their eventful, soul-baring Christmas celebration. She wore her silver necklace every day, feeling the skates tickle her skin. Breathing the cool air, heavy with the familiar rink smells, she swung backwards into smooth crossovers and flowed into a giant figure eight.

The last two months had flown by in a whirlwind of activity to produce the successful ice show, find good homes for the puppies, and spend as much time as possible with Tate, Ella, and Gracie. Tate gave in and allowed Ella and Gracie to choose one of the females from the litter, and they became the proud mommies of Poppy. In the midst of it all, Krista invited her parents to watch the ice show and, more importantly, meet Tate. Even Mom approved, and Krista enjoyed an almost stress-free visit.

Now, a future in Blue Sky was a real possibility. Imagining her future as Tate's wife and as Ella and Gracie's stepmother, she felt endless excitement and anticipation spin through her middle faster than a loop jump.

Today was a banner day, and she couldn't wait to tell Tate.

This morning, Janine had arrived in her office with a contract in hand. As the faint sounds of the ice resurfacing machine rumbled a background soundtrack, she fixed her sharp gaze on Krista. "I admit I had concerns at first, but the skaters are thriving. The difference in Olivia's attitude and her work ethic is amazing. And the ice show! I still question a Mexican fiesta in January, but apparently, it was just what this sleepy town needed. We set a record for ticket sales, and the revenue means the rink will meet its budget for the year."

Krista nodded and pictured the colorful costumes, lively music, and glowing faces of all the skaters. "Everyone pulled together and made the show pretty special." Janine still wasn't her favorite person, but Krista had learned how to keep her happy.

"As you know, Lauren resigned to become a full-time mom," said Janine. "On behalf of the club board of directors, I'd like to offer you the role of permanent head coach."

"Thank you, Janine." Smiling, Krista bounced out of her chair and shook hands. She had a feeling the offer was coming, and she didn't need to mull it over for even a second. "I'm pleased to accept."

"I expect Tate Harris will be happy to hear the news." Janine smirked and raised her eyebrows.

"I'm excited to stay." Janine was famous for her snide humor, and she would never change. Krista had ignored the slight dig.

Now, she arced into a graceful spiral, and the sight

of Tate behind the boards at the rink gate pulled her focus back to the present. Pulse jumping, she swooped and curved. She couldn't wait to spin into his arms.

"Wait at center ice and close your eyes," called Tate from the sidelines.

"Really?" Excitement fluttered in her middle. He was the man of her dreams, and she'd do almost anything he asked. What had he planned for Valentine's Day?

"Really."

"Okay, I guess." She looped and stopped with a spray of snow. Hard as she wanted to peek at her surprise, she squeezed her eyes shut and waited. The ice crackled as he glided to join her. "Can I look yet?" Her knees quivered, and she sensed his presence close by. He was the guy she'd waited for all her life. He was her man for today, for tomorrow, and for always. Love and gratitude filled her heart so full it might burst.

"I'll tell you when." Silence fell over the rink. "Okay, now."

Opening her eyes, she faced him.

Grinning, he extended his arms, overflowing with red roses.

"Two dozen roses?" She breathed the fragrant bouquet and hugged it gently to her chest. They're beautiful! Thank you, my dear Tate. I love them, but you shouldn't have." Always so thoughtful, he knew roses were her favourite.

"I didn't."

She tilted her head and stared deep into his eyes, glimmering with light and humor. He couldn't resist teasing—just one of the countless qualities that made *him* irresistible. What did he mean? "But..." She

289

glanced down, starting to mentally count.

"I didn't get you two dozen roses." He paused and smiled, showing his perfect white teeth. "I got you seventeen." He swooped a finger back and forth overtop without touching the blossoms. "A dozen for this year. And one for every month I've known you."

Krista blinked and swallowed. Starting with Amy's wedding, the past five months falling in love with Tate had been the best of her life. She pictured the rocky life she left behind, the bumpy road she travelled, and the winding path ahead, and her breath caught somewhere deep in her chest. No matter what the future held, she knew for certain who she wanted by her side throughout it all. "I…what can I say…?"

"Say *yes*." Tate set the roses on the ice and dropped to one knee. Reaching into his jacket pocket, he retrieved a blue velvet box and snapped open the lid. "Krista, I love you. Will you marry me?"

Krista gasped, and her eyes filled with tears of joy. "Yes! Oh, Tate, I love you too. Of course, absolutely, without a doubt, yes!" With each word, her voice grew stronger until she practically shouted. She wanted more than anything to become Tate's wife and the mother of his children. Maybe Ella and Gracie would even have a little brother or sister someday soon.

The sapphire-and-diamond ring glinted under the rink lights, and he slipped it onto her finger.

Throwing her arms wide, she spun once, pulled him up to face her, and nestled into his arms. He cupped her chin and kissed her with his warm lips, gently at first and then with an intensity that could melt the ice.

Finally, they dropped their arms and, still holding

hands, slid apart ever so slightly.

"I can't wait to blend our lives forever. Let's set the date," he said.

"Yes." She gazed up past the stubble on his chin to his gentle eyes and drank in the hope and promise reflected there. "Is tomorrow too soon?"

Acknowledgments

I always dreamed of becoming an author, and this is now my seventh book! As a former figure skater, I spent many hours on ice, so I enjoyed creating a story set around a local skating rink.

Thank you to all the family and friends who encourage me to keep writing. I hope you know how much I love and appreciate you.

A special thank you to Rick, my biggest supporter, for your humor, patience, insights, and even occasional proofreading. All errors are mine!

My editor, Leanne Morgena, has worked with me on all seven books. Thank you for sharing your expertise once again.

A word about the author...

Margot Johnson writes feel-good stories about women who chase their dreams and find romance along the way.

She is the author of six romances--the novels Some Other Way, Love Takes Flight, and Love Leads the Way and three novellas in the Merilee Tours series--Let it Snowball, Let it Melt and Let it Simmer. Her characters can't possibly find their happy endings...or can they?

Before turning her focus to the fun writing life, Margot held leadership roles in human resources and communications. When not writing, she loves to connect with family and friends, volunteer with SK Writers' Guild, and walk at least 10,000 steps a day (except when it's minus 40!)

She lives with her husband in the Canadian prairies.